BRIGHT
RUINED
THINGS

ALSO BY SAMANTHA COHOE

A Golden Fury

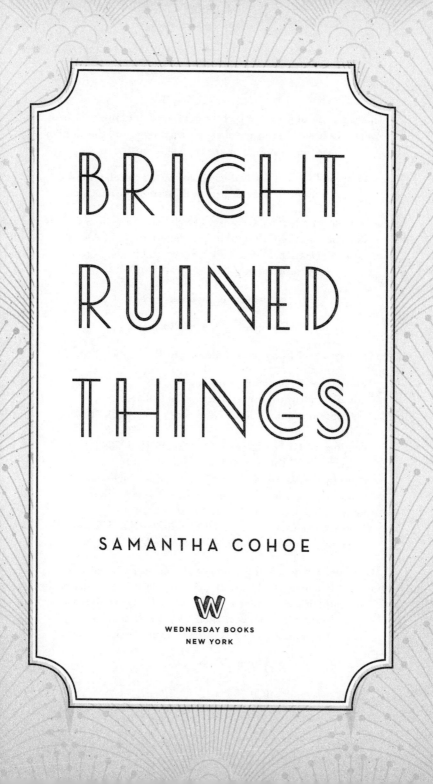

BRIGHT RUINED THINGS

SAMANTHA COHOE

W

WEDNESDAY BOOKS
NEW YORK

First published in the United States by Wednesday Books, an imprint of St. Martin's Publishing Group

BRIGHT RUINED THINGS. Copyright © 2022 by Samantha Cohoe. All rights reserved. Printed in the United States of America. For information, address St. Martin's Publishing Group, 120 Broadway, New York, NY 10271.

www.wednesdaybooks.com

Designed by Devan Norman

Library of Congress Cataloging-in-Publication Data

Names: Cohoe, Samantha, author.
Title: Bright ruined things / Samantha Cohoe.
Description: First edition. | New York : Wednesday Books, 2022.
Identifiers: LCCN 2021016066 | ISBN 9781250768841 (hardcover) | ISBN 9781250768858 (ebook)
Subjects: CYAC: Magic—Fiction. | Ghosts—Fiction. | Islands—Fiction. | Families—Fiction. | Love—Fiction. | Secrets—Fiction. | LCGFT: Novels.
Classification: LCC PZ7.1.C64255 Br 2022 | DDC [Fic]—dc23
LC record available at https://lccn.loc.gov/2021016066

Our books may be purchased in bulk for promotional, educational, or business use. Please contact your local bookseller or the Macmillan Corporate and Premium Sales Department at 1-800-221-7945, extension 5442, or by email at MacmillanSpecialMarkets@macmillan.com.

First Edition: 2022

10 9 8 7 6 5 4 3 2 1

FOR MY GRANDMOTHER,
JOAN ALICE CORBIN SMITH.
STILL THE MOST GLAMOROUS WOMAN
I'VE EVER KNOWN. I MISS YOU, GRAMA.

THE PROSPER FAMILY

LORD ALPHONSUS PROSPER

+

LADY IMOGEN MONTJOY PROSPER
(DEAD)

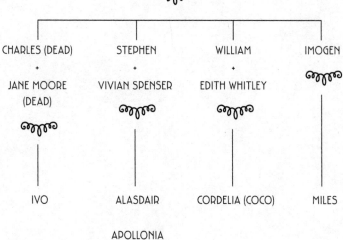

CHARLES (DEAD)	STEPHEN	WILLIAM	IMOGEN
+	+	+	
JANE MOORE (DEAD)	VIVIAN SPENSER	EDITH WHITLEY	
IVO	ALASDAIR	CORDELIA (COCO)	MILES

APOLLONIA

BRIGHT RUINED THINGS

CHAPTER ONE

I ran up the path as dawn broke. I didn't need the light for my feet to land sure on this trail. Light or dark, I knew every step of this island.

My island.

Their island.

They were all coming home today, all the Prospers. The ones I loved and longed for and the ones I did my best not to. It was First Night. Every last lovely, loathsome one of them would be here soon, sipping whatever they felt like and settling into their beautiful rooms. Breathing in the familiar scents of the island, listening to the gentle music of the spirits above the crashing of the sea, and thinking how good it was to be home.

Home. Even though they were only here a few times a year.

I had never left.

I ran along a cliff face. The path was narrow and cut down sharply into white rocks. Below, waves smashed against them with enough force to send the mist thirty feet up, where it clung to my already damp and salty skin. The rising sun's lavender light spilled across the water, and the spirits' morning music swelled at Lord Prosper's command. The path went upward, steep, but my breath was as steady as my pace. I was good at this, unquestionably. Even if no one cared but Coco, it steadied me to do something I knew I could do well first, before I plunged into a day full of things I wasn't sure I could.

Like make Miles notice I had grown up and wasn't just a dirty kid he was nice to in the summer.

Like convince him he wanted me at his side when he asked his grandfather to train him.

Like convince him to ask.

I wasn't sure I could, but I had to. I had to find a way to make a place for myself here, before it was too late. Before Lord Prosper noticed his promise to my dead father had expired, and they finally sent me away from their island.

From my island.

The thought of it spiked my pulse more than the running could. I turned a corner, and the house came into view below me. My heart clutched at the beauty of it. Familiar as this scene was, I never grew tired of looking at it. The house rose out of the soft green spring grass, tall and white and elegant. From here, the swimming pool shone as blue as the sea, surrounded by pink bougainvillea. I could see Apollonia's balcony overlooking it, and above that, the fifth floor, topped with its glinting glass dome.

Lord Prosper and Ivo would be under that dome now, working the morning's magic. If I could be there with them—helping Lord Prosper, as essential as Ivo, or more—I would never have to worry about losing all of this. If I were a magician, I would never have to worry that the rest of me wasn't impressive or interesting enough. What could be more interesting and impressive than doing magic? I would do anything to be under that dome every morning. Calming the sea and taming the storm that had kept humans away from the island and its secrets for so long.

This patch of ocean had been a dead zone, once. Ships had sailed around for miles to avoid it. Cartographers had marked it with the image of a storm and the word *tempest*.

Lord Prosper had changed all that. Now, I rarely saw a cloud.

My steps slowed. I tried to imagine tonight, if everything went as I hoped. I'd find Lord Prosper, maybe after the fireworks. Miles, his grandson, at my side. His strong hand in mine.

Unbidden, Ivo's scowling face rose in my mind. I grimaced and banished the thought. We would just have to find Lord Prosper when he was alone, without his eldest grandson. It shouldn't be that hard tonight. Ivo always made himself scarce on First Night. He wasn't one for parties.

I turned from the house, pushing Ivo from my mind, and stared out toward the mainland. There was a black spot on the lightening horizon. A ship, already? It was early for that. The only Prospers who got up early were the ones who lived here year-round: Lord Prosper, Ivo, and Lady Vivian. The rest of them stayed up late and slept later. Even Coco rarely made it up in time to run with me in the summer, despite her promises. What she really wanted to do was lie in bed and eat breakfast off a spirit-borne tray, like the rest of them. I didn't blame her for it. If I had her room and the spirits served me in it, I would do the same.

The black spot moved quickly, and in a few moments, I was certain it was a Prosper boat. It moved through the waves against the wind without sail, steam, or smoke. Aether-powered. It flew the island's gold pennant flag, fluttering back toward England.

I picked up my pace again. Then a wind blew against me, pushing me toward the cliff face.

My foot slipped. My feet never slipped.

I wasn't running anymore, but the ground wasn't right. Wasn't there. I rose, pushed up by the wind, limbs kicking and grasping and finding only wind and air. There was a high-pitched giggle in my ear.

Aeris.

His wind hit me, knocking me sideways off the path. I reached for the cliff face, caught nothing.

I couldn't believe this. My mind was a blank scream of terror and denial.

The pounding waves rushed toward me.

And then they didn't.

The same wind that had blown me off the trail now blew up from the sea. It caught me just as my feet broke the surface and flung me quickly up and over a towering wave. It pushed me toward the bluff, then dropped me unceremoniously back in the dirt, where I landed in a tangle of long, skinny limbs.

"Aeris!" I screamed, jumping to my feet. I pointed a trembling, furious finger at his nearly human form standing a few feet away. "You aren't allowed!"

"Not allowed to save a silly girl who falls into the water?" asked the spirit in an innocent tone. "Should watch your feet,

Mouse. What would have happened if Aeris had not been near?"

Aeris shuddered, his human form dissolving in a ripple into pure light, then rearranged into false flesh again.

"You nearly killed me, you wretched sprite!"

"Didn't," said Aeris.

"I'll tell Lord Prosper," I said. My voice shook with powerless rage. Aeris was always an irritation, but he'd never terrified me like this before. His binding shouldn't have allowed it. I might be the least important human on the island, but I was still a human. I started down the path, toward the big house.

"Oh, yes, go tell Lord Prosper," said Aeris. "Go tell the good, wise wizard how wicked Aeris almost hurt the dead steward's brat. Lord Prosper will care. Lord Prosper won't be angry that Mousy Mae comes into his magic room to tell tales on his loyal spirit."

Mousy Mae. I ground my teeth whenever Aeris said it. It was the perfect name for everything I feared I was and wished I wasn't.

"I told you never to call me that!"

And if I had magic, I could have made him obey.

Instead I stalked toward the house. But it didn't take long for my footsteps to slow. I had never interrupted Lord Prosper's magic before, and he did favor Aeris. He was the most humanlike of the spirits, the only one who showed will and intelligence, and despite binding Aeris, Lord Prosper allowed him a great deal of freedom.

But surely he would want to know if the spirit had tried to hurt a human, even if it was only me?

Perhaps he would. I closed my eyes and imagined myself climbing up the spiral stairs to the fifth floor, knocking on the deep-blue door. The perplexed look on Lord Prosper's face when he opened it. The long moment it would take him even to remember who I was, even though I was one of only five humans who lived on the island all year long. Even though I had lived there all my life. Even though I had never left, not even once.

I stopped walking. No. I was not going to tell Lord Prosper for the same reason I'd never asked him to train me in magic. I couldn't bear the look of pity he would give me, the kind words that would go along with it when he put me gently back in my place.

A soft breeze blew past me, raising the hairs on my arms. "There, there," said the spirit. "Aeris wouldn't have let you fall. Aeris is sorry to have frightened you."

"Don't do that again," I muttered.

"Aeris almost forgot," said the spirit, suddenly appearing in front of me. "Lady Vivian wishes to speak to Mousy Mae. She is in the house. In Lady Apollonia's room."

"What?" I asked. "Why?"

"Don't know," said Aeris. He shrugged, and his form blinked light at the motion. "Why would Lady Vivian want to speak to little Mae? Why would anyone? Who knows? Only Lady Vivian."

Aeris stood in front of me on the footpath. I could have gone around him, through the rock roses. I strode through him instead. Aeris's yelp of displeasure was worth the skin-crawling tingling that passed over me. The spirit dissolved back into light, then winked high above me.

"Wicked little mouse!" The spirit's voice was disembodied

now. It echoed through the air, then suddenly was small again, whispering in my ear.

"Mae should go around the back. Mae will see what Lady Vivian wants of her if she does."

I clapped my hands over my ears to push him out, but there was no need. He was gone.

CHAPTER TWO

I followed the dirt footpath that led to my cottage and tried to think of a single reason Lady Vivian would want to talk to me that would bode well. None came to mind. Instead, a host of possibilities that ranged from unpleasant to extremely worrying presented themselves. Lady Vivian might simply have some chore she wanted me to perform, something the spirits couldn't do. That happened once or twice a year, most recently when Ivo and I were still friendly and Lady Vivian thought I might convince him to write a letter to some archipelago girl she hoped he would marry. I didn't convince him, and he didn't marry her.

Or she might have found out about the dress I had nicked from the back of Apollonia's closet, to wear for First Night. Or worst of all, it was possible Lady Vivian had realized I had recently turned eighteen and the Prosper family's promise to my dead father that they would care for me until I came of age had expired. My pulse raced again. The thought was almost as terrifying as falling off that cliff.

I opened the door to the cottage and slammed it shut

behind me. I needed to change out of the ragged clothes I wore to run in before I could possibly face Lady Vivian and whatever she wanted me for. The cottage was two rooms: a larger living area, complete with a tiny kitchenette; a table and two chairs, only one of which was ever sat in now; several overstuffed bookcases; and the daybed that had been mine before my father died six years ago, and which I still slept on. My father's room contained a bigger bed, but I didn't use it. I didn't use the bedroom at all, except to store clothes in. I stepped in there now, shed my running things, and changed quickly into a pair of camel-colored trousers and a white button-down. Hand-me-downs from Coco, who never wore anything more than a few times. I was grateful for them, though Coco's style wasn't the one I would have liked for myself. I would rather have had Apollonia's cast-offs, but Apollonia wasn't generous enough to give away even what she no longer wanted.

I toweled off my damp hair and went back into the main room. I kept my training logs tacked to the wood-paneled wall, along with some of my favorite poems—copied out in my best penmanship—and assorted clippings from the Chelton School paper. All the Prospers went to Chelton, the most prestigious boarding school on the mainland, and Coco sent me the school newspaper. Officially, this was so I could compare my running scores to the best of the track team, but unofficially, the newspaper was my most engrossing entertainment when they were all away. I read anything about Miles and Coco, of course, but I also devoured the stories about Alasdair's polo victories, Apollonia's fashion glamor shots, the breathless tales of their social lives in the gossip pages. I wouldn't have admitted it, of course. Sometimes I imagined myself in similar stories. Wild horses couldn't have dragged *that* out of me.

I grabbed a stubby pencil from the table and hastily jotted down this morning's sprint times on the log, which hung beside a clipping of Miles. I lingered on it for a moment. It was an action shot from his last rugby game. He was running, a ball tucked under his arm, and a look of intense concentration on his extraordinarily handsome face. I let out a small sigh. No one had ever taken a picture of me when I was running, but if they did, I was sure I wouldn't look half so attractive as Miles did. Fortunately, Miles wasn't going to see me running tonight. He was going to see me cleaned up and glamorous.

But first, I had to see what Lady Vivian wanted. I took a deep breath and headed toward the big house. My feet fell into step with the air spirits' music. It came from their voices, I thought, but they sounded like a chorus of strings. Their song was gentle and quiet in the morning but with a slowly swelling energy that made you feel like getting up, getting going, doing something great. I wondered if Lord Prosper noticed that his magic music only seemed to work on me. His own grandchildren stayed stubbornly in bed.

I looked up and caught sight of the air spirits, just a streak of lavender against the pale blue horizon. The well spirits stayed at the wells. The house spirits went where you told them. But though their music was everywhere, the air spirits were always just on the edge of sight, fast and nearly free. No one's to command but Lord Prosper's. As soon as I saw them, they were gone again. I went on.

The footpath wound around toward the house from my cottage and led straight up to the front stairs, which rose in tiers to the front fountain. It burbled low now, the little aether-fueled jets rising only a little higher than my head. Tonight, at the party, those jets would cut high into the sky, and the spirits would fill them with glittering light to look like gigantic erupting champagne bottles. The fountain was the first thing the guests saw as they came up from the docks, and Lord Prosper like to make a good impression on First Night.

I stopped at the bottom of the stairs and looked up at the gleaming white house. Apollonia's room was on the third floor, facing the back balcony. It was beautiful, of course, like the rest of the house, but it was more than that, too. It was Apollonia's. It breathed out her perfume, her taste, her style. I had been in there before, though never by invitation. I wiped my damp hands against my pants.

Aeris had told me to go around the back to see what Vivian wanted. It wasn't wise to take advice from Aeris. I had eighteen years' worth of experience to tell me that.

Still, I needed any clues I could get about this summons, even if the clue came from Aeris. I did as he said and followed the footpath around the house. The back of the house was perhaps even more splendid than the front. Staircases curved down from balconies on each floor to a broad, beautiful terrace. Tonight it would be a dance floor, lit by spirits, filled with people who were here once a year and yet walked around like they had more right to it than I did. The richest, highest-class people from the mainland who didn't long for magical power, because they didn't need it. They had their places at the top in the world they came from. They were happy to take the island's magic—processed into aether— and add its clean, powerful energy to their luxurious lives.

Enjoy a magical party that commemorated its discovery. First Night.

Tonight, I had to do more than enjoy it.

I approached the back door with slow, quiet steps. No one appeared to be here, which for a moment sent my pulse racing, suspecting some trap of Aeris's. Then I saw him.

Ivo.

He stood with his back to me, facing an alcove under the sweeping staircase. He wore a suit coat that had been beautiful and new a couple of weeks ago yet somehow was already shabby. His hair was long, greasy, and unkempt. Lady Vivian would have to take him in hand before tonight. They couldn't have Lord Prosper's eldest grandchild and heir looking like an eccentric hobo, even if everyone already knew he more or less was.

I took a quiet step backward. I'd done my very best to avoid Ivo since our last conversation—if you could call it a conversation when one party had screamed furiously at the other, who had silently run away. I cringed, remembering it. I wish I'd at least managed to scream back.

It occurred to me that Lady Vivian might want help with Ivo. Again. My stomach clenched. Lady Vivian had seemed mildly pleased with the awkward, halting friendship that had started to form between Ivo and me those months ago. She had smiled when she saw us walking behind the house and hadn't complained when Ivo brought books to my cottage. Maybe Lady Vivian was under the impression that I might have some influence over her nephew. If so, then Aeris must not have told her about our near friendship's abrupt and decisive end.

I started to back away. Then I noticed.

Ivo's shoulders were hunched forward, as usual. He had terrible posture. But there was something strange about the way he was standing, so still, with his hands steepled over his nose and mouth. He was in silent distress, staring at something.

I couldn't help myself. I came up behind him, just close enough to see, and then I gasped.

It was one of the house spirits, lying in a dissolving pool of its own translucence, a faint purple puddle on the tiles. A breakfast tray lay beside it. The china cup had shattered, soaking the eggs and toast with chocolate.

Ivo whirled on me. I stepped back, instinctively, but forced myself to look at him. Not to quail quite so completely as I had the last time.

"Is it . . . ?" I asked.

Dead? But spirits couldn't die. Not even the small, silent house spirits, bound to their bodily forms. I had never heard of one even being injured or sick. And yet something was wrong with this one. It lay still, its gnomelike body leaking something soft and glowing, like liquid. I stepped closer and reached toward it.

Ivo seized my arm.

"Don't touch it!" he exclaimed.

I jerked my arm away, but he held me tight. His hand was unnaturally hot on my skin, almost burning. A jolt of fear shot through me.

"You have to tell Lord Prosper," I said.

"I know what to do," he said, but there was a flicker of doubt in his eyes. Like he didn't believe his own words. His breath smelled like metal, as though he'd just drunk a bowl of melted tin. The scent brought me back to that day in his shack, the last time he'd been this close.

My heart sped up. He didn't look quite as angry as he had those weeks ago. He had seemed even taller then, towering over me with magic sparking between his fingers and violence in his eyes.

"Let go," I said, as firmly as I could muster.

Ivo's face changed, and he let go, whipping away his hand like I was the one whose touch burned like fire.

"Just don't touch it," he said in a low, gruff voice. "Go."

I obeyed as quickly as I could without running.

"Wait—" commanded Ivo. I stopped. My hand shook on the doorknob. "Why are you going in there?"

"Aeris said Lady Vivian wants to speak to me."

Ivo opened his mouth to reply, then to my surprise, he flushed a dark crimson. He turned away, back to the puddled spirit.

I hurried into the house and up the servants' stairs. I saw two house spirits at the top of the third floor, carrying empty breakfast trays.

"Do you know your friend is sick?" I asked them.

The spirits looked up at me with no sign of understanding in their wide, vacant eyes. Sometimes, on First Night, I heard the guests exclaim at how odd the spirits' eyes were. Pale gold, and without pupils. I was used to them. They weren't odd to me, but they certainly weren't human, either.

I spoke to the spirits sometimes, usually deep in winter, when the days were short and it seemed an empty age until Coco and the others would come home for First Night in the spring, and then for summer break. I had to be very lonely indeed to find any comfort in their blank attention. And yet there were times when theirs was the only attention I could command.

"Is that what it looks like when you die?" I asked.

They said nothing, of course. Aeris was the only spirit on the island who spoke, and talking to him was like trying to argue with the cruelest thoughts in your own head. When I spoke to the other spirits, it was only to hear the sound of my own voice and imagine someone listening. I didn't think about them much; no one did, except visitors. Mainlanders. People who weren't used to their shimmering, translucent bodies and silent stares. They were dim and empty and unchanging. Perhaps that was why the broken spirit on the terrace affected me so. It was the only time I ever saw a house spirit do anything unexpected.

They stared at me, waiting for an order. I tried giving them one.

"Nod your head if you can die," I said.

The spirits didn't move. I hadn't really expected them to.

I sighed. "Go. Go do whatever you were doing."

They moved on, and I continued down the hallway. I passed Coco's room and smiled. Empty still, but not for long. She would arrive later, probably around teatime.

I stopped in front of Apollonia's door and stared absently at the multitone wood, cut into rising triangles, like a star bursting upward. I wiped my damp hands on my trousers and tried to arrange my mind into a subservient blank. Lady Vivian preferred me that way, as close to a house spirit as I could manage to make myself. I knocked.

"Come in," called Lady Vivian.

Walking into Apollonia's room was like walking into my

own fantasy: the room was all sunlight, glinting metal, and cloudlike fabrics. It smelled like Apollonia's ruinously expensive French perfume and like the sea breeze that came in through the wide French doors, thrown open to the balcony. Lady Vivian stood fussing with a sumptuous bouquet beside Apollonia's morning table, a particular object of my desire. It was wasted on Apollonia, who received many letters but returned few of her own. They were always hastily scrawled, short, and probably trivial. Romantic rejections, I imagined, or gossipy little notes. If I had Apollonia's life and anyone to write to other than Coco, I would sit at that beautiful table for hours. I would write lovely letters on that creamy, thick stationery in my well-practiced script. They would be full of careful observations and literary allusions. Once I was a trained magician, initiated into the secrets the Prospers kept so well hidden, perhaps I would get letters from the universities on the mainland. They would beg me to tell them what I had learned. Coco told me there were whole academic disciplines dedicated to studying the island from afar. Departments of Spiritology. Books trying to explain why magic only existed here, and to a lesser degree, on the few islands close by. Dissertations on aether: what it was, why it could only be found on the island, and how it could provide power a hundred times more efficient than oil, gas, or coal, without any smoke or dirt. All that speculation, all that work, and none of them really knew.

But I wouldn't tell them. If Lord Prosper told me his secrets and trusted me to keep them, I would. To the grave.

"Oh, Mae," said Lady Vivian. Before she married Stephen, Lord Prosper's second son, Lady Vivian had been the most beautiful debutante of her year on the mainland. She was still lovely in late middle age, always elegantly dressed, with luminously pale skin and long dark hair knotted elaborately behind her head. Lady Vivian had been quite irritated when mainlander ladies conceived a fashion for short, blunt bobs. She had forbidden Apollonia from cutting her hair, which meant that Apollonia surely had. "Thank you for coming. I thought you might be able to help me with something."

She smiled at me—not a particularly genuine smile, but pleasant enough. Wearing it, she looked a little less like Apollonia. The tension in my chest loosened by a fraction.

"Of course, Lady Vivian," I said. I trained my eyes on the stenciled wood floor. The intricate pattern of gold lines pulsed ever so slightly with a faint light, as though the floor were breathing. It was spelled with some kind of protection, though what kind, I didn't know. It didn't protect against the steward's daughter sneaking in and taking a torn dress, though. I did know that much.

Lady Vivian walked to the closet and opened it, revealing a silk dress the color of champagne hanging from the back of the door. I had spent my life admiring and envying Apollonia's clothes. They were always impeccably made, impeccably fashionable. They were things I had never known to want until I saw them and realized I wanted that, and nothing else would do. It wasn't just that Apollonia bought only the very best and the most expensive. She found the most beautiful thing, but no one realized it was the most beautiful until she put it on. She did it every season, and every season all the rich mainland girls hurried to add Apollonia's latest look to their wardrobe.

This was Apollonia's wedding dress. I couldn't stop myself from gasping.

Lady Vivian touched the fabric with a light finger, a slight smile on her face.

"Yes, beautiful, isn't it?" she asked.

It was a thin, tight sheath of pale golden silk, overlaid with a drape of shimmering lace. The lace hung down in loose, fluttering sleeves and cut into a deep V in front. A silk sash was tied around the waist, inlaid with sparkling clear stones that looked like actual diamonds.

"Oh," I breathed. "It's . . ."

"You're about her size," said Vivian. "Help me see how it looks on."

"On . . ." My mind went blank. "On . . . me?"

"Yes, my dear," said Lady Vivian with a smile. "You don't mind putting on a dress every once in a while, do you? Or are you like Cordelia—mortally opposed to any clothing you can't scramble up rocks in?"

"No, ma'am," I said, flushing red. "But—Apollonia's wedding dress—"

As much as I longed to try it on, I couldn't help quailing a little. Once, when we were children, Lady Vivian had given me a doll Apollonia had thrown away. It was a few months after my father had died, when Lady Vivian was still maudlin enough over it to pay me a few small kindnesses. The doll was beautiful, porcelain with shiny black hair and silk dresses. I'd never had a toy so lovely. I took her everywhere and was even unwary enough to let Apollonia see me with her once. She took the doll from my hands and threw her over the cliff, into the sea.

"You don't think she will mind?"

"Oh, certainly she would," said Vivian. "We simply won't tell her."

I stared in disbelief. Was it some kind of trap? Lady Vivian had never shown this degree of interest in me before. She had never asked me questions about what I liked, or offered to let me wear anything of Apollonia's, or proposed that we keep a secret together. Something was definitely wrong. But not so wrong that I could resist a chance to wear Apollonia's wedding dress, even just for a few moments.

Lady Vivian snapped, and two house spirits appeared. I hastily unbuttoned my shirt and stepped out of my pants. At Lady Vivian's command, one of the spirits lifted the gown from the hanger and slipped it over my head. I shivered at the silken touch of the fabric. The other spirit tied the diamond-inlaid sash around my waist. Lady Vivian looked me over with half a smile.

"Lovely," Lady Vivian said and gestured to an ornate standing mirror in the corner. I turned to it.

Longing shot through my body like a fast-acting poison. Even with my wind-burned cheeks and messy brown hair, I looked like another person in this dress. I had never worn anything so beautiful and couldn't imagine I ever would again. But it fit me perfectly. It was almost cruel that Apollonia and I should be precisely the same size, when our lives and our futures were so different.

"You're almost Apollonia's age, aren't you?" asked Lady Vivian.

"Not . . . not quite," I said. My palms started to sweat. Lady Vivian didn't seem to have called me here to discuss my eighteenth birthday and whether I should leave. I had never dared to ask, and none of the older Prospers had ever mentioned it. For all I knew, they would put me on a boat to the mainland tomorrow, though it was much more likely that they wouldn't do anything at all because they had no idea when my birthday was. They would figure it out soon enough, but I didn't want Lady Vivian to stumble on the information.

Lady Vivian nodded and smiled at my reflection. "You'd like to get married, wouldn't you?"

I started and stared at Lady Vivian in alarm. I caught myself quickly and lowered my gaze. But too late—she had noticed.

"Oh, my dear! You needn't be worried," she said. "If you feel what I suspect you might feel, I wouldn't dream of telling anyone your secret. You might even confide in me. I could help you. I think we might have the same goal."

The same goal? My chapped cheeks flushed an even deeper red. How could Lady Vivian know how I felt about Miles? He and I had spent so little time together since the summer when we were ten, when his mother had left him on the island with no word of where she was going or if she would come back. Lord Prosper had sent him to boarding school on the mainland that fall, and since then, our friendship had slowly weakened until it consisted mainly of my secret longing from afar. Miles didn't come back for the summers anymore, just for First Night. And then, he seemed so distracted. He smiled at me if he saw me, but he never sought me out. If he remembered that summer fondly, scampering around the island and reading adventure stories in the sun, he didn't show it.

"The same . . . goal?" I asked. "I . . . I'm not sure . . ."

Unless . . . but it wasn't possible that Lady Vivian was talking about magic. Even if Ivo had told her that I'd been sneaking a look at his magic books, there was no chance Lady Vivian would want me to learn it. She would find it as impossible and insulting as Ivo did. No, she had to mean Miles. My eyes went back to the mirror and the wedding dress.

Did Lady Vivian want me to marry Miles?

Hope thrilled through me, in spite of myself. I could hardly dare to believe it, and yet what else could she mean? It wasn't impossible. Miles was a Prosper grandchild, true, but he was the least of them. Almost an outcast, with his wild, unmarried mother and his anonymous father. And Miles hadn't been born on the island, so he wasn't entitled to the full Prosper inheritance. Even with Lord Prosper for a grandfather, none of the families who lived on the nearby islands would be keen to offer their daughters to an illegitimate, half-rich grandson. He was the only Prosper who knew some small part of what it was like to be me, to belong here and yet not belong. I met Vivian's knowing smile, eyes wide.

I was suddenly, viscerally reminded of the time when I was eleven and Apollonia had told me Alasdair was sweet on me. She'd even faked a letter in his handwriting.

"Perhaps you've guessed that we face some difficulties in arranging a match for him." Vivian's smile vanished, replaced with a hard look that was more like her. "Even with all that the other island families owe my dear father-in-law, still they act as though they would be doing us a favor by marrying his grandson! If Lord Prosper asked me, I'd tell him to stop their allowances of aether for a few months and see how haughty they are then. None of them would have anything but the fumes of magic if Lord Prosper hadn't been brave enough to make a way here. All they did was stay back and wait while he did the hard work."

Lady Vivian was working herself up into a rant, one I'd

heard many times before. It never ceased to infuriate her that the families on the few nearby islands didn't acknowledge her unquestioned superiority over them, as mistress of the island where all the magic originated. She was certainly right that they gained their wealth from Prosper generosity. The spirits made the aether here, and Lord Prosper distributed it to the other island families in raw form for processing and sale on the mainland. Before Lord Prosper came to this island and tamed the spirits, this had been a place no one dared to come, even though the little magic that filtered to the other islands came from here.

Lady Vivian sighed deeply.

"Unfortunately he is even harder to please than they are," she said. "He won't accept any of the other island families' daughters."

"Have you been trying to arrange his marriage?" I asked. It seemed soon. Miles was only just eighteen, and though Apollonia was going to be wed at that age, the other grandsons weren't engaged. Alasdair was twenty and officially unattached, though there were probably many girls who imagined otherwise. And, of course, Ivo wasn't married, though he was nearly twenty-five.

"Oh, yes," said Lady Vivian. "He needs a wife—I'm sure you see that. We worry about him. He is so unsociable and, well . . . to be frank, so unhappy. But you don't mind, do you?"

I didn't mind. Miles was reserved and gloomy, yes. Always angry, like one more insult would push him over the edge. They never did, though. Not that I had seen.

"No," I said. "I don't mind."

"And he likes you very much, we have all noticed that," said Lady Vivian.

I shot another startled glance at her. "You have?"

"Of course!" she exclaimed. "Now, my dear, don't get your heart too set on the idea just yet. I haven't spoken to Lord Prosper about it. He might take a little convincing. Ivo is his grandson and heir, after all. But you're the only name we've given Ivo that he's even considered. And we do owe him so much."

Lady Vivian kept talking. My face still burned but for a different reason now.

Ivo. Of course. They wanted me to marry Ivo. Not Miles.

"Once I thought of it, it makes perfect sense. You've always been just a little . . . Oh, how should I put it . . . A little 'at loose ends' here, since your father died." My mouth twitched as I tried to hold back a sob of mortification, but Vivian continued, heedless, "Your role has never been very well defined, has it? I suppose that's our fault—we should have put more thought into it. And you're not a child anymore, are you? It's not right for you to keep spending your days scampering over the island with nothing to do."

I shook my head. I wasn't a child. And Vivian was right. Eventually, whether they knew my birthday or not, they would realize I had grown up. I did need my own role on the island. Or else I needed to leave. I wasn't like the Prosper grandchildren. They could leave for school, for parties, even for marriage, and then come back. They could always come back, because the island was theirs. It belonged to them, to all of them. They took it for granted, even Miles.

It wasn't so simple for me. They had gone away to their

mainland boarding schools while I stayed behind. The island was all I knew. And yet unlike them, if I left, I might never be able to return.

But Ivo.

The things that bothered everyone else about him didn't bother me. I didn't much mind his odd habits or unkempt appearance, the way he stalked around the island when he wasn't closeted away performing the island's magic with Lord Prosper. I didn't mind the little things he collected in his little hut behind the hill or that he preferred to spend his time in that dirty hovel rather than in the big, luxurious house. It wasn't that he glowered at everyone he saw. None of that really bothered me when we started becoming friends a few months ago. That strangeness wasn't all there was to him. He was interesting, sometimes. He read books, different ones than I did. History and political theory. The few times I'd gotten him talking about them, it had surprised me how thoughtful he was.

But Ivo wasn't just odd and quiet. He was dangerous. I thought of his hand on my arm, how unnaturally hot it had been. He always smelled strange. Not unwashed or dirty as you would have expected, but worse. Wrong. Like metal, chemicals, or sometimes, horribly, like blood. I had seen him truly violent only once, throwing Alasdair against a tree with an outstretched hand and a fiery blaze in his eyes. He had screamed when he did it, his head thrown back, as though it hurt him more than it hurt Alasdair. Though it couldn't have. He broke three of Alasdair's ribs and might well have done more if Lord Prosper hadn't intervened. That was two years ago. I had let myself forget about it until the day he found me in his shack, and I was sure he would do the same to me.

Ivo was strange, powerful, and prone to anger. I could have accepted any one of those traits separately, but together? I thought of the broken spirit he'd been standing over. He must have been the one to do that. No one else on the island had that power and that rage.

I looked at Lady Vivian. Her eyes were narrowed slightly.

"What is it, my dear?" Vivian's smile was thinner now. I wasn't acting as delighted as I should have. I opened my mouth to say I wouldn't marry Ivo, but other words emerged.

"I saw something strange, before." My breathing had become shallow. "On the terrace, on my way here. It was—it was—well—"

"Yes?" Lady Vivian prompted, all warmth gone from her voice.

"Ivo was standing over a house spirit who was . . . it was . . . there was something wrong with it. I think it was dead."

"That's impossible," said Lady Vivian. "Spirits don't die."

"It was either dead or very sick," I continued. "It was . . . leaking."

"What?" snapped Lady Vivian.

"I don't know what it meant, Lady Vivian, but I thought I should tell you."

Lady Vivian narrowed her eyes and frowned.

"Take the dress off," she said. The spirits flew at the sash and buttons, and in half a moment, they lifted it over my head and handed the beautiful gown to Lady Vivian. I hurriedly put on my clothes again.

"I shall have to go tell Lord Prosper about the spirit, though if what you say is true, he probably already knows." Lady Vivian fixed a hard look on me. "While I'm there, I'll speak to him about what we have discussed here."

I meant to say no. I meant to tell Lady Vivian she had made a mistake and that I would never marry Ivo.

Instead my head went up and then down in a submissive nod.

Sometimes I hated myself.

Lady Vivian gestured to the door in dismissal, and I left Apollonia's room.

I closed the door behind me and let out a long, shuddering breath. I clapped my hand over my mouth to keep any sounds of distress from emerging. Lady Vivian might be listening. Something turned over in my stomach, and for a moment, I thought I would be sick on the polished parquet floor.

The sun was scarcely up, and yet somehow tonight had already gone completely awry.

I had just agreed to marry the wrong Prosper.

CHAPTER THREE

Lady Vivian, I will not marry Ivo.

It shouldn't have been difficult. This was my own life, after all, my own future. Any of the heroines in the many novels I read would have been brave enough to say no to a marriage she didn't want or at least say yes for reasons of her own, not simply because she couldn't bring herself to refuse.

And if I couldn't quite muster bold defiance, I could at least have managed an apologetic refusal.

I'm sorry, Lady Vivian, but I cannot marry Ivo.

Would that have been so hard?

I stared behind me, up the stairs, and thought about going back. I tried to imagine myself saying the words and the look on Lady Vivian's face. My heart sank.

Perhaps it shouldn't have been so hard. Maybe it wouldn't have been for someone else, someone who hadn't lived their whole life on the edges of Prosper benevolence. But I couldn't make myself take a single step back toward her.

I went out the back stairs, my face flaming with shame, past where the broken spirit had been. It was gone now, along with the translucent puddle that had oozed from it. Ivo was gone. I looked up toward the fifth floor, where Lord Prosper's magic room was. A window was open, and I heard voices filtering down—Lord Prosper's and Ivo's.

What if he had killed that spirit? The possibility suddenly seemed more likely than not. Maybe he had tried some new magic on it, testing out its strength. It might have been an accident.

Or it might not.

I would prove it. I would find out what he did and why, and I would tell Lord Prosper. They couldn't expect me to marry him if I proved he was a murderer.

Could they? I wasn't certain. Come to think of it, I wasn't sure Lord Prosper would consider the killing of a house spirit to be murder. He would be alarmed, surely, but perhaps only because it was supposed to be impossible. It was as Lady Vivian had said: spirits didn't die.

Murder or not, it was wrong. I hurried past the pool and out along a path that led to the interior of the island. If I could prove it, it wouldn't be the same as refusing outright. I would have something solid I could point to, something that he did that wasn't about me. Something other than, *But I'm afraid of him, and actually I'm in love with Miles.*

I definitely wasn't going to say that.

I followed the footpath up into the hills behind the house. They were lush and green now after the winter rain, covered in soft spring grass. In another month or two, the grass would be scorched gold by the sun. I didn't mind that. Every season on the island was beautiful in its own way, but spring was my favorite. It was the green season, the season of First Night.

The magic was thickest around First Night, and lately, it was the only season when Miles came home.

The path wound between and behind the hills, and I followed it until the house was out of sight. Ahead of me, the faint plume of yellow smoke rose from the aether wells. I'd never been able to get into them. There was magic that pushed me away, even curious as I was. From outside the gate, I'd heard nothing but strange, eerie silence. The spirits made no sound as they went about their work, and there were no birds or lizards or crickets there. Like me, they were kept away. It smelled wrong, too. Like metal and magic. Like Ivo.

But they made the aether. And aether was the source of the enormous Prosper fortune. It was the reason anyone lived on the island at all.

I left the path and cut directly up a hill, following a stretch of trodden grass to a shack at the top. When I reached the crest of the hill, I turned and looked back toward the house and the sea. I had been up to Ivo's shack twice before, once by invitation, and once not. But I had never lingered outside it long enough to notice everything he could see from here. Bits of the trails I ran along branched off in several different directions. To the west of the big house was an oak tree I liked to sit in and watch the sea, and not too far inland from that was the cottage where I lived. I could even see the patch of grass behind the cottage where I lay reading through many empty hours of the day.

From here, Ivo could have watched me live most of my life, and I would never have known it.

I shivered.

Maybe Lady Vivian was right. Maybe Ivo really did have

feelings for me. He had a strange way of showing it, if he did. But then, Ivo *would* have a strange way of showing that. And if he wanted this marriage, how could I refuse? Ivo wasn't the most favored grandchild. He didn't sparkle and shine in society like the others. He didn't have their glamor or assurance. But he was the most needed. They tried to keep him happy. When Lord Prosper was gone, Ivo would be the only one who could do the magic. And they needed the magic. Without the magic, there would be no aether. The Prospers had a very good reason to give Ivo what he wanted.

I would need a very, very good reason to say no.

I scanned the footpath one last time. It was empty. Ivo would still be in the big house for most of the morning, working the magic with his grandfather. Though you could never be quite certain what Ivo would do or where he would show up. I glanced around nervously. The second to last thing I wanted— just before having to marry Ivo—was for him to find me sneaking around his shack again. I would have to work quickly.

I pushed the door of the shack open, took one step, and froze.

Miles stood in front of me, his arm raised. There was a gun in his hand and violence in his eyes.

We stared at each other, not breathing. The violence changed to surprise.

I hadn't seen him in a year. He was a little taller, a little broader. His curly black hair was longer and messier, and his well-tailored clothes were rumpled, like he'd slept in them. There were dark shadows under his deep-brown eyes.

He was still beautiful. More beautiful. I hadn't thought that was possible.

"Miles," I whispered. I reached out and pushed the gun gently away so it wasn't aimed at me. I knew he wouldn't use it, but the sight of it aimed in my direction still sent a bolt of terror through me.

"Mae?" he asked. His perfect, tanned face creased in confusion. "What—what are you—?"

"I'm—what are *you*—?"

"I was just—"

Miles slowly lowered the gun and stared down at it as if he hadn't realized what he was holding. I tore my eyes away from Miles and scanned the room quickly. It was a mess. Stacks of books lined the walls. A table pushed against the wall was covered in little piles of moss and seaweed. Several long pieces of rope were coiled in the corner. I didn't want to think about what those were for.

"I came to look for . . . something," I said. Now that I tried to put it into words, I wasn't exactly sure what I had hoped to find. What kind of proof of Ivo's wrongdoing did I think would present itself here? I was having a hard time putting my thoughts together. My heart thundered distractingly in my ears, whether from the terror of finding the gun pointed at me or the nervous pleasure of seeing Miles, I wasn't sure. "Ivo . . . did something. Or, I think he did. I guess I was hoping there might be proof here."

"Did something?" Miles looked up at me sharply. Violence sparked in his eyes again. "Ivo did something to you?"

"No, not to me," I said hastily. "I saw him near a house spirit that was . . . well . . . I think it was dead."

"Dead?" asked Miles. "But spirits—"

"Don't die," I finished. "I know. But something was wrong

with it. It wasn't moving. It looked—" I gestured helplessly. "It looked dead."

Miles frowned and looked back down at the gun in his hand.

"So . . ." I opened my mouth to ask what he was doing here, then closed it. There seemed to be a pretty obvious explanation for why Miles was here. Why would he stand in Ivo's shack with a gun pointed at the door and a murderous look on his face? But I couldn't think of a way to ask him about it other than, *So . . . why do you want to kill Ivo?* And I couldn't just say that.

". . . the gun?" I said instead. It wasn't a great deal better.

Miles looked away, a slight blush darkening his cheeks.

"I have some questions to ask Ivo about my mother," he muttered. "The gun was to make sure he answered truthfully."

I nodded. "But . . . he could just use his magic to take the gun from you."

"Ivo isn't the only one with magic," said Miles. He switched his gun to his right hand and reached with his left toward one of Ivo's stacks. Books scattered around the room, flying open, landing on their spines or open faces. One of them flew toward Miles, who barely caught it. I gasped, and Miles looked quite surprised as well.

"Whoa," he said, staring down at the book in his hand.

"How . . . ?" My voice came out a rough whisper. "How did you learn to do that?"

"Last time I was here, I stole a book out of Grandfather's library," he said. "When we were here last spring. I practiced this spell for hours, but it didn't work this well."

I stared at him, my mind racing. Here it was, the first step of my plan, already successful before I even knew it. Miles wanted to learn magic. He might already be planning to ask Lord Prosper to train him.

Miles put the gun into a leather satchel and then reached toward a thermos on the moss-covered table. It flew into his hand.

Miles had done it. A thing I'd dreamed of and schemed for and not yet managed.

"Does Lord Prosper know you can do magic?" I asked.

Miles let out a small sigh. The bravado went out of his posture like air.

"I can do one spell," he said. "It's not much, really. I haven't told him yet."

I recognized the hesitation in his voice. I didn't have to ask why he hadn't told him.

Lord Prosper hadn't taught any of his grandchildren magic except Ivo. He had tried Alasdair, but Alasdair was a terrible student. I could easily imagine how he had sulked, whined, and generally refused to learn. The rest of them never got a chance. Lord Prosper didn't say why, exactly, as far as I knew. But it wasn't hard to speculate. Apollonia and Coco were girls. Miles was illegitimate. No one seemed to question it.

Except Miles, it seemed.

"I want to learn, too," I said.

The statement jumped from my lips before I had time to consider it, like my mouth was braver than I was.

Miles looked at me, surprised.

"Still?" he asked.

Still. I couldn't calm my racing mind enough to answer right away. That single word showed so much. It showed that he remembered our summer together, well enough to remember what I'd confided to him.

And it showed what he thought of it. His surprise that I was still holding on to this childish dream. My desire to do magic was something I should have outgrown by now. I shouldn't want to learn it, still.

Even though he did.

"Yes." I was pleased to hear my voice was calm and steady. "Still."

Miles looked at me thoughtfully, like I'd said something worth considering. Something that gave him pause. Hope swelled in my chest. I'd planned to be wearing a pretty dress when Miles noticed me. Maybe do something different with my hair. But here he was, noticing me, despite my trousers and tangled curls. The next step in my plan. I met his eyes and tried to look serious. Like someone he could take with him to ask Lord Prosper for what we both wanted.

Then he raised his eyebrows and took a swig from his thermos.

"Good luck," he said, a bitter smile twisting his beautiful mouth.

My mind went white. My hopes crashed and then cowered, ashamed of themselves for ever having been.

Good luck. There was even more in these words. Rejection. Disbelief, not just that I would succeed but that I even dared aspire to it.

I swallowed down hard and blinked harder. I had to wipe the pain off my face, quickly, before he could see it.

But Miles wasn't looking. He set his thermos down on the table. I knew he didn't drink coffee, so it must have been full of alcohol. Miles turned his attention to the book in his hand.

It was leather bound and handwritten. Ivo's journal. I'd often seen him write in it—not the way I did, carefully and slowly, like I was thinking something out, but hastily. Like there was something he had to write down before he forgot.

I didn't know what he wrote in it, but I knew it mattered to him. Seeing the journal in Miles's hands made mine itch with nervousness.

"This is in code," Miles muttered, flipping through the rough-cut pages.

"You should put that back. He'll notice you took it."

"You seem to know a lot about him," said Miles. He looked at me again, eyes slightly narrowed. Suspicious. The thought occurred to me, sudden and horrifying, that he might somehow know I'd agreed to marry Ivo. But no. He couldn't. Could he?

"There aren't many people on this island most of the time," I said, ignoring the slither of shame snaking down my spine. "And I pay attention."

"Then what can you tell me about him? That I don't already know?"

"I don't know what you know," I said slowly.

"You told me about the spirit you think he killed, but has he ever tried to hurt . . ." Miles hesitated, his mouth forming a word that didn't emerge. ". . . anyone else?"

"There was that time he threw Alasdair into a tree," I said. "Broke his ribs."

Miles nodded and looked impatient. "Yes, but anyone would throw Alasdair into a tree if they could. I meant . . ." He looked away then back up at me. "Has he ever hurt you?"

It had hurt a little when Ivo grabbed my arm that morning. But that didn't answer the strangely intense, furtive look in Miles's eyes.

"Not really," I said. "No."

Miles stared at me another moment. When he looked away, it was almost as if I'd disappointed him. My stomach squirmed. I had a sudden, insane wish that Ivo had done something to me worth mentioning to Miles, though I wasn't sure what, exactly, he had in mind.

"I thought he would once," I blurted out.

I had his attention again. Miles's gaze fixed on me expectantly. I savored it, even while the unpleasant memory clawed its way to the front of my mind.

"It was here, actually." I glanced around the room, remembering. "I was . . . well . . ."

Snooping was the most accurate word. Ivo had loaned me books before but not his magic books. And he'd glowered so fiercely the one time I'd mentioned borrowing one that I hadn't dared ask again. But I knew he kept some in his shack, though he'd moved them all back to Lord Prosper's library since that day.

"I wanted to read his spell books," I said. "I knew he wouldn't let me, so I came up when I thought he was sleeping."

"But he found you?" Miles asked.

"Yes."

I cringed at the memory: how he had thrown the door open, ripped the book from my hands with magic, and hurled it against the wall. The look in his eyes was just like the day he'd thrown Alasdair against the tree.

"What did he do?" Miles asked.

"Just . . . yelled," I said. Though that didn't really cover it. I had never been yelled at like that before. If there was a word for a kind of yelling that felt like taking a beating, I would have used that instead. "He was *so* angry."

"What did he say?"

I didn't remember the specifics, but the general idea had been burned into my heart.

"To stay away from his magic books," I said. "And that magic isn't for me."

As if I didn't already know. Even Miles thought it was absurd that I thought they might teach me. Learning magic was the special realm of Prospers—and not even all Prospers. Male Prospers. Male Prospers born to the right fathers.

I was so far from that, I might as well have been a spirit.

Miles frowned. He was a Prosper, but still he'd had to steal a book to learn a spell instead of learning real magic from his own famous grandfather. He stared at me another moment, as if expecting more, and then looked back down at the journal.

"What did you want to ask Ivo about your mother?" I asked.

Miles looked back at me blankly.

"You said . . . Ivo . . ." My throat closed on the explanation. I'd known it would be hard, reminding Miles that we'd been close once, never mind making him feel for me some part of what I felt for him. But this was even harder than I expected.

"Oh. Yes. There's something I—I think he might have done to her. I have to ask him."

I blinked. That sounded ominous and unlikely.

"Why don't you ask your mother?" I asked.

"She left a few months ago. Wasn't there when I went home from school. The landlord said she hadn't left any word."

"Doesn't she do that, sometimes?" I asked. From what I

could tell, Imogen was always disappearing. She'd run away from the island and had Miles when she was younger than me and hadn't settled down anywhere for longer than a few months since.

"She always tells me where she's going," said Miles. "Or, she always has before now."

"Oh," I said. "I'm sorry."

Miles tucked the journal into his satchel and looked around the room with distaste. He picked up a small, polished skull and frowned at it.

"Is this a rat?" he asked. "Do you think he killed it himself?"

"I don't think you should take Ivo's journal," I said again. "He'll be back from Lord Prosper's study soon. He'll notice it's gone."

"You're afraid of him," said Miles, looking at me. "Why are you afraid of him if he's never hurt you?"

The answer to this was so obvious that it took a moment to find words for it.

"Because he could," I said.

"Yes, he could," said Miles with a frown. "Do you think he's on the fifth floor now?"

"Yes," I said. "They usually spend most of the morning there, doing magic."

"How do you know they're doing magic?" asked Miles. "Do you watch them?"

I used to, when I was much younger. The magic room was topped with a glass dome, and I would sometimes climb onto the roof and peer in the top. But I didn't do it anymore.

"No," I said, shaking my head. "No."

Miles shouldered the satchel. "I'm going to."

He walked past me, out of the shack. I followed. Dread pooled in my stomach, slowing my movements. I forced my legs into a run. I was a good runner—better than good. But just now I could barely jog.

"It's not a good idea," I said, catching up to him on the footpath. He didn't slow down.

"Everyone knows there is something wrong with him, but no one will say it. It's not right."

"Miles—" My breath was short. It wasn't from the running. I ran every day, sometimes the whole length of the island. I felt ill. Something was wrong. Really, really wrong. "Don't climb up there. Don't watch them. Don't."

Miles didn't respond, except by walking faster. I stopped and bent over, breathing hard, panic flaring up above the pain. My stomach had started to churn. When I forced myself upright, Miles had disappeared down the path. I swallowed hard against my nausea and hurried after him.

CHAPTER FOUR

I caught up with Miles when he had almost reached the house. He approached it from the east side, the side with the tallest trees and the branches that hung over the fifth-floor roof. Those were the trees I had climbed. The ones I didn't climb anymore.

Miles started up the tree, but I couldn't follow him. My legs melted beneath me, and I dropped to my knees, gasping for air and fighting not to vomit. Miles stopped climbing and looked down at me.

"Mae?" he asked. "Are you all right?"

I shook my head. I was shaking all over and afraid. Desperately afraid. Something was terribly wrong with me. I cast about for explanations—maybe I'd run too much this morning. I hadn't eaten. I tried to believe it was something as simple and comforting as that. But I knew it wasn't. I fell forward onto my hands. Miles touched my forehead gently, and I was too terrified to enjoy it.

"I don't know," I gasped. "I feel sick. I don't know . . . I don't know what's wrong with me. I'm sorry . . ."

"It's okay," he said. "Let's get you up."

He lifted me to my feet. I could barely stand. He slung my arm over his shoulders, put another around my waist, and walked us away from the trees.

As we walked away, the nausea slowly started to ease. My legs became steadier under me, but Miles didn't let go. By the time we reached the garden behind the swimming pool, I had almost forgotten all the horrible feelings that had been so overwhelming only minutes before. There was a fuzzy kind of confusion in my head. I wasn't sure if it was from the strange sickness or Miles's side pressed against mine, his arm around my waist. He lowered me onto a bench and sat beside me.

"Do you feel better?" he asked.

I nodded. "Much better, thank you."

Miles looked at me thoughtfully and pressed his thumb to his lower lip. It was a mannerism of his that I had always particularly loved. He was the only person I had ever seen do it, and I loved everything that set Miles apart from the other Prospers. His absent father, his difficult mother, all the little slights the other Prospers sometimes gave him.

"I think we should tell Grandfather about this," Miles said. "Something wasn't right about that."

"About what?" I asked.

Miles stared at me. His high forehead creased slightly in concern.

"About how sick you just felt," he said slowly.

"Oh."

I nodded, to cover my confusion.

Yes, of course. I remembered it now. I'd felt very sick a moment ago, but I was better now.

"I think I just need something to eat," I said. "I didn't have breakfast."

Miles squinted a little, skeptically, and pressed his thumb to his lip again.

"Hmm," he said. "Maybe. But still, I'd feel better if we told Grandfather about it."

I could hardly say no to that. I would have done just about anything to make Miles feel better. And anyway, this feeling—Miles worrying about me—was too intoxicating to brush off lightly.

But the thought of going to Lord Prosper put a different worry in my head. What if Lord Prosper said something about my possible engagement to Ivo? I looked at Miles again. I should tell him now. I should have told him already, really, at the shack, when we were talking about Ivo. I half opened my mouth to say it, but the thought of telling Miles I had silently agreed to marry Ivo sent a twist of shame straight down my spine and into my toes. No, I would fix it myself, before he had to know.

Miles helped me to my feet, and we passed through the garden, its citrus trees and pink bougainvillea magically kept in constant bloom. We circled the pool and climbed two sets of curving stairs to the third-story balcony. I paused at the top. I wanted to prolong this impossible moment, when in the space of less than an hour, and without planning it, I'd made Miles care about me.

"What is it that you think Ivo did? To your mother?" I asked almost without thinking, just to hear him talk again. He turned, a forbidding look on his face.

"I—I'm sorry," I said. "You don't have to tell me if you don't want to."

Miles looked at me again. He hadn't looked at me this much in years, so perhaps it made sense that he seemed so perplexed by me, like he was figuring me out from scratch.

"Things are very different here than on the mainland." He stopped, pressed his thumb to his lip. "I'm not sure if I can explain the way my mother is . . ."

I swallowed. He thought I was sheltered, of course he did. And of course I was, but I had always done everything I could to make up for it.

"I read a lot," I said. "If it's in a novel, I probably know about it."

Miles frowned.

"They don't put everything in novels."

He turned back to the door and didn't try to explain any further.

We climbed the last two sets of stairs inside the house. The outside balcony stairs didn't go all the way to Lord Prosper's floor. By the bottom of the last stairway, a tight spiral that narrowed as it rose, we heard shouting. We hesitated outside the door.

"—have no reason to accuse him of this."

This was Lord Prosper's voice, tremulous but louder than I was used to hearing it, even through the door. Ivo spoke more quietly. We each leaned an ear against the door to hear him, spies by a shared instinct.

". . . have no reason to trust him," Ivo said. "You shouldn't allow it. She doesn't want to marry him. You don't know what else he will do if you let him into the family."

Miles raised an eyebrow at me in question.

"Rex," I mouthed at him. Apollonia's fiancé.

"Apollonia doesn't want to marry him?" Miles mouthed

back. I nodded, though I wasn't exactly sure. Over Christmas, I'd overheard Lady Vivian delicately suggesting that Apollonia could delay the wedding if she wished. Apollonia hadn't taken her up on it, though. She did treat Rex with a coldness that sometimes seemed like hatred, true. But she treated everyone that way.

"He's the only one besides us who could do it," said Ivo. "It's the only explanation!"

Instead of a response, I heard the sound of footsteps. Footsteps that were coming up behind us.

"Mae?"

Lady Vivian peeked her head around the stairway beneath us. She was whispering, apparently as little eager to be discovered as we were.

"Miles!" she whispered. "Come down here, both of you!"

We glanced at each other, then followed her down the stairs. She stopped on the landing, a turquoise-papered jewel box of a space, lit by the sun through a round window that opened onto the day like a porthole to the sea.

"What is this about?" Lady Vivian whispered, louder now. She didn't wait for a reply. "Is this about our conversation earlier, Mae dear?"

I stared at her. Panic blossomed in my chest. I glanced at Miles and started to shake my head, but Lady Vivian plowed on.

"But I've already taken care of that!" she said. "Lord Prosper has agreed to the match. The only question is when the wedding should be, but now is not the time to bother him with the details. If you pester him, he might change his mind altogether about allowing you to become his granddaughter-in-law!"

"His . . . what?" Miles asked, not bothering to whisper.

"Oh—no—" I took a step back, into the papered wall.

"Did she not tell you?" Lady Vivian asked. I kept shaking my head, but Vivian had a determined glint in her eyes. "She and Ivo are going to be married. Lord Prosper has given them his blessing."

CHAPTER FIVE

Miles drew back from me, eyes widening.

"You're going to marry him?" he asked. The disgust in his voice lodged like a bullet in my belly. I braced my hands on the wall behind me. I wanted to deny it, but the look on Lady Vivian's face silenced me. I stared at the ground instead.

"Congratulations," he muttered and started down the stairs.

"Miles," Lady Vivian called after him. "I haven't seen your mother yet—where is Imogen?"

"I don't know." He kept walking.

"What do you mean, you don't know?" Lady Vivian pressed. "She can't have gone very far since you arrived!"

"She didn't come with me," said Miles, without turning his head. "She's not coming at all. I haven't seen her in months."

Lady Vivian's mouth dropped open. She gaped after Miles in obvious alarm. She shook her head slightly, regaining control of her expression, and patted me lightly on the arm.

"Excuse me, dear. I must see what Miles means." She

started down the stairs after him. "Not coming at all. Surely not . . ."

I stood against the wall, listening to the skittish, wild sound of my heart thudding in my ears. My gaze went to the window and the sea beyond. I drew in a breath and let it go, then did it again. The sun shone down on the sea, turning it from the frothy gray of the sunrise into a sparkling blue. A sense of unreality had settled over me. This was all too much for a single day in my life, even the day of First Night. Since my fight with Ivo, weeks and weeks had gone by with nothing in them that I hadn't planned myself. Nothing more exciting than a longer run, faster sprint, or rereading a favorite book. Now there were all these revelations, fears, changes. My greatest hopes raised and immediately crushed. I needed someone to tell, someone who would know the right thing to say, and more important, could tell me what I had done wrong and how I could fix it.

Because I had to fix it. For part of an hour, Miles and I were friends again, on a mission together. It was too precious a thing to lose simply because I hadn't been able to tell Lady Vivian I didn't want to marry Ivo.

The door above creaked, and heavy footsteps echoed toward me. Ivo's. He wasn't a very large man, but every ounce of his weight seemed to fall when his feet did. I considered hurrying down the stairs ahead of him, but Lady Vivian's voice floated up, followed by Miles's reluctant response. I stood still, eyes glued to the window. He might walk past me without saying anything. That was what he usually did.

But Ivo's footsteps slowed a few steps before the landing.

"What are you doing here?" he asked.

I turned. His cheeks were flushed, and his eyes were

unusually bright. His shaggy brown hair fell into his face where it contrasted with his unkempt beard. I lifted my chin.

"I came to speak to Lord Prosper."

"Why?"

I had to stop and think about this. It had been Miles's idea, I remembered that much. Something to do with me, I thought, though it was hard to imagine what that might be.

I made something up.

"I had a question for him about—about what happened to the spirit."

"Oh," said Ivo. His shoulders lowered slightly, and he let out a long breath. "Never seen anything like it. Shouldn't be happening."

If he was responsible for whatever happened to the spirit, he was showing a surprising talent at hiding it. I had never seen Ivo lie, as far as I knew. The perplexity I had felt only a few hours ago—before Lady Vivian and the wedding dress, before Miles and the gun—came back.

"But what did happen?" I asked. "Was it dead?"

Ivo shook his head. "Not dead, but close to it. They could wake up." He scowled, like he hated the idea.

"They?" I repeated. "Are there others like that?"

He nodded. "At the wells."

The aether wells. It was a bigger problem than I'd known, then. The wells didn't produce aether without spirit labor. If enough of the spirits went sick, the wells might not work. And if the wells stopped producing—

"But why? Do you know?"

Ivo's scowl deepened, and I thought of what he'd said to Lord Prosper, about Rex. *He's the only one besides us who could do it. It's the only explanation!*

"Do you think . . ." I hesitated. Ivo looked angry enough to blow up any moment, but it didn't seem directed at me. I pressed my luck. "Do you think someone is doing something to them? Another magician?"

The frown lines on Ivo's face loosened, and he stared at me with a closer attention.

"Why're you asking about this?" Ivo asked. "What do you care what happens to them?"

"Of course I care." My heart beat faster at the challenge. "This is my home, too."

Ivo looked down at the ground and shook his head. He looked back up at me with a strange emotion on his face. It was sadness, almost—though that alone wasn't unusual for him. There was something wistful about it, too, and that I didn't understand.

"You live here," he said. "That doesn't mean it's your home."

It took a moment for the words to land.

"What?"

He didn't reply. Beneath my disbelief, fury gathered, rising up against my self-control.

It was what they thought, I knew that, but none of them had ever been cruel enough to say it in so many words.

"I've lived here all my life," I said, anger choking my voice. "I've never lived anywhere else. I care what happens here even if I'm not a—"

I caught myself before the name escaped my lips.

"A what?" asked Ivo. "A Prosper?"

Ivo hadn't moved, but he seemed closer now. I couldn't look at him. For just a moment, I had forgotten that I'd agreed to become a Prosper, even with the man I was supposed to marry standing a foot away. My anger dropped back into my stomach and became something squirming and shamed. I wanted to melt into the turquoise wall at my back.

I glanced up. He looked away as soon as my eyes found his.

"It's not your concern," he muttered and continued past me down the stairs.

As soon as he was out of sight, the anger returned. My breath came tight and shallow. A new, horrible thought occurred to me. What if this marriage was his idea and not Lady Vivian's at all? He knew I wanted to belong here. What if he threw it in my face to convince me to accept him? Did he really think he could shout and rage at me and then arrange with Lady Vivian to marry me? Without even asking me first?

I clenched my teeth so hard, my jaw ached. If that were true, it was obvious what kind of marriage he expected it to be. One where I did as I was told. Owed him everything. Left the magic, and the power, to him.

I waited on the landing, my breathing thinned out with anger, and gave them all enough time to move on before I went down. Even so, Vivian was at the foot of the stairs, pacing, a hand pressed to her mouth. She looked up at my approach, startled.

"Oh, Mae dear. It's you." She seemed to have entirely forgotten she had left me a few flights up and was quite likely to see me descending. "Have you—has Lord Prosper come down?"

"I don't think so," I said. "I didn't see him."

"Ah." Lady Vivian stared at me blankly for a moment, knitting her fingers together across her chest. "It's just—it seems Imogen—"

"Isn't coming," I said. "I know. Miles told me."

Lady Vivian's mouth worked silently.

"Yes," she said eventually. "Well, I should tell him."

I had never seen Lady Vivian like this. Anxious. Frightened, even. What did you have to be anxious about when you were richer than god, and in fact, god was your father-in-law?

Lady Vivian paused her pacing, then looked up the staircase with evident dread. She was definitely frightened, and all because Imogen wasn't coming to First Night.

It occurred to me that now was the time to tell her I wouldn't marry Ivo. She was distracted enough that she might not even react at first. I had let it go too far already. It wasn't going to get any easier to call it off.

I watched her pace. The moment stretched out, slow and viscous with my reluctance.

"Lady Vivian," I began.

She turned to me, and her anxious expression changed to a frown.

"Yes?"

All of a sudden, she didn't seem distracted at all. In fact the look on her face was so forbidding, I suspected she knew just what I intended to say.

"I—"

I didn't stop, exactly, I only hesitated. But Lady Vivian took the opportunity to break in.

"Actually, Mae dear, I do feel I should mention something to you." She took a step toward me and lowered her voice. "I know you're not used to giving much thought to what is appropriate to your station, and there has never really been any need for you to before. But now that you're engaged to Ivo, it's not seemly for you to run around the island with Miles, unchaperoned."

"Oh," I said. Heat rose in my cheeks. "We—we weren't exactly—"

Lady Vivian waved her hand in dismissal.

"I don't need excuses. You didn't know. But Ivo wouldn't be happy about it, you see. And after all—" She laughed a little, joylessly. "That's what this engagement is for. To make him happy."

"Ah," I said. My stomach turned over. "Well. I . . ."

"You do see, don't you, how important that is?" Lady Vivian pressed. She looked at me closely, eyes slightly narrowed. "And not simply for Ivo's sake! It would be very sad for all of us, I'm sure, if this didn't work out, and we had to say good-bye to you."

There it was. She'd come out and said it. Made it a threat, if not in so many words.

Marry Ivo. Make him happy. Or leave.

"We've grown very fond of you, dear," said Lady Vivian. She reached out to pat my arm. "None of us want to see you go."

I swallowed hard.

"I don't, either," I said. "Not at all."

That was all there was to say, which was just as well since my throat was too tight to force anything else out. I'd been right to be a coward and not to refuse. I looked at the ground and wished I could sink into it.

Then an unfamiliar sound cut through the ever-present susurrus of the waves and the delicate hum of the spirit music. It was loud and mechanical, and drawing nearer. Lady Vivian glanced at me, and we both hurried to see what was coming.

We ran through the cavernous entryway, down the front

stairs, and skidded to a halt on the marble-tiled dais before
the fountains, our faces turned up.

"It's an airplane!" said Lady Vivian, shading her eyes at
it with her hand.

The airplane was flying low and sinking fast. One wing
tilted down below the other, giving it a wild, out-of-control
look. The plane passed by the house with the roar of a conventional, non-aether engine—close enough for me to get a
glimpse of the pilot as she waved at me.

I groaned. "Coco."

"It's Cordelia?" asked Lady Vivian. "Where in the heavens did she get an airplane?"

I ran down the footpath after Coco and her madly tilting
aircraft. Coco would have to be making for the north beach,
since it was the only stretch of flat ground on the island long
enough to land on. I didn't like the look of her erratic flight
path. An unwelcome image of her crash-landing into a cliff
flashed in my mind, sending my heart into my throat.

The plane zoomed out far ahead, past the northern reaches
of the island. Then it turned around, making a jagged arc in
the sky and approaching the north side of the island at an even
lower height. My run turned to a sprint, and I cursed under
my breath. The last time I had seen Coco, she didn't know
how to fly. She couldn't have gained very much experience
landing one since then.

The plane passed low out of view. I braced myself for
an explosion or at least a column of smoke to rise up over
the tree line. There wasn't one, so the plane hadn't ignited,
at least, but it was still possible Coco had crashed. I didn't
slow my pace. My legs and arms pumped like a well-primed

engine, propelling me up the path like I practiced for this every day, which I did. Though I'd never imagined sprinting to see if my best friend had survived an airplane trip into the ocean.

I sped up on the final incline to the last grassy ridge overlooking the north beach nearly half an hour later and stopped, bent double, gasping for breath both from terror for Coco and from the sprint.

The airplane was parked quietly on the beach, propellers still, with long, deep tracks behind it and its wheels buried in mounds of churned-up sand. The glass roof over the cockpit was thrown open, and the plane itself was empty. Behind the plane, clothes, aviator goggles, and a leather jacket were discarded in a haphazard trail leading to the water. Coco emerged from under a frothy white wave in her underthings. She threw her arms above her head and let out a howl of pure exaltation, then dove under the surface again.

I straightened with a grin and a frustrated laugh. Coco was better than fine, as usual.

I scrambled down the ridge to the beach. I kicked off my shoes and peeled off my socks, slowing as I approached the water. I was warm enough from my run, but I knew what the ocean would feel like.

"Mae!" screamed Coco, emerging from under a wave. "Did you see me fly?!"

"I did!"

"Come on, Mae, swim with me!" Coco cried.

I reluctantly unbuttoned my shirt and stepped out of my pants, leaving them in a heap with Coco's clothes. I waded into the water up to my knees and then stopped with a scream. The water was bitterly, viciously cold in the spring.

I never chose to subject myself to it unless Coco was there. Then, somehow, I could never say no.

Coco joined her hands above her head and caught a cresting wave. She barreled with it through the water toward me, then jumped to her feet and seized my warm hand in her icy, wet one.

"Come on, Mae! It's glorious!" she cried.

I let Coco drag me deeper into the water. Every wave crashing higher on my midriff was like a punch to the gut, and I gasped for the air it knocked from my body.

"Come on, come on!" Coco laughed. "Once you go under, you won't feel anything but alive!"

I dove under the next wave that rushed at me and came up spluttering and shrieking. But it was true, what Coco said. I felt nothing now but the piercing, thrilling cold. Every worry was knocked clean out of my mind. Every nerve in my body sparked to life. I screamed at the top of my lungs and dropped under the water again. This was why I always did what Coco dragged me into. It was the only way I knew to feel the way Coco must feel every day. Coco laughed and threw her wet, cold arms around me.

"Mae, you beautiful creature! I've missed you!" She kissed me on the cheek and then threw herself under another wave, which I attempted to jump over, ending up pummeled.

"Coco," I said, through chattering teeth. "When did you get a plane?"

"Do you like it?" Coco asked. "It was the cheapest I could find that I thought could make the trip, and it was still beastly expensive."

"But—" Another wave crested above us, and we dove under and came up shrieking again at the cold. "But—" There were too many questions to choose only one. How did Coco afford a plane? She had a reasonable allowance but wouldn't get any control over lump sums until she turned twenty-five or married. And then, why did she want one? When did she learn to fly? And my initial, least interesting question, still unanswered: When did she get a plane?

"Have you heard of Bessy Coleman?" Coco asked.

I shook my head. I hadn't heard of anyone who wasn't in the magazines Coco gave me when she came home from school, and the last time she came home from school, her magazines had all been about silent films, not airplanes.

"She's a pilot! She's incredible, and beautiful, and she's Black, Mae! I saw her fly one weekend, and I just knew I had to fly, too. And you know those ridiculous aether-stones mother gave me for my birthday?"

That I did know. The stones had been fitted into a necklace. Lord Prosper hadn't approved—said it was a frivolous application of his magic. But no one could deny they were beautiful. Like opals, if opals were full of something real and alive and struggling to escape.

"Well, I sold them! They were worth a fortune, and I would never have worn them anyway. I used the money to pay for the plane and flying lessons. I'm quite good! I'm going to have my pilot's license by the fall."

"You flew here from the mainland without a pilot's license?"

We dove under another wave and came up screaming again.

"Let's go ashore," said Coco through chattering teeth. "I've been in here so long, I'm actually starting to feel cold again."

We rode a midsize wave to shore, Coco gliding much farther than I did, and picked our way across the shell-littered beach to our abandoned clothes.

"So, how's the running going?" asked Coco. "Any new records?"

It had been Coco who first told me about competitive running and brought me the training schedules I now followed religiously.

"Nothing on the short distances," I admitted. "I'm afraid I might have reached my limits there, at least without a proper trainer. But my long-distance runs are still getting stronger. I cut almost a minute off the—"

"Oh, look, it's Miles!" Coco cried in delight and waved up at the ridge. I barely had time to register my disappointment at Coco's inattention before diving for my clothes and clutching them over my bare midriff and camisole. I owned a nice brassiere, the kind with lace, ordered from a catalog, but I was wearing an old, yellowed undershirt instead. I'd been saving the brassiere for the party, when I planned to see Miles for the first time. It was a good plan. I wished it had worked as I hoped. Meeting Miles early at the end of a gun hadn't proved better at all.

"Hello, Miles!" Coco called. "Do you like my plane?"

Miles (for it was Miles, I confirmed this with one quick, mortified glance) had already turned away and walked out of view.

"He's here awfully early, isn't he?" Coco said. Miles and his mother always arrived for First Night at the last possible minute and left as soon as the sun was up.

"Yes." I struggled into my shirt. Loose as it was, it was difficult to get on when soaking wet. "He's here without Imogen."

"That's odd," said Coco. "She's coming later, then?"

"Miles doesn't think she's coming at all."

Coco stared. "But she can't miss First Night!"

I wrestled my legs into my trousers. The elation I had briefly felt at Coco's arrival and our reckless swim was already starting to fade. Now I was just anxious again—and cold.

"I know," I said. "Lady Vivian seemed downright frightened about it when she heard. And that isn't the only strange thing that's been going on. Coco—" I wondered whether to mention the dead spirits first or my accidental engagement and decided for the latter in case concern over the aether wells swallowed her concern for my plight. I told her.

"What?" gasped Coco. The shock on her face at the idea was both upsetting and deeply satisfying. "Is she serious?"

"She is," I said. "She already spoke to Lord Prosper about it, and he agreed."

"No!" gasped Coco again. She had put her clothes back on—high-waisted camel-colored suit pants and a white button-down much like the one I was wearing. She had fixed her aviator goggles onto her forehead, where they somehow made her shocked green eyes bulge even wider.

"She said he likes me," I said despondently. "He's refused everyone the family suggested. They want to make him happy. And here I am, serving no purpose, nowhere else to go, nothing better to do with my life . . ."

"Don't say that, Mae," said Coco earnestly. "You can do anything you want, you know."

"I can't," I said. "You're thinking of you."

"Well, if I can, why can't you?"

I stared at her.

"Well, why not?" Coco demanded. "If you mean money, I can pay! You can come with me! I'm going to fly all over the world and maybe do shows like Bessy Coleman does. I could buy you lessons, too! Wouldn't you like to fly, Mae?"

"Maybe," I said. In fact, I wouldn't. But I would pretend to, as long as Coco was still mad for flying. Coco didn't know it, but she wasn't offering to let me do whatever I wanted, just whatever she did.

I thought of telling her about Lady Vivian's threat, but the awful possibility occurred to me that she might not see it as such a terrible thing. She was always telling me I needed to see the world. I couldn't bear to hear her make light of my possible exile.

"In any case, you don't have to marry anyone you don't want to," said Coco. "Though, to tell you the truth, if you wanted to marry one of my cousins, Ivo might be the one I'd pick."

"What!" I cried. "Why wouldn't you pick the one I'm in love with?"

"Miles?" Coco scrunched up her face. "Would you really want to marry him? He's good for a crush, but for a husband? He's so miserable and brooding all the time."

My jaw dropped in outrage. "And Ivo isn't?"

"He is," admitted Coco. "But somehow it feels less . . . I don't know . . . less put-on with him. Ivo is just odd, and no one's ever really liked him, he has no friends. He never knew his mother, and then his father—" Coco grimaced and drew a line across her neck, which was not a very good representation of Charles's death. He had killed himself by jumping off a cliff onto the rocky shore. She continued, "So of course he acts miserable all the time. But Miles isn't like that. Miles is handsome, and everyone likes him, or at least they would if he ever bothered to be civil. He chooses the Heathcliff act."

I knew Miles could choose to act pleasant and friendly. Of course I knew it—I had to do it all the time. I liked that he didn't pretend. It was what I would do if I had the freedom he did. Not all the freedom of Prosper acceptance and full inheritance, but more than enough to live without ingratiating himself to anyone.

But I couldn't explain that to Coco.

"Not everyone likes him," I said instead. "Most of your family doesn't like him much."

"Oh, those snobs," said Coco. "They don't like anyone much. I meant everyone else. Girls talk about him all the time, at school, because of his looks." She rolled her eyes, like his looks annoyed her. "And his birth gives him a bit of mystique, really. Illegitimate, but still rich enough. It's an attractive combination. He'd notice that if he didn't spend so much time sulking over every little insult."

I shook my head. It made my chest tighten to disagree with Coco, but this I couldn't agree with.

"Miles is only getting half the money you will—just because he wasn't born here! He has much more cause to brood than Ivo does. And not just because he's illegitimate. His mother . . ." The word the Prospers usually used of Imogen was *flighty,* but it wasn't particularly accurate. *Flighty* conjured up a picture of a featherheaded woman prone to mislaying her purse or forgetting her evening plans. *Opium-eating whore* was what Lady Vivian called her, and it wasn't kind, but it wasn't exactly untrue, either. Imogen abused every drug her allowance could buy, which was quite a few, and cycled to a different man every month.

"Ivo's mother is dead," said Coco. "And his father, too. And Ivo is kind, sometimes. Miles only thinks of himself."

"Miles was kind to me today," I said.

And that was true, though only by half. He was kind enough until he wasn't kind at all. I shook off the uncomfortable memory of Miles's look of disgust and sarcastic congratulations. It was nothing compared to Ivo's raging at me and possibly murdering a spirit.

"There's something else I haven't told you yet, something I think Ivo might have done."

Coco cocked her head in anticipation, and I paused longer than was strictly necessary. Now that it came to it, I wasn't sure I should tell Coco my suspicions about Ivo or my hopes that exposing his possible crime would free me from this marriage. It occurred to me that it was a dangerous proposition, trying to prove ill-doing on the part of my supposed fiancé. What if Coco told him? She wouldn't do it on purpose—at least, I didn't think she would—but she wasn't always so careful in what she said.

Still, Coco was my best friend. If I couldn't tell her, I had no one.

"I saw Ivo standing over a spirit this morning," I said. "It looked dead. Ivo said it wasn't dead but almost. I'd never seen a spirit look that way before. It wasn't moving. There was something terribly wrong with it. I think . . . I think he did something to it."

Coco's face contorted into a look of deep skepticism.

"Why would Ivo hurt a spirit?"

I had no idea, really, but the look on Coco's face stung me into speculating.

"He might have done an experiment on it—or—"

"No way." Coco shook her head. "He wouldn't do that. Did you talk to him?"

"Just a little," I said, flushing.

"Does he know about . . . you know . . . the plan?"

I flushed deeper. "It's not *the* plan. It's not my plan, anyway."

"I know, I know," said Coco. "You know what I mean."

"I think he does," I said, anger again gnawing at me.

"Well, he does fancy you," said Coco. "I've known that for a while."

"Then why didn't you ever say anything?"

"I didn't want to make you uncomfortable around him, at least not more than you already are. I figured he deserved a chance to tell you on his own."

I stared at my friend. A miserable, sinking sensation filled me.

Even Coco wanted me to marry Ivo.

And of course she did. Of course. Because it was inevitable. Because Miles didn't want me, and Ivo did, and even Coco knew the only way for me to really belong here was to marry one of them.

"Don't do anything you don't want to do," said Coco. "But he's not all bad."

A prickling feeling. An unnatural breeze tickling the hairs on the back of my neck.

"Not all bad, not at all," said Aeris. "Not too bad at all for Mousy Mae."

"Don't call her that, you wretched imp," snapped Coco. "I've told you a thousand times not to call her that."

"Don't want me to say it, then bind me not to," said Aeris. His voice was in our ears, but his corporeal form slowly materialized on the wing of the plane. "Oh, but you can't. Poor Cordelia. Prospers with magic are bad enough. But a Prosper without it is a sad, useless thing."

"Get off my plane, Aeris!" cried Coco, running toward him. "If you so much as scratch it, I will not rest until Grandfather stuffs you back in that tree he rescued you from!"

Aeris vanished right before Coco arrived.

"Grandfather Prosper would not stuff Aeris," said Aeris, standing beside me now. "And if he did, who would deliver Lord Prosper's messages and bring the wind to gently land Cordelia's flying device? Cordelia should be more grateful."

"I don't need you to land my plane!" Coco shouted. She wheeled around, standing between Aeris and her airplane with her arms out, as though she could protect it from him that way. A wind blew against her, one of Aeris's, whipping her hair back and forcing her to close her eyes against the flying sand.

"Stop it, Aeris, please," I said. "You said you have a message for us?"

The wind stopped abruptly, and Coco coughed and wiped at her eyes.

"Lord Prosper would like Cordelia and Mae to join him in the big house for lunch."

"Tell him we're not hungry!" snapped Coco.

I looked at her in alarm. "Who else will be there?" I asked Aeris, to keep him from immediately relaying Coco's ill-advised retort. Even his grandchildren didn't just turn down invitations from Lord Prosper.

"Your intended," crooned Aeris into my ear in a breathy,

horrible voice. "And your beloved. And you know what that means! Poor little Mae will be in such distress! What will she do, what will she say?"

And then he was gone. No sound of his voice, no trace of his corporeal form. But you never knew if Aeris was really gone, of course. Anywhere you were on the island, he could be listening to you. He probably was.

CHAPTER SIX

Coco walked back to me, glancing around angrily, as though Aeris might appear at any moment and then she could punch him. She walked in a twitchy way, usually, her gait stuttering and starting up again, her shoulders bunching occasionally at some unwelcome thought or feeling. I didn't know what it was Coco had to twitch about. She hated school, true, but when that depressed her, she could simply buy a plane and fly it across the channel. She didn't even have to be good at it, it seemed. Lord Prosper would see to it she landed safely one way or another.

I realized I was frowning and carefully relaxed the lines on my face. Coco could frown. Coco felt free to defend Ivo, whom I hated, who yelled at me, and tell me I should marry him, and attack Miles whom I had always loved. Coco could tell me her true feelings, whatever they were. Coco didn't know it, but it didn't go the other way. How could it, when I depended on her so much, and she didn't have to depend on anyone? No one except her grandfather, anyway.

"I didn't need him to land the plane," Coco muttered.

"Of course you didn't," I agreed at once. "He just said that to annoy you. You know what he's like."

"True," Coco said. She picked up her leather bomber jacket from the sand and shook it out, then flung it over her shoulder. It looked like a practiced gesture, and I wondered who Coco had copied it from. "I suppose he was telling the truth about lunch, though."

"He'd never lie about a message from Lord Prosper," I said.

"We don't have to go," said Coco. "Let's go up into the hills, have a picnic. We can talk about how to get you out of this, if that's what you want."

If that's what you want.

The words landed on my heart with a dull, final thud. Coco would help me get out of marrying Ivo, but not because the idea was unthinkable, or awful, or absurd. Because it wasn't what I wanted.

And that wasn't good enough at all. Coco didn't realize that, either. Sometimes I couldn't believe she could be so smart, know so much more of the world than me, and yet understand so little about what it was like to be me.

We started walking up the narrow stairs that led to the cliffside. It would be quite a long walk to the big house. Goose bumps pricked on my arms under the damp shirt. I shouldn't have plunged into the water simply because Coco wanted me to. The whole experience was much less thrilling on this side of it, when I was cold and wet and trudging across the island. We might not even have time to change our clothing before the meal. Perhaps if I showed up looking wet and unsuitable in secondhand trousers, Lord Prosper would change his mind about approving the match. But no, whatever we looked like, Ivo was sure to look worse.

I was frowning again. Once more, I smoothed out my face.

"How was your term?" I asked.

"Oh, fine," said Coco. "Apollonia was much too busy with wedding and graduation plans to waste any time torturing me, so I'd say it was a bit better than usual, actually."

"I saw her wedding dress," I said. "It's breathtaking."

"That's lucky for the dressmaker," said Coco. "If it weren't, Apollonia would hunt her down and have her boiled in oil. I'll tell you something, I've never seen a crabbier bride. And the few times I've seen her with Rex, she acts like the very sight of him makes her sick."

"He's too handsome for that—it must be the smell of him that makes her sick," I said. Coco threw back her wet, goggled head and shouted her laughter. Rex wore an enormous amount of horrible cologne. Rex had no taste of his own; he simply chose whatever cost the most. Coco and I had decided there was a cabal of luxury peddlers who had figured this out and marked various kinds of trash with outrageous price tags just for Rex. Under this theory, the cologne was probably some kind of exotic animal excrement. When she stopped laughing, Coco shook her head ruefully.

"I don't understand why she's in such a hurry to marry a man she clearly hates, even if he is disgustingly rich. She's plenty rich enough on her own without marrying at all—or at least she will be when she turns twenty-five. And until then her parents will give her anything she asks for."

"I suppose she has her reasons," I said. "He runs the second-biggest island. Rex is his family's only magician. It's what everyone wants her to do."

"Sure, but since when does Apollonia do what *anyone* wants her to do?"

"Since now, I guess," I said and shrugged. I saw what Coco meant, but it wasn't at all difficult for me to imagine why Apollonia was marrying whom Lord Prosper wanted her to marry. The Prosper money and reputation relied on united, decisive maintenance of the archipelago's magic. Intermarriage between the magical families of the archipelago strengthened those things. And after all, no one enjoyed the Prosper money and reputation more than Apollonia did. Abruptly, I remembered what I had overheard Ivo saying about Rex.

"I heard Ivo say—I think he might have been accusing Rex of something to Lord Prosper."

"You heard that?" Coco asked.

"I was on my way to tell Lord Prosper something, and I heard them arguing through the door." I blushed and snuck a nervous glance at Coco. But I needn't have worried. Coco grinned at me.

"Go on, then," said Coco. "What else?"

"I think . . ." I hadn't had much time to reflect on what I overheard. Vivian had been there so soon after, and then Miles's muttered *congratulations* had knocked everything else out of my mind. "He seemed to think Rex had done something bad—something magical, maybe." I sorted through my memories until I found the one that had given me the impression Rex's ill-doing was magical in nature. "He said, 'He's the only one besides us who could have done it,' or something like that. I thought he meant because Rex is the only other magician."

"Interesting," said Coco, and then her face lit up. "Oh! That makes perfect sense! He must have meant the strange thing that happened to the spirit! I didn't think a spirit could be hurt at all, even a house spirit, but maybe you can do it with magic, if you want?"

"But why would Rex want to hurt a house spirit?" I asked. "He's horrible, but the spirits are harmless. It's not like one of them could have set him off in some way."

"That's true," Coco agreed. "But I'd believe it of him sooner than Ivo."

I bit the inside of my lip too hard and tasted blood. Ivo's guilt was the only defense I could see against marrying him, and Coco refused to even consider it.

"It could be anything, really," said Coco, shrugging. "It's just one house spirit."

"No, it's bigger than just one house spirit," I said. "Ivo said there have been some going the same way at the wells."

"At the aether wells?" Coco stopped for a moment, then doubled her pace to catch up. "How many?"

"He didn't say." I had finally hit a real nerve. Coco had gone pale under her freckles, and she bit the side of her mouth.

"Are they worried, do you think? Ivo and Grandfather?" she asked after a moment.

"I don't know," I said. I felt a small, horrible squirm of satisfaction that Coco finally knew what it felt like to have her future threatened and immediately hated myself for it.

"It's amazing you learned to fly so quickly," I said, to atone for my secret, disloyal thoughts. "You looked incredible, soaring toward the island like that. And you should have seen Lady Vivian's face when we realized it was you."

Coco half smiled at that. "I thought about flying in later, after most of the guests had arrived, but I didn't want them all to see if I crash-landed."

So she had been relying on Lord Prosper's magic to salvage

her landing after all. Otherwise she would have been more concerned about dying in the crash than embarrassing herself.

"Maybe you could take it for a spin around the island just after sunset," I said. "Now that you know you can land it."

"I could do it when Grandfather is about to give his toast to Apollonia and Rex's engagement—or just after—"

Apollonia and Coco had this much in common: they both loved to steal a dramatic moment. Especially each other's.

The path we followed led up a green hill and down again through a grove of tangerine trees. The sun was high in the sky now and beat down on our wet clothes and hair. The last traces of morning mist were banished. I finally started to feel warm again. My thoughts drifted ahead of me, across the valley to the eastern side of the island, into the big house.

I had never been invited there for a meal before. I'd gone to the First Night party, of course. Never as a guest, though, simply because no one would keep me out on First Night. The invitation was a small taste of what I could have if I agreed to the path laid before my feet. I could live in the big house, with my own sparkling light fixtures and polished morning table and spelled patterns on the floor. I would have my own wardrobe—Ivo had as much money as the rest of them, though he didn't use it, and it could all be mine. I could go to the mainland with Coco, perhaps go to the glittering parties Apollonia went to. And then, best of all, I could come back. Finally, *finally*, it would be my island as well.

But only because I was Ivo's.

I shuddered.

"Well, hello, Miles," said Coco. She took hold of my arm, and we slowed to a stop.

Miles was leaning against a tangerine tree, peeling a fruit. He stared down at the tangerine then up at me.

The problem with the idea that Miles was a fake Heathcliff was that he looked the part so perfectly. Every time I saw him, his beauty struck me like I'd never seen him before. And now he was looking up at me from under his long, silky lashes with his beautiful deep-brown eyes full of something that looked almost like remorse. My legs wobbled a bit at the impact. I quite literally went weak in the knees. So it wasn't just something that happened in books.

"Hi, Coco," said Miles to his cousin, who was raising her eyebrows meaningfully at him. "Nice plane."

"Why, thank you, Miles," said Coco. "We were just talking about you."

Miles's eyes darted back to me, suspicious again. So quick to suspect me of telling Coco his secrets.

"What were you saying?" he asked, eyes on me.

"Nothing much," I replied flatly. "Nothing new or exciting."

"Right," said Miles. He dropped the shredded tangerine peels and clutched the fruit in his hand like a ball. "I just wanted to say I'm sorry for snapping at you earlier. On the stairs."

Coco was staring back and forth between us, barely keeping her nosy questions inside.

"Oh," I said. "No, I understand. I wanted to explain, but . . ."

"But . . ." repeated Miles. He looked at me, then down at the peels at his feet, then back at me. "But it's true? You're engaged . . . to him?"

Coco let out the breath she'd been frantically holding in a long stream that sounded distractingly like a whistle. She'd figured out what we were talking about.

"Not . . . not exactly," I said. "Lady Vivian approached me about it this morning. I wasn't sure how to say no, so I just . . . said nothing."

"That makes sense," said Miles, like it didn't. He split the tangerine and put a segment in his mouth.

"You really should have told her you didn't fancy the idea right away," said Coco.

"I never said yes!" I said. "I just . . . nodded."

"She knew exactly what she was doing, if you ask me," said Coco. "You didn't say no, and now she wants to make sure you don't feel like you can. She pounced on it the moment she had the slightest murmur of consent from you, and now Grandfather has signed off, and the whole family is coming to lunch . . ."

"Well, you can't go, then!" Miles exclaimed. "You can't marry him."

An angry, choking sound came out of Coco's mouth.

"She—what? What's that now? She *can't*?" Coco glared at him. "You think you get to tell Mae what she *can't* do?"

"No—I just meant—there's something wrong with him!" said Miles. "I know there is! And Mae doesn't even like him!"

Coco knew very well that I didn't like Ivo, as she'd just been doing her best to talk me out of feeling that way. But she skipped over this point.

"Now you're just being mean," she said. "Ivo is a little strange, yes, but that doesn't mean there's anything *wrong* with him. He's a magician. He can be a little eccentric."

"He isn't just eccentric," Miles said. "He did something bad. He and . . . and maybe his father before him. Something magical. My mother told me."

"Uhhhh, all right," said Coco slowly. "So you're saying your mother told you Uncle Charles and Ivo did some kind of bad magic on her, but she wouldn't tell you what it was?"

"I'm going to find out," said Miles. "Today. Tonight."

"Great," said Coco. "You let us know when you do that. Until then, Mae can make her own decisions without you telling her what to do."

"What about the spirits?" I asked.

Miles and Coco both stared at me like there were slugs coming out of my mouth instead of words. Like the last thing they expected to happen in this conversation about me was for me to contribute.

"What do you mean?" asked Coco.

"What I told you earlier," I said, carefully smothering my frustration. "The spirits are sick or something, and I think Ivo might be causing it."

"Oh, right," said Coco. "That's probably Rex. I thought we agreed. It fits, right, Mae?"

It did fit. It could be Rex. But I didn't want to say so. I didn't want to let go of the only weapon I might have to prove I shouldn't have to marry Ivo. And although Miles's suspicions weren't particularly concrete, he did seem very certain that something bad had happened to his mother. But I didn't know how to argue with her.

"Ivo did something to my mother," Miles insisted. "I know it was him. She told me."

"It doesn't sound like she told you much." Coco's eyebrows were raised with pointed skepticism. "You don't even know what he's supposed to have done."

"I know enough," said Miles. Color rose in his cheeks.

"You don't know enough to prove anything, that's for sure."

This hit a nerve. Miles clenched his jaw shut.

"You don't have any *proof* that Ivo did any of those things," said Coco, more calmly. "You're telling Mae she can't marry Ivo, with *no proof*."

"What, you *want* her to marry him? *Ivo?*"

"I want her to do whatever she wants to do!" cried Coco. "And I want her to do it without any unfounded accusations mixing her up!"

"She doesn't want to marry him!"

"Did you ask her what she wants?"

"Did *you?*"

"I'm right here, you know," I said with a touch of irritation. "You could ask me what I want instead of fighting about whether you already did."

Miles and Coco looked at me in surprise again, still obviously on the verge of hurling more accusations at each other. Miles recovered first.

"Fair enough," he said. "What do you want, Mae?"

I met Miles's deep-brown eyes and imagined answering him truthfully, giving the answer I'd planned on.

I want you to look at me the way I look at you. I want you to take me with you and ask Lord Prosper to train us both. I want you to love me and take me with you to see the world and then, most of all, I want to come back.

I looked down.

"I don't want to marry Ivo," I said instead.

And I didn't. But Ivo was offering me something I did want, desperately. Something I needed.

A place on the island.

But I couldn't take it. Not like this. Not when he shouted at me and kept me from what I wanted. Not if he did violence to the spirits. And not while I still might have a chance with Miles.

Could I?

I thought of Lady Vivian, the smooth, easy way she had threatened me with exile, like it wasn't a threat at all. Just the obvious next step on my path. And it was. No one would find it strange if I had to leave, any more than they found it strange that Ivo wouldn't let me read his spell books. Coco could insist all day long that I was free to do what I wished, but that didn't make it true.

I needed more time. I needed more information. I wasn't ready to decide.

"I want to know the truth," I said. "Something is wrong on the island, and I want to know what it is before . . ." I glanced at Miles, whose jaw was hinged tight again. "Before I make any decisions."

"So . . . how do we help you find out what you need to know?" Coco asked.

"What if—" I had an idea. The words filled me with terror but escaped my mouth before I could think better of them. "Since I'm already more or less engaged to him—what if I played along?"

Coco figured it out first. Her mouth turned down into a slight frown. "And you talked to him? Asked him questions?"

"Hmm," said Miles. "I don't know if that's a good idea."

"Do you want to find out what's going on or not?" demanded Coco. "We need more information. And anyway . . . Mae shouldn't do anything rash."

Like call off my engagement to Ivo. I agreed completely, and yet it still made my heart sink into my damp shoes to hear her say it. I waited for Miles to disagree.

He didn't.

I looked up at Coco and forced a smile.

"Then it's a plan."

CHAPTER SEVEN

We arrived at lunch with the bones of a plan. Actually, the bones of three different plans, which, combined, were not quite enough for a full skeleton. Miles's plan was for me to play along with the engagement just long enough to prove the various wicked things Ivo had done and then immediately break it off. Coco's plan started the same and ended up opposite: she wanted me to consent to the engagement, discover that Ivo had done nothing wrong, and live happily ever after.

I wanted to live happily ever after, too. Preferably with Miles. It seemed possible, now that he was speaking to me again and looking at me with gratitude instead of disgust. And for now, this plan let me put off making the fateful decision of whether or not to refuse Ivo and face what came after. I could go to this lunch without disappointing anyone, angering Ivo, or defying the Prospers. I could have Miles's and Coco's approval and the feeling that all three of us were in this together. And really, what were my other choices? Refuse to go to lunch? Impossible. Go to lunch and call the whole thing off? Unimaginable. But go to lunch and pretend?

That sounded easiest. And just now, with my head racing and my heart roiling with all that had already happened, I couldn't face anything but the easiest option.

"Look, make sure it's not too obvious you're trying to get information from him." Miles was frowning, nervous. "He's dangerous. We don't know what he might do if he finds out what you're after."

Coco rolled her eyes. "What he'll do is wander off into the hills with very hurt feelings."

"Are you sure about this, Mae?" Miles said. "You don't have to do it. It's not too late to find Grandfather and tell him what we know—"

"What we *suspect*, you mean?" Coco said. "Because, remember, we have no proof, which is exactly why Mae suggested we do this."

"But—"

"This is the best way," I said gently, though it sent a thrill of pleasure down to my toes to see Miles worrying for me.

"Just make sure he doesn't find out what you suspect," said Miles.

But what *would* Ivo think? I had to wonder. Before today, he hadn't said a word to me since chasing me from his shack. If this engagement had been his idea, he certainly hadn't tried to win me over. What would he think when I sat down next to him as his fiancée? Did he really expect that I would?

Maybe he did. Maybe he really thought I had that little spirit in me, that little pride. My anger rose. Yes, he probably did. In fact, it probably hadn't even occurred to him that I might say no. I was just Mousy Mae, after all. He was doing me an unthinkable honor.

I ground my teeth together. At least I had a plan, or something like one. Some small way to prove I wasn't as spineless as they thought.

We fell silent as we approached the house. The spirit music filled the quiet space between us. I let it calm me, loosen my jaw, settle the anger pricking under my skin. I looked up, but the trees obscured my view of the sky.

There was no spirit music on the mainland. I couldn't imagine what that was like. When she'd first gone away to boarding school, Coco had written me that it nearly drove her wild. Her parents had sent her a Victrola, which she played constantly just to fill the emptiness. The thought of that much quiet made me shudder.

Sometimes, when I was waking up, I put my fingers in my ears and tried to imagine I was on the mainland, in London maybe. I didn't have a very clear picture of it, but I knew that without the music, without magic, it would be gray. It would sound gray, look gray, feel gray. Everyone seemed to think that gray world was where I belonged. And maybe they were right. Maybe, in some ways, it would be easier to be there, away from the Prosper magic and money. Maybe it wouldn't be so hard to make a place for myself there. But I couldn't imagine any place away from the island that was worth having.

I was so lost in my thoughts, I almost didn't notice the other voices murmuring in the garden until one of them was suddenly raised.

"I've been patient, Apollonia! Show me any man who's been as bloody patient as I've been with you!"

We stopped. The footpath we followed led into the thickest part of the garden before opening onto the rear patio and pool. We couldn't see them, but Apollonia and her fiancé were evidently only a few hedges away.

Apollonia replied. Her voice was too low and quiet to make out the words, but the icy tone was unmistakable. For half a moment, I felt sorry for Rex.

"I've had enough," he said. "You'll do what I say, and you'll do it tonight."

"Take your hand off me." Apollonia raised her voice this time, enough for us to hear. Miles made a move forward, but Coco and I both seized his arms. I couldn't imagine Apollonia actually needed help.

"Tonight, Apollonia," said Rex. "You know what I can do to your family. No more excuses."

There was a rustle of leaves followed by a heavy tread on the cobbled path. A few moments later, Apollonia's lighter steps followed.

We stared at each other.

"You know what I can do to your family?" I quoted in a whisper. "Like hurt the spirits and shut down the aether wells?"

"I'd say this is a significant piece of evidence for the case that Rex is the magician running amok," said Coco.

"It's a significant piece of evidence that Rex is a bastard and someone should beat him," muttered Miles.

"What do you think he wants Apollonia to do?" I asked.

Coco and Miles both looked at me with something like pity.

"What?"

Coco and Miles looked at each other.

"Well . . ." said Coco. "Rex . . . has a certain reputation."

I waited, with the sinking sensation I sometimes had

around Coco that I'd missed something obvious. Something everyone who hadn't lived on an island their whole life knew.

"I see," I lied.

"Do you?" Coco asked.

"No," I said.

"He wants her to go to bed with him tonight," said Miles flatly.

I couldn't look at either of them. My face felt as hot as the sun at noon. Once he said it, it was obvious, and yet so sordid, I could hardly bring myself to believe it.

"No," I breathed. "I mean . . . it could be something else, couldn't it? That's not the only explanation for what he said . . ."

But nothing else occurred to me, and Coco and Miles looked at the ground.

"Heavenly spheres," I muttered. "I never thought I could feel sorry for Apollonia."

"What are we going to do about this?" Miles asked.

"We'll find out what Rex is threatening to do," said Coco. "*Before* he can force Apollonia into anything. Then we'll tell Grandfather."

"Why not just tell Grandfather after lunch?" asked Miles. "If Rex is threatening Apollonia—"

"If the solution were as simple as telling Grandfather, don't you think Apollonia would have done it already?"

Miles grimaced.

"We have to find out what the threat is. But first, we have to get Mae through this lunch. Actually—" Coco looked up, her face brightening. "You could ask Ivo what he knows about it, Mae. This has nothing to do with"—she glanced at Miles—"the other thing, so it would be a good way to get him talking."

I nodded. I felt a small measure of relief. It had been hard to imagine starting a conversation with Ivo before, but I knew he hated Rex. *Rex threatened Apollonia* seemed an excellent opener.

"Fine," agreed Miles. "But don't forget, Mae, Rex isn't the only thing wrong on this island. I know it."

This time Coco managed not to roll her eyes, though the strain of the effort showed on her face. We emerged from the garden to find Lady Vivian running toward us on the path.

"There you are! What took you so long?" And when she was close enough to take in our appearance: "And what on earth happened to your clothes?"

"We went swimming on the north beach," said Coco. "Before we knew we were invited to lunch."

"Oh, dear," Lady Vivian replied with a deep sigh. "Lunch is in ten minutes. Cordelia, dear, do you have anything . . . ?"

She trailed off, eyeing Coco's high-waisted pants and aviator goggles. The corners of her mouth turned down slightly in answer to her own question. She turned from Coco with a despairing sigh and looked me over.

"Come with me," said Lady Vivian. She seized my hand and walked toward the house.

"I'll see you at lunch," I said over my shoulder.

* * *

Lady Vivian knocked on the door to Apollonia's room.

"Yes. What." Apollonia's voice from the other side of the door was chillier than the ocean.

"Darling, I'm here with Mae," said Lady Vivian. "She's coming to lunch in a few moments and has nothing at all to wear. Is there something in your closet you're finished with for the season?"

Apollonia opened the door. Whatever she had been wearing during her meeting in the garden with Rex, she'd shed it and put on a midnight-blue kimono. It was belted across her narrow waist but hung open in front enough to show the low, delicate lace of her slip.

There were some people who said Apollonia wasn't beautiful. Coco told me so. They were mostly women, she said, or the sort of men Apollonia would never say a single word to. Her eyes were too widely spaced they said, or they might complain that the bones of her face were too sharp. I was amazed when Coco told me this and thought about it when I looked at the catalogs and magazines Coco brought me from the mainland, comparing Apollonia to the models and actresses in them. Apollonia didn't look like them, but the truth was that she was more beautiful than those blank-eyed women, not less. She had an unusual sort of beauty, but it was true beauty. The Prosper eyes were just green in most of the Prospers. Apollonia's cut into you like emeralds. Her hair was as dark and shiny as a spill of her expensive ink. She had the kind of face artists wanted to capture. I even wrote a terrible poem about her once, which I had destroyed the moment I considered how many smitten men must have done the same. She leaned lightly against the doorway and looked me up and down with a cold smile, like she'd read it.

"I don't know why you think any of my things might fit her," she said.

We were exactly the same size, except in the bust, but I

understood the sentiment. It was hard to believe that Apollonia and I had even that much in common.

"Perhaps something with a little give?" said Lady Vivian, though she knew perfectly well that I could fit into Apollonia's least forgiving dresses. Her wedding gown, for instance. "From last season?"

Apollonia lifted one shoulder in something like permission and went to her morning table. A page of her creamy, monogrammed stationery lay under a fountain pen on the desk. She hadn't written much yet. Just a name.

Seb,

That was it.

Lady Vivian opened the closet and rummaged in the very back. I looked at Apollonia's arms, covered by the kimono, and wondered if Rex had left any marks where he'd grabbed her. Apollonia glanced up and found me peering at her. Her already hard expression turned to stone.

"What does she need a dress for?" asked Apollonia.

"I told you, darling," said Lady Vivian. "Lunch."

"Lunch? What do you mean, *lunch*?" Apollonia said. "Since when does a servant come to lunch?"

"She's not really a servant, darling," said Lady Vivian from the back of the closet. "And Mae and Ivo are engaged now, so she'll be family soon enough."

Lady Vivian poked her head out of the closet and gave her daughter a slight look of warning.

"Really?" Apollonia turned in her chair until she faced me. She propped her elbow on the chair back and rested her chin in her hand. "Mousy Mae and Ivo? Did the oldest Harcourt girl finally say no, then?"

"She was willing. But when we took Ivo to meet her—" Lady Vivian sighed. "Well, let's just say he didn't behave himself and leave it at that."

Apollonia laughed. She had a very pleasant, melodic laugh. To listen to it, you wouldn't guess how much cruelty was underneath.

"I can't say I blame him. The Harcourt girl is a cow, and stupid, too. She almost didn't graduate last year because her grades were so terrible." She laughed again. "Can you imagine failing finishing school? And she was *trying*, too, that's the worst part."

"But she did graduate in the end," said Lady Vivian mildly.

"Only because her father bribed Mrs. Wiltshire with a new building. And all for nothing. If even Ivo won't marry her, then no one will."

Lady Vivian emerged from the closet with a clutch of dresses, all of which I recognized at once and longed for.

"Now, I haven't seen you in any of these all year long, Apollonia, so I think—"

"Not the green one," said Apollonia sharply.

The green dress was the best of the bunch by far; it had been Apollonia's signature look last year. As stylish as it was, I wouldn't have chosen it. Wearing a dress Apollonia had worn to such effect would invite comparisons I would rather not have made.

"Or the gray silk," added Apollonia. "Or the red one."

That left a cream-colored, low-waisted day dress. I'd never seen it before, which meant Apollonia had never worn it outside of school. It was a pretty dress—Apollonia didn't wear anything that wasn't at least pretty—but that was all that could be said for it. The color would have set off Apollonia's striking eyes and dark hair nicely, but I doubted it would do anything much for me. Lady Vivian held the dress out.

"Put this on, then, Mae dear." She actually sounded disappointed. I was almost touched that Lady Vivian had wanted the nicer dresses for me, even though she hadn't been willing to press her daughter for them. Lady Vivian snapped for the spirits again.

I took the dress and glanced at Apollonia. She had turned back to her letter and picked up the pen, but she hadn't written anything else. She started tapping the pen against the table at an irritated, rapid speed. The spirits helped me out of Coco's castoffs yet again and into Apollonia's.

I couldn't help looking in the mirror once it was on. Even though it was the least attractive thing in Apollonia's closet, it was far more beautiful than anything in mine, except the torn dress I'd stolen for tonight. I smoothed it down, pleased with the feel of the thick fabric under my fingers. Then I looked at my reflection and patted helplessly at my hair.

"Hmm, yes," agreed Lady Vivian and took a comb from Apollonia's morning table.

"You'll never get it through that mess," said Apollonia.

Lady Vivian slowly put the comb back down. Apollonia heaved a put-upon sigh, and I wondered if she knew how much she sounded like her mother when she did that. Apollonia opened an abalone shell box and rummaged for some pins. Lady Vivian reached for them, but Apollonia ignored her hand and stood. She approached me slowly, with a critical eye.

"It doesn't look so bad on you, actually." She didn't sound particularly pleased about it. "You have a better figure than I realized. I suppose I never noticed because you were always wearing Coco's ridiculous costumes."

"Costumes?" Heat rushed to my cheeks. It made me nervous to disagree with Apollonia, but I couldn't let her insult Coco. "They aren't costumes. They're her clothes."

"Oh, please," said Apollonia. She approached me with pins in hand, like weapons, and reached for my head. I tried not to flinch. Apollonia was a predator. She could smell fear. If you ran, she'd chase.

Apollonia ran a cold, painted fingernail down my scalp, parting the hair and almost, but not quite, drawing blood. Apollonia flipped the excess hair across my head and started to pin.

"When you wear them, they're just clothes," she said. "When Coco wears them, they're costumes. Picked for the role she wants to play."

"And what role is that?" I asked.

I had hoped to sound challenging and strong, but there was a slight tremor in my voice. Apollonia smiled.

"Well, she couldn't be me, could she?" she asked. "That role was already filled. Coco didn't want to be a cheap copy."

My heart stuttered at the audacity of this. For a moment, I forgot to feel nervous.

"You are not why Coco is who she is," I said.

Apollonia stepped back, the same smug smile still playing on her wine-colored lips.

"Not terrible," she said and turned me back toward the mirror.

Instead of a halo of unmanageable frizz, my hair had been tamed enough to look almost like curls. The new part was to the left, and Apollonia had pinned one side and left the other free. The resulting asymmetry was stylish. Apart from my sunburned face, I almost looked like a girl from one of my mainland catalogs.

"Come by my room before the party tonight. I can really fix you up," said Apollonia. "If you like."

"Thank you," I said.

Coco and I had plans to get ready together, but I didn't mention those. After all, Coco might want me to take Apollonia up on this offer. Perhaps I could get her talking about Rex and what he was threatening her with.

And anyway, if Apollonia could do so much with my hair in three minutes, I wanted to know what I'd see in that mirror if Apollonia really fixed me up.

"Very nice, darling, thank you," said Lady Vivian. "Now put something on, and we can all go down to lunch together."

Apollonia slung herself back over her chair. Her kimono gaped open, showing an intentional amount of bust. "I'm not going to lunch."

"But darling, Rex is here! I'm sure he expects—"

"I don't need you to tell me what Rex expects, Mother," snapped Apollonia. "Tell him I have a headache."

Lady Vivian glanced at me, and I had the distinct feeling there were quite a few things Lady Vivian would have said if I weren't there.

"I'll go," I said. "I'll tell them . . ."

I wasn't sure what I would tell them, in fact, but Lady Vivian didn't seem to mind. I went out the door, closed it firmly behind me, and walked away.

Then, with much quieter steps, I came back and put my ear to the door.

CHAPTER EIGHT

"—entirely pleased with Rex, darling, but—"

"I don't want to talk about this."

Silence. I listened carefully for footsteps. If Lady Vivian had given up and was coming for the door, I needed to high-tail it down the hallway. But there weren't any.

"I know you don't want my advice about Rex, Apollonia," said Lady Vivian. "I know you don't want my advice at all. But you do trust that I always have your best interests at heart, don't you? Yours and Alasdair's? Above all else."

Another long silence. Perhaps Apollonia nodded, because Lady Vivian went on:

"Good," she said. "Then I need you to trust me. You must not break things off with Rex tonight."

"I'm not going to—"

"And you mustn't let him break it off with you. Not tonight."

"Why not tonight?" asked Apollonia. She sounded as puzzled as I was. "What's so important about tonight?"

"It's First Night," said Lady Vivian.

"If you're worried about the party—"

"Darling, haven't I just told you? The party is nothing to me. Nothing compared to you."

"Me and Alasdair." There was something probing about the way she said this.

"Yes," agreed Lady Vivian. "But tonight I'm worried about you."

"You're being dreadfully mysterious," said Apollonia, again voicing my thoughts.

Lady Vivian sighed.

"I know, darling," she said. "I would say more if I could. You must trust me."

"Fine." Apollonia's voice was heavier than I had heard it. "I will. But you must trust me as well. I know how to handle Rex, and I will not be coming to lunch."

"Good," agreed Lady Vivian. "Fine."

There were footsteps now, coming to the door. I started down the hall but didn't have time to get around the corner before Lady Vivian emerged. I threw myself into the next room down and closed the door quietly behind me, then pressed my ear to it, listening for Lady Vivian's steps going past.

"Shhhhhhhhh," came a whisper in my other ear. Aeris, though not in his corporeal form. "He's sleeping. And you're not the kind of girl he's used to waking up next to."

I slowly turned around. I was in Alasdair's room, and Alasdair was asleep in it, one arm thrown over his head and his pants in a crumpled heap on the ground. Dread rose up in my throat like acid. The last time I'd seen Alasdair, he told me Coco's clothes made me look like a chimney sweep. The time before that, he'd pulled a surprised expression and said he thought I had died. Apollonia had laughed and said no, that was my father.

Coco had told them both to go to hell.

There was a wink of light by the bed, and a light, unnatural breeze fluttered Alasdair's messy brown hair.

"Don't wake him, Aeris," I breathed. "Please don't wake him."

Lady Vivian's footsteps passed down the hallway, then stopped in front of the door.

Panic flooded me. This was Alasdair's room, and Alasdair was her son. Of course Lady Vivian was going to wake him for lunch.

But the footsteps moved on, and I breathed a quiet sigh of relief. She had decided to let him sleep.

"Uh-oh," came Aeris's voice in my ear again.

I glanced back toward the four-poster bed. Alasdair's handsome mouth was slightly open, and a small thread of drool hung out of it. Inexplicably, the standing brass lamp beside his bed began to tip toward him.

"Don't!" I whispered again to Aeris. I thought about hurling myself out of the room, but Lady Vivian wouldn't be quite out of sight yet. The lamp rocked back and forth, gaining force. I saw the moment when it had rocked too far, and making a quick choice, I ran across the room and caught it before it hit Alasdair in the face. I tilted the lamp back up and set it firmly down, only to have my feet knocked from under me. I fell onto the bed—and Alasdair.

"Well, hello there, Mae."

I rolled off him until I was on my side, facing him. I tried to roll farther, but his arm was around me. For someone who'd been drooling onto his pillow a moment ago, he had awoken with a firm grip.

"I knew you'd eventually awaken to my charms, though I have to admit, I didn't expect you to be this forward about it."

"I'm so sorry," I muttered breathlessly. "I didn't mean to wake you."

"Why not?" Alasdair deftly snaked his other arm under my waist and pulled me toward him. He ground his hips into mine, and even with the covers between us, I could feel the details of his hard body against mine. "On the whole, I prefer to be awake for this kind of thing."

My face burned. He lifted himself onto one elbow so that he was slightly above me and ran his other hand down my side and under my skirt. I jerked back with an embarrassing squeak.

"I'm sorry," I said, scrambling off the bed. "I'm sorry— I—"

"S'all right, you're allowed to change your mind." Alasdair lay back with a grin. He stretched his arms over his head and yawned extravagantly. He'd always loved embarrassing me, but I'd never given him an opportunity like this before. "Try me again some time."

"Uh, no. I don't think I will." I backed slowly into the brass lamp, then spun quickly to catch it before it fell. I suspected my face was the color of bougainvillea. I backed slowly toward the door now, smoothing my dress. If I didn't get down to lunch quickly, Lady Vivian might come looking for me, and that would be a disaster. "Would you mind not . . . mentioning this to anyone?"

"I might not be good for much, but I do know how to keep a lady's secret." He winked at me and then yawned again.

"Yes," I said without thinking. I opened the door and peeked out. Lady Vivian wasn't in sight. "Well . . . see you."

"Thanks for dropping by, Mae."

I hurried down the hall, putting the cold backs of my hands to my cheeks in hopes of cooling them down. I took the stairs two at a time and arrived outside the archway leading into the dining room with unacceptably short breath. I stood just out of sight for a moment to settle myself. I gulped down air and listened to the clink of silver on china, the rustle of clothing. But even when I had my breath back, I hesitated. Though it had seemed like the easiest option half an hour ago, it now seemed impossibly hard to go in there, sit down beside Ivo, and smile.

"So, Cordelia." The bluff, masculine voice belonged to Rex. "I take it that was your plane that circled me when I was coming across."

"Oh, was that your boat?" said Coco innocently. "I saw Alasdair on deck, so I decided to say hello."

"I can't believe your parents bought you an airplane," said Lady Vivian. "I may have to speak with Edith about that."

"Mother didn't buy it for me," said Coco. "Or, not intentionally. I sold that aether-stone necklace she bought me to pay for it."

A shocked silence fell.

Lady Vivian cleared her throat nervously.

"I do hope Mae hasn't gotten lost," she said. "Perhaps I should go find her?"

I smoothed my dress again, wiping my sweaty palms

against the delicate fabric and realizing, too late, that I had left damp marks at my sides. I simply had to go in and sit down. They wouldn't expect me to say much—maybe anything. I tried to make myself move but stood frozen.

"I'll go," said a low, rough voice.

Ivo. My feet finally lurched forward. The only thing more nerve-racking at the moment than facing a whole room of Prospers would be facing Ivo alone.

I wasn't quite fast enough. Ivo turned the corner just before I did and pulled up short.

"Oh," he said, eyes widening.

"I was just—"

"Right."

Ivo had changed into a pale gray suit that he had surely not chosen but nevertheless fit him quite well. He had tied his dirty-blond hair back, but the front pieces had already escaped and fallen in his face, which was flushed. It wasn't the worst look I had seen on him.

In fact, did he look handsome?

I peered at him. Did he? I was shocked that it had even occurred to me. I had never considered it before. He was always so disheveled, his clothes so ill fitting, his hair so wild, expression so grim.

His expression wasn't grim at all now. Though he wasn't smiling. I tried to remember if I had ever seen Ivo smile and couldn't.

"You look very nice," he said and then flushed deeper.

"Oh," I said, surprised. "Thank you."

Ivo nodded, looked down at the ground, then back up at me again.

"New dress?"

I blinked. It was hard to believe he noticed, despite the fact that he'd never seen me in a dress before.

"Yes," I said, then shook my head. "I mean, no. It's Apollonia's."

"Oh," said Ivo. He frowned a little. "Do you like it?"

"Yes," I said. "I didn't pick it, but yes."

Ivo nodded again, frowning. I couldn't tell if he was unhappy about something or just thoughtful. Ivo frowned so much, it was sometimes hard to tell his frowns apart.

"But you like . . ." He gestured at me. "That sort of thing."

I squinted at him questioningly.

"Clothes," he supplied. "You like clothes."

I did, of course, though I didn't quite like to admit it. It was usually the mark of good character in a novel's heroine when she cared less about clothes than her sisters, friends, or rivals did. I wondered if Ivo hoped I would deny it. He certainly didn't care about his own clothes. He probably found it frivolous.

For half a moment, I thought about giving him the answer I thought he wanted. But no. I'd done more than enough of that today. I raised my chin.

"Yes," I said. "I like nice clothes. Though I haven't had much chance to indulge in them."

Ivo nodded again, apparently satisfied. His frown was gone. He held out his bent arm to me, and I stared at it a moment before realizing he meant for me to take it.

"Oh," I said. I stepped toward him and only hesitated another moment before slipping my arm through his. He looked down at me, and for a quick moment, a smile crossed his lips. I stared at him. The fleeting smile had changed his face. It came to me again, unwillingly, that Ivo might actually be handsome.

He looked away. We walked into the dining room together.

It was a beautiful room. I'd been in it before, but never as a guest, to have a meal. One side was lined with windows that looked out toward the sea. The other side was papered with a pale green botanical print. An aether-powered chandelier hung over the long table, where it sparkled even though it wasn't turned on. The room was bright with sunlight. House spirits stood at attention, pouring drinks and clearing plates when needed. Their lavender forms were nearly transparent in the full light of midday.

Despite the silence, the table was quite full. They all stood when we entered. Lord Prosper was at the head, white-haired, spindly, and austere. To his left was Lady Vivian, then Rex, then Miles, who looked up and caught my eye. He gave me a small, worried smile, which died immediately when his eyes traveled to Ivo. I shook myself. What had I been thinking? Ivo wasn't handsome; Miles was. Ivo was just . . . well . . . not as grim and untidy as usual.

Lord Stephen, Lord Prosper's eldest living son and Apollonia and Alasdair's father, was the first to sit again. He was at the foot of the table, with Coco at his right hand. Ivo pulled out the empty chair next to Coco for me and pushed it underneath me as I sat. He took his seat on my other side.

"You found us, Mae dear!" cried Lady Vivian, with obvious relief. "I was beginning to think you'd gotten lost!"

Lord Prosper still stood. He cleared his throat. It took more time than one would usually allot for such a task, and when he'd finished, every eye at the table was turned expectantly toward him. He reached for his glass of very pale rosé.

"I propose a toast," he said. His voice was very low, but recently he had grown an old-mannish quaver that made my heart skip a beat. I didn't see him often, since he kept mostly to the house and I mostly kept out of it. But his presence on the island was an underlying fact of all our lives, one I couldn't imagine losing. Every day he did the magic that made this island a paradise instead of a storm-ravaged wasteland. He gave us everything we had, and even if I didn't have as much of it as I wanted, the thought of losing him was terrifying. "To the union of these young people, and of our families. Wilson was a good friend to me in the difficult early days of the island. He came here with me when it was a wild and dangerous place, and he served me through many heartaches and tragedies. I am sorry he is not here to see this day. His daughter deserves all that is good. May this marriage bring it to you. To Ivo and Mae."

"To Ivo and Mae."

My father had never talked much. We had lived together in near silence. I'd never doubted that he loved me, but most of the time, this didn't seem to amount to much more than an occasional word of thanks or an awkward pat on my shoulder. Even when he was alive, I hadn't known what my father thought of much, myself included.

But I knew exactly what he would have thought of this. He had worshipped Lord Prosper like he was some kind of god. *The things I've seen him do,* he had said more than once, a look of awe on his face.

If he'd lived to see this, my father would have been overjoyed. He would have been proud enough to weep. It was more than he'd ever imagined for me—to be the Prosper family's last choice for their least marriageable son.

My father had certainly never imagined for me what I had dared to imagine for myself: my own magic. My own place here in my own right.

I picked up my glass of rosé and took a deep drink, swallowing hard against the bitter bile rising in my throat.

I'd imagined something like this many times. A seat at the family table, a toast to my future from Lord Prosper. But in my mind, he'd been toasting to my progress in magical studies, and Miles had been sitting next to me, and Ivo hadn't been there at all.

I glanced at Miles. He hadn't raised his glass or taken a drink. He stared at his plate, his mouth set in a grim, tight line. I wanted to signal him somehow, to remind him that we'd all agreed on this plan and that it wasn't real. I leaned forward just far enough to see Coco, who was staring into her glass and looking unusually sober. Perhaps it had occurred to her, too, that a fake engagement wasn't really so fake once everyone had drunk a very real toast to it.

Beside me, Ivo was still and quiet. He didn't look at me, though not in the way people usually didn't look at me, without even noticing I was there to be looked at. Ivo's eyes weren't on me, but his attention was. I felt it in his unusually straight posture and the careful way he held his spoon and trained his eyes down while he ate his soup.

"Well," said Lady Vivian. It was an awkward silence, and somebody had to break it. "It will be lovely to have you in the big house more often now, Mae dear. I hope you won't mind if I fill in a bit helping you plan your wedding?"

She meant "fill in" for my mother. She'd died in childbirth, so I had never known her. Even so, the thought filled me with aversion, strong enough that I might have actually proposed an alternative if this were really going to be my wedding.

"Oh, of course," I murmured instead. Everyone but me had begun eating their soup. It was a delicate green, cold, and smelled like onions. I picked up the correct spoon—I knew which was which from a book of etiquette I'd studied—and carefully spooned the soup away from myself and then into my mouth.

"It won't be until after Apollonia's and mine," said Rex. Even from the far end of the table, I smelled his musky cologne. He was the biggest man at the table by far. As tall as Ivo, muscular like Miles, but with an extra layer of beefiness all around. He had the commanding tone of someone used to being the richest, most important, most powerful man in the room. This island was the only place he ever went where he wasn't.

"I hadn't thought about that. I suppose it would be best to have it after," said Lady Vivian. "What do we all think?"

"There's no hurry, is there?" asked Coco a bit too quickly.

"No reason to wait, either," said Lord Stephen. "It's not as if she has to finish school."

I placed my spoon on the edge of the plate beneath my soup dish but didn't let it go. It was true. I wasn't in school. I had no training that couldn't be interrupted. Nothing better to do at all. I gripped my spoon and said nothing.

"No, but we do have our hands full planning Apollonia and Rex's wedding," said Lady Vivian.

"I'm sure Mae doesn't want to be a bother," said Lord Stephen.

"Of course not," I murmured. The hard edge of the spoon bit into the inside of my hand.

"It's no bother at all!" exclaimed Lady Vivian. "Especially since Apollonia's wedding will come first. We can use all the same decorations, the same basic plan—but on a smaller scale, of course."

"Why, 'of course'?" asked Coco abruptly.

"Our wedding is going to be the event of the season," said Rex. He'd finished his soup already and turned in his chair to signal the house spirits for the next course. "The richest mainland families won't be having a party as big as ours. You think theirs is going to match it?"

Coco glowered at him. Her jaw shifted back and forth, like she was clamping down a retort, probably one that involved heavy hinting at Rex's unproved misdeeds.

"I don't want anything elaborate," I said quickly.

"But we will make sure it's lovely," said Lady Vivian. "Modest and tasteful, just like you, Mae dear."

Modest. I rolled the word around in my mind for a moment, which was all it took for me to decide I didn't like *modest* any better than *mousy*. One was just a thinly disguised form of the other.

"And of course you'll need some new clothes. Pick out whatever you like from those catalogs of yours, and I'll order it for you," said Lady Vivian.

"Will you take her to Paris?" asked Ivo.

There shouldn't have been anything shocking about Ivo contributing to the conversation during his engagement lunch, but nevertheless a brief, shocked silence followed.

"To do the shopping," Ivo continued. "You took Apollonia to Paris for that."

"Oh," said Lady Vivian. "I don't think that would be quite Mae's sort of thing."

"Is it?" Ivo asked.

"Well, of course—" Lady Vivian continued, but Ivo cut her off.

"I was asking Mae," he said.

I didn't look up at first, but I felt their eyes on me like a physical pressure. Ivo had given them all no choice but to watch and wait until I had spoken. I could hold their silence by holding mine, if I wanted. I was usually quiet, but usually nothing much hinged on it. Ivo had given me this power. It wasn't the power I wanted, but it was something. A sliver of gratitude slid into my heart amid everything else.

Of course I wanted to go.

"I would love to go to Paris," I said.

Lady Vivian's lips parted, but nothing came out. I suppressed a smile of satisfaction at the dawning alarm in Lady Vivian's eyes as she realized she couldn't undo this with a word.

"That's settled, then," said Ivo.

I realized then that Ivo hadn't been asking me if I liked clothes to judge me for it. He simply wanted to know. And once he did, he made sure I could have them.

I turned my face slightly toward him, and the corner of my eye met the corner of his. I couldn't help it. I smiled.

CHAPTER NINE

When lunch was over, Coco, Miles, and I couldn't look at each other. Our plan felt childish now, like a play monster that had suddenly turned real. I watched Ivo walk out of the dining room, toward the back door. It didn't feel right, watching him walk away. There was too much unsettled between us. I followed him, averting my eyes from Miles and Coco. I was supposed to talk to him, after all.

I followed him through the French doors. Ivo stopped and looked down. He was standing where the broken spirit had been this morning. I took a step backward, and Ivo turned to me.

"Would you go for a walk with me?" he asked, rather abruptly.

"Oh." My nerves lit up like fireworks. I tried to remember what it had felt like to talk to him when we had almost been friends. He'd always made me feel a little jittery, even before he'd made me afraid of him. "Um, yes. Of course."

He nodded, and we went up the hills of soft green grass and down through the valley that led to his shack. But we passed that hill and went deeper inland than I usually went. The sun got hotter as we went farther from the cool, coastal breezes. Just past the hill where his shack was, Ivo stopped and took off his pale gray jacket. He dropped it on the ground and undid the top button of his shirt.

"I want to show you something," he said, looking past me, into the hills. He rolled his white shirtsleeves up past his elbows. I tried not to look at his arms, which were very tanned and corded with lean muscle, another thing I'd failed to notice about him before.

"What?" I asked.

Ivo shook his head.

"I have to show you," he said.

I did not much like the sound of that. I looked at Ivo's hands. They were calloused and strong. Nails bitten down to the quick. I had seen magic sparking between those fingers. I'd felt the power of the spell he had thrown at me from across the shack. All it did was pull his book from my hands, but it could have been anything. Anything at all. If there were limits to what Ivo could do, I didn't know what they were.

"Please," he said.

It was the first time he'd said *please* to me. I met his eyes, let myself search them. There was nothing frightening there this time. No anger, no coldness. Nothing that warned me away. And I had my plan to execute. I nodded, and we went on.

After another few minutes, we came to a section of the footpath that narrowed as it wound along the edge of a canyon. We were walking very close to each other, close enough that we bumped every once in a while. Ivo slowed and held out his arm for me to go ahead.

"We're going to the aether wells," I said. Ivo nodded.

No one went to the aether wells. I used to get close, driven by my curiosity, but once I had run into the faintly purple shimmer that arced over the canyon entrance, I felt the power of its prohibition from crown to toe. Whatever spell was on that place had both ordered me out and made me want to obey it. I slowed my steps, and Ivo walked into me.

"It's all right," he said quietly. "It won't hurt you."

"What won't hurt me?" I asked. I turned half toward him but stopped when my shoulder grazed his chest. This close to him, I felt the heat coming off his body. I smelled his burnt-metal magic scent.

"You don't need to be afraid of the magic," he said.

"I'm not afraid of magic," I said.

It wasn't true. Not quite. Magic was the silent, constant power behind everything I knew, stronger and stranger than the sea. And it was good to fear the sea, wasn't it? Even if you loved the sea, learned about the sea, swam in it, and lived off it. Even more, then. If the sea threatened a storm, you stayed out of it. I didn't fear magic, exactly, but I respected it.

"No—" Ivo shook his head. "I mean—you should fear it. But not when you're with me."

I wouldn't need his protection from magic if he would let me learn it. But I kept the angry retort in my thoughts and tried one more time:

"What are you showing me?"

But Ivo shook his head and gestured forward. And I went.

"I overheard something today," I said. I had almost forgotten why I had agreed to this walk in the first place.

We were nearly at the aether well gates, and I hadn't even attempted to get any information from Ivo. "Something that worried me."

Ivo grunted. "You were listening in on Grandfather and me. You and Miles."

I whipped my head around to look at him and tripped on a root growing across the footpath. Ivo grabbed my arm and steadied me. His face was smooth. If there was anger there, I couldn't see it, and in my experience, his anger was easy to spot.

"Yes," I admitted. His hand on my arm was still hotter than a normal man's would be, but I found myself disliking it less than I had this morning. He seemed friendlier now. Less threatening, at least for the moment. "You were talking about Rex, I thought. And then before lunch, I also overheard Rex and Apollonia in the garden."

"And?"

"And it seemed like he was threatening her," I said. Ivo still hadn't let go of my arm, but his grip had gone from steadying and functional to something looser, almost affectionate.

"Threatening her how?"

"He wanted her to do something tonight, or else he would do something to her family."

"Do what?"

"He didn't say what. I think he said, 'You know what I can do to your family.' Something like that."

Ivo's hand dropped at last. His scowl returned. He looked more familiar with it on his face, and this reminded me that he hadn't been wearing it for the entirety of our walk until that moment.

"What did Apollonia say?" he asked.

"Not very much," I said. "But it sounded like she planned to do . . . whatever he was asking."

"And what do you think that was?"

"I had no idea, but Miles and Coco thought . . ." I blushed furiously again and looked down. "They thought he wanted her to go to bed with him."

Ivo was still, and after a moment, I glanced up at him, expecting him to show the same rage Miles had. He was still scowling, but not much more angrily than he usually did. He shook his head.

"No," he said. "They'll be married in a month. He'd be willing to wait that long, I think. And there are plenty of other women if he really wanted—"

Ivo glanced down at me and then straightened.

"Sorry," he said.

"It's all right," I said. "Coco said . . . well, she said Rex has a certain reputation."

"What do you think?"

As nice as it had been of him to ask for my opinion at lunch, it didn't make much sense to ask me about this.

"I don't know Rex, and I don't know men," I said. "What I think about it isn't worth much."

I started walking again, faster this time. I couldn't tell if my heart was beating fast in my throat from anger or nerves.

"You know more than you think," he called after me. "You listen. You watch. The rest of them don't know anything about this island."

I stopped and turned to look at him. I met his sad green

eyes, and I was suddenly certain there was something he wasn't telling me.

"What do I know about it that the rest of them don't?" I asked.

Ivo was still. He didn't answer.

"You're right that I listen," I said. "I watch. But where has it gotten me?"

Ivo looked startled. He stared at me for a long moment, searching my face. Looking for something particular, I thought.

Whatever it was, he didn't seem to find it. He looked down and walked toward me, then past, managing somehow to get around me on the narrow path without touching me at all.

"We should keep going," he muttered.

"Ivo," I said. "What's going on?"

I watched him press ahead, ignoring me. I thought about turning around, going back to the house, and telling everyone it was over. Letting Ivo come back alone and find out from someone else.

Instead I took a deep, shaky breath and started after him. There was the plan to think of, and afraid or not, I wanted to see what he would show me.

We went deeper into the canyon in silence. The silver plume of smoke that rose from the wells grew thicker as we came closer. The metal, magic smell thickened, too, and my unease along with it. The canyon felt dead. There were no creatures here, no birds or natural sounds beyond the wind. Even the insects stayed away.

We stopped a few yards before the shimmering lavender barrier. My breath was shallow, and not from the hike.

"We're not going in," I said, reassuring myself and the wards that pushed against me.

Ivo walked forward, much closer to the magic barrier than I could make myself go. He turned toward the canyon wall and knelt by a small hollow.

"Here," he said quietly.

I approached slowly and stopped a few paces behind Ivo when I saw it.

"Oh," I breathed.

It was another spirit, broken and leaking like the house spirit I'd seen in the backyard. This one was a well spirit, of course. The form it was bound to was larger than the house spirit's, and there was a golden tinge to it rather than a purple one. But it looked just as sad and just as dead. Ivo had said there were others.

He moved his hand over the dead spirit and held it over the blurred, flattened head. The few inches between the spirit's head and his fingers crackled and lit. I took a step forward.

"What are you doing?"

Ivo muttered under his breath. Low, foreign words, not addressed to me. The answer was obviously "magic." I took another step forward just as Ivo put the meaty part of his thumb into his mouth and bit until blood dripped down onto the prostrate spirit.

My stomach turned. Blood magic.

Ivo resumed muttering, with his own blood smeared across his lips and teeth. My shoulders heaved, and I tried not to retch. He squeezed his bitten hand into a fist, wringing a few last drops of blood.

With all my watching and listening, I had managed to

learn just a few things about magic. First among them was that it was powerful, beautiful, frightening, and kept only to a few. And second, blood magic was forbidden.

Nausea roiled my stomach. The blood on Ivo's face and hand repelled and disturbed me. I didn't want to look at it. I really didn't want to look at it.

No, I mustn't look at it. I wasn't allowed—

I jerked my head up and stared at the sky. There was a round blur of lavender, and then another. The air spirits were circling above us. I had never seen them do that.

Ivo wiped the blood from his mouth and fell quiet. The crackling light between his hand and the spirit sparked and then went out. He sat back on his heels and placed his hands together in front of himself while he watched.

The spirit started to dissolve.

It happened slowly at first, like a continuation of whatever sickness had taken it. It was as if its corporeal form were made of golden ice that was suddenly melting all at once. Ivo stood and stepped backward. Then the puddled spirit erupted into flame.

Ivo backed toward me, both his arms extended outward to the flame where the spirit had been. The fire was growing, not in width but in height, taller and taller until it was half again as tall as Ivo. The fire spoke in a language I didn't understand. It was hissing and angry and not much like a human voice, yet I knew it was making words. Ivo spoke back in what sounded like the same language, awkward with his human tongue. The fire spoke again, then pulsed with a furious, threatening heat. I stumbled backward, sweating and gasping in the thick, hot air. Ivo turned his palms toward each other, and a fire-like substance of his own spread between them. Then the spirit attacked.

It went for me, vaulting over Ivo and his defenses. I had no time to flee. The spirit moved faster than I knew a thing could move. It was over me, on me. I dropped to the ground screaming into the roar of the flame.

Then the roar of the fire spirit retreated behind Ivo's voice shouting the strange language he'd been muttering before. I rolled on the ground smothering the remains of the fire on my burning clothes.

"Aeris!" Ivo screamed. *"Arcesso te!"*

"WHAT DID YOU DO?"

It was Aeris's voice, but not like I had ever heard it before. This wasn't the voice of a sly and malicious spirit but of something strong and deep, not like the ocean but like the crash of a hurricane.

"Deal with it!" cried Ivo.

I pushed myself back, scuttling like a crab, until I was flat against the opposite canyon wall. Ivo backed toward me, his arms stretched out, magic sparking between his hands. Above us, the fire spirit careened toward Aeris, who took on the form of silver light. Then, with a scream of wind and a flash that nearly blinded me, they were both gone.

Ivo dropped to his knees, gasping.

I stared at the sky where the spirit had crashed into Aeris. It was gone for now, but I couldn't quite bring myself to believe it wouldn't reappear there at any moment and plummet back toward me.

"Mae."

I didn't want to look at Ivo. I looked down at my dress

instead. Apollonia's dress. The cream fabric was singed and smoking. I didn't feel any pain, except on my palms, where I had beaten the last of the fire from my skirt. I held them up. They were blistered and trembling.

"Mae," said Ivo again. He stood over me, then lowered himself to my level. "It's gone. You're fine."

I met his eyes.

"I'm not fine." The tremor in my voice said more than the words.

"You are," he said. "It's not coming back."

I shook my head. "You said you would keep me safe. You said I didn't need to be afraid."

"You were safe," he said.

"I was on fire!" I pushed myself to my feet and winced when my burned hands touched my knees. The low throb of pain in them was starting to grow stronger. Tears welled in my eyes.

Ivo took my hands in his, turning them over so the palms were facing up. He started to mutter again, but I jerked away.

"I don't want your help!" I started back down the footpath, out of the canyon, away from the smell of the wells and the suffocating heat. I needed the sea breeze and the sound of the waves. Even the spirit music was fainter down here.

"Wait—" Ivo hurried after me, panting to catch up. I was fast, but he was usually fast, as well. His magic fight had drained him. I started to run. I had forgotten every goal I had except that I needed to get out of this awful canyon, away from the terrifying spirit.

I ran until the dusty canyon was behind me and the footpath wound its way back into hills of soft grass. I kept running, a sprint I knew I couldn't sustain, until it all caught up with me. The run that morning, the swim, the rosé at lunch, the hike, the spirit's attack. My calf muscles started to seize. My body demanded rest. I threw myself onto a patch of grass in the shade of a cypress and hoped Ivo would simply pass me by.

The music of the spheres was louder here than it had been in the canyon, though still fainter than it was at the big house. I quieted my breathing and tried to ignore the pain in my hands, forget everything but the music.

Instead, my mind crowded with anxieties.

So far, my plan to learn more about what Ivo might have done to Imogen or the spirits was not going well. I hadn't learned anything about Rex, either, except that Ivo doubted he was threatening Apollonia into going to bed with him. I had asked him almost nothing, and he had answered even less. But I wasn't entirely without information. It was hard, somehow, even to think of it, but Ivo had shown me something. If I could only make any sense of what it meant.

Ivo had nearly caught up with me, walking slightly bent over, like he had a terrible cramp. I pushed myself into a sitting position, and after briefly toying with the idea of running away again, I stood to wait for him. He came up to me and stood awkwardly, holding his side and panting.

"Did you know that would happen?" I asked.

"No," said Ivo, then winced a little, like the lie hurt him. "I wasn't sure."

"What made it so hostile?" I thought of it swooping down on me. Its heat had felt like fury. "Why did it attack?"

Ivo stared at me and said nothing.

"They can't hurt humans," I said. "The binding prevents it—so—did you do something to its binding?"

Ivo didn't reply. My anger rose.

"Why did you want to show it to me?" I demanded.

"You don't understand?"

His eyes bored into mine like he was willing some knowledge into my head. Beads of perspiration slid down his face. I thought it through—the dead spirit, the muttering and magic, and then the spirit's revival in homicidal form. But no, I didn't understand.

"No."

Ivo looked away, his face closing down like fog rolling over the coast.

"So explain," I said.

Ivo shook his head. He started to walk away, back on the path toward the big house.

"Where are you going?" I asked.

He kept walking. He didn't even turn his head. It was like I had disappeared.

It stung, his turning away, ignoring me. Worse than I would have expected. It hurt, that all the regard he'd been paying me, that I hadn't even realized I cared about, could be turned off so quickly and completely.

"Do you even want to marry me?"

Ivo stopped.

"I didn't even think you liked me," I said and was mortified to hear my voice break. I tried to remind myself that I didn't care if Ivo liked me or not. It wasn't very convincing when I couldn't even bring myself to look up and see the expression on his face. I clenched my hands, forgetting the burns, and then winced in pain.

Ivo walked back to me quickly. He took my burned hands in his, and before I knew it, he had hastily muttered the incantations, and a lovely, tingling cold was spreading through the painful burns. He withdrew his hands, stuffed them in his pockets, and stared down at the grass.

"I told you not to do that," I said.

"I'm sorry," he said. "I won't have you in pain because of me."

And the pain was gone, but tears spilled down my cheeks anyway.

"I won't hold you to this engagement," said Ivo. His voice was rough and quiet, just above a whisper. "If you change your mind. I will tell them I broke it off."

I thought about this. It was a way out, no doubt. If the Prospers believed Ivo had broken it off, they couldn't blame me. They would feel sorry for me, not angry with me. They might let me stay, for a while longer. I wouldn't have exiled myself from the island.

But I wouldn't have made a place for myself here, either.

"I'm sorry I lost my temper," he said. "In the cabin. About the spell book."

I wanted to say it was all right, that I forgave him. I forced my mouth shut, stomping down the instinct to ingratiate. I didn't forgive him. For that, or any of the rest of it. I looked away, and Ivo went on.

"There are things about myself I can't change. About the past—not just the past. Things that might be hard to live with."

He trailed off and stared back toward the wells.

"I've always liked you, Mae. That's never been the problem," Ivo said and walked away.

CHAPTER TEN

I sat back down under the tree and did my best to think.

What had Ivo been trying to tell me? What things about him would be hard to live with? Was it just his odd habits? His strange unsociability? Or was it something else, something worse? Maybe Miles was right. Maybe Ivo really did have something to hide.

The way out Ivo offered me beckoned. This pretense at an engagement had been a terrible joke, but not on the Prospers. On me. There were forces at play here much too strong for me to bend into my own game.

I looked back down at my perfectly healed hands. They were milky white and pink, softer than I could remember them. Even the callouses I'd earned from climbing trees and scrambling up rocks were gone. My stomach twisted with longing. Magic had done that. Magic no one wanted me to have.

I had two choices that I could see. I could accept Ivo, his magic, and the things he'd done that might be hard to live with. I could stop stirring things up, let them rest, and lay a cover over it all. I could have this life and everything that came with it. I would never be a magician, but I would have all the privileges and luxuries magic could procure. I could take this much and stop wanting more.

And the second choice—refuse Ivo. Take a chance for something better. Leave the island, probably, with no way to learn magic and no certainty that I could ever come back.

A life I knew, or a life I couldn't even imagine.

"Mae!" Miles's voice, frantic, calling for me. "Mae!"

"I'm up here!" I called back, and he came running up the hill.

"Mae! I couldn't find you after lunch! Are you all right?"

He ran toward me and knelt down in the grass next to me. I felt very cold then very hot. He took my hand in his own, which was shaking.

"I'm fine," I said.

"You don't look fine!" Miles exclaimed. "Mae, did he do something? I didn't know where you had gone—I thought—was he with you?"

"He was," I said. "But he left."

Miles scanned my burned clothes and then stared into my face, searching for something. I looked back at him as steadily as I could. There was real fear in his eyes.

"I'm all right," I said again. He took a deep breath and nodded.

Miles helped me to my feet. I was shakier than I'd realized. I wobbled, and Miles pulled me into a fierce, completely unexpected hug. Then, before I had time to recover from the surprise enough to enjoy it, he pulled back, hands on my shoulders, and stared into my eyes again.

"What happened?" Miles repeated.

"We went to the aether wells, stopped just outside," I said.

"The aether wells? Why?" asked Miles.

"He said he had something to show me."

We started to walk, his arm around me, and I described the sick spirit; how Ivo had revived it with magic, how it had flown at me and been taken away by Aeris.

"Did he explain why he put you in danger like that?" asked Miles.

"No," I said. "But I think he was trying to tell me something. He acted disappointed when I said I didn't understand."

"Disappointed?" exclaimed Miles. "Then why didn't he just tell you what he wanted you to know?"

"I don't know," I said dully. Miles's anger flattened my own. I'd been angry enough to hit Ivo a few moments ago, but now I just felt tired. Even Miles's arm around my waist didn't invigorate me.

"He must have known it would attack you," said Miles. "Maybe he set it on you so he could save you. Make you feel grateful."

"Maybe," I said. "If so, it didn't work. I don't feel grateful."

"Good," said Miles. "He put you in danger and wouldn't explain why."

"Yes," I said. "And he admitted that he would be hard to live with. He said there were things in his past he couldn't change."

Miles stopped walking. He looked down at me.

"Did he say what?" he asked in a low voice.

"No," I said. "But he said he'd let me out of the engagement if I wanted."

"But he admitted—he admitted he'd done things, wrong things—"

I looked up at Miles's beautiful, furious face. I was used to seeing him like this, seething against the wounds of his life. Sometimes, before, it had been at his mother. Now it was at Ivo, on his mother's behalf and on mine. I wished I could make him feel something other than rage. I wanted to make him smile.

"We've waited long enough," said Miles, looking down at me but seeing past. "If you tell Grandfather what Ivo said, and I tell him what my mother said, and what I suspect—"

"Then what?" I asked. "What do you think your grandfather is going to do, even if he believes us? Ivo is his heir—he's the only one who can do magic—"

Miles let me go.

"Ivo is *not* the only one who can do magic," said Miles. "And he doesn't have to be the heir."

I stared at him.

"You want to take Ivo's place."

"Why not?" Miles demanded. The edge to his voice, the set to his jaw, his wound-tight posture—everything in him was defensive. "I can do magic—you've seen me! Not much, but that's without training. Grandfather never tried to teach me, because he had Ivo. But once he knows what Ivo really is, it'll be different!"

Conflicting emotions tangled up in my chest. This was what I had wanted. Miles, admitting his ambition. Willing to go after it, even if it was likely to mean rejection. Taking a chance and taking me with him.

I should have been delighted. Excited, or at least hopeful. Instead what I felt was an unwelcome, sinking certainty that both our dreams were nothing more than that. Dreams. Fantasies I had used to keep myself sane through the long, empty months. Ivo was the reality—the real heir, already trained, already so powerful.

And mine. If I wanted him.

"But—" I didn't want to argue. Yet I needed Miles to convince me that he was right. "Ivo isn't the only reason Lord Prosper never trained you in magic."

Miles spun on his heel and took two hard steps away from me. Then he stopped.

"Say what you mean," he said, without turning around.

"He tried with Alasdair, even though he already had Ivo," I said. "He could have tried with you, but he didn't."

"And?" said Miles.

"What do you want me to say, Miles?" I said quietly. I hated this. I hated saying things that would hurt him. "I wish he had trained you, but he didn't."

"And you think you know why."

I didn't answer. We both knew why, even if he wouldn't admit it.

"Maybe you do," he said. "So why, Mae? Because no one knows who my father is? Because I'm illegitimate? Because I wasn't born here? Because my mother—"

He broke off. I took a step toward him, put a hand on his arm. It was warm and strong and exactly what I wanted. Almost.

Miles looked down at my hand.

"He's always been good to me," he said.

"I know," I said.

He went on as if I'd contradicted him. "I've always been welcome here. He sent me to school. It's not his fault that the rest of them—"

"I know," I said again, because it wasn't Lord Prosper's fault that Alasdair called Miles foul names or that the older generation tilted their heads away when he spoke, as if avoiding an unpleasant sound. And however he was treated at the school he and Alasdair both attended—that wasn't Lord Prosper's fault, either. He couldn't have stopped any of that. Probably.

"I could show him what I've already learned," said Miles. "If he knows that it was Ivo's fault, and Charles's—what happened to my mother, what she became—"

"But we don't know that it was."

"I know it!" Miles yelled, pulling away from me again. "She has spent every day of her life for as long as I've lived trying to forget what they did to her! The parties and the drugs, the men—all of it was to shut it out! She wanted to do better by me, all this time she wanted to and she couldn't, because of them! Because of Ivo! He's the one who should be ashamed of what she became, not her, not me—him!"

"I don't understand." I tried to imagine standing next to Miles when he took these vague accusations to Lord Prosper. It wouldn't be good enough. "What is it you think he did to her?"

"He did blood magic, Mae!" Miles wheeled on me. "He bound her—I don't know why—but I know he did the same thing to you!"

I stepped back. The words landed like punches.

"No," I said, shaking my head. "What? He wouldn't."

"It's the only thing that explains it," said Miles. "For as long as I can remember, she avoided him, couldn't stand hearing about him. When I tried to ask her what had happened, all she could say was his name, and even that was nearly impossible. It made her sick, frightened—just like you when we went to that tree this morning."

My hands had started to shake. I didn't know what he was talking about—and yet, did I? It sounded familiar, somehow. It sounded true.

"What tree?" I whispered. I could hardly get the words out past the terror tightening my throat. "What—this morning?"

"You don't remember," said Miles. "I know. She didn't, either. The binding makes you forget everything, even trying to go against it."

"Binding?" I repeated. "Why would they bind me? I can't do anything they don't want me to do, anyway."

Miles smiled, rueful and fond. I couldn't appreciate it. I hardly even saw it.

"But you did," he said. "The tree. I think you climbed it. Watched him. I think you saw something Ivo didn't want you to see. Then he used blood magic to bind you from remembering and from ever climbing that tree again."

"No," I said again. I feared Ivo—yes. But not for that. I shook my head, banishing the thought. It couldn't have happened. It was too terrible to contemplate. It was bad enough that they controlled my life in the ordinary ways, setting boundaries on my ambitions and hopes. If Ivo had come into my mind? Set limits on what I could even think?

I thought of his face when I asked him what he was hiding and he stared at me, looking for something. Had Ivo looked guilty, or was I only imagining it now?

"This was why I was so worried when you went off with him. I'm sorry. I should have warned you. I should have kept a closer watch—" Miles stepped toward me, but I edged back.

"You can't marry someone who would do that to you. You could never trust him. You could never know what else he might do."

"You don't know," I whispered. My head was spinning. "Even if it happened—you don't know it was him."

"I know he watches you," said Miles. He reached into his messenger bag and pulled out Ivo's leather journal. He flipped to the back and held it out to me. It was a simple sketch, of me. I was lying on my stomach in the grass behind my father's cottage. A book was open in front of me. My chin was resting on my stacked hands, my legs stuck into the air at the knees.

"That doesn't prove that he . . ."

I couldn't even say it. My stomach heaved at the attempt.

"No, it doesn't prove that he bound you. But—"

"Stop!" I cried. "Stop saying that!"

I pushed past him on the trail and walked as quickly as my exhausted legs would take me. All I wanted was for Miles to stop talking. My whole body and mind screamed against him. But was it really me who wanted him to stop? I couldn't tell which was more sickening—the things he was saying or the magic they put on me to make me not want to listen.

Because he was right. I knew it. I could feel it.

"You can't just ignore this, Mae." Miles had followed along behind me.

"I could," I said. Nothing would be easier. It was a fight even to hold on to the words he was saying. "I could do just that."

"Is this what you want to be, Mae?" Miles called after

me. He was falling behind. "What kind of life can you have, married to a man who won't even let you have your own mind to yourself?"

I stopped walking. I forced myself to face it. To think it.

He was right. I couldn't let myself forget this. Not with the rest of my life at stake.

I ran through every interaction I'd ever had with Ivo in my mind. The few quiet walks. The borrowed books. The brief, halting conversations about whether I had enjoyed them. I'd been a little afraid of him even then, before he had exploded at me, but that was because of the magic. Because of what he could do with magic.

Like break into my mind. Take out something that had displeased him.

Miles caught up with me. He reached toward me, tentatively. His hand brushed my shoulder and fell back to his side. I turned away and started walking again.

"I didn't mean to upset you," said Miles.

"Yes, you did," I said. "That's exactly what you wanted to do."

"I wanted to put you on your guard."

"On my guard? On my guard?" My voice was growing too loud. I didn't want to shout at him, but I couldn't stop myself. "Then you should have put me on my guard before you let me stay engaged to him!"

"I didn't let you do anything!" Miles said. "This was your idea!"

"And you approved, even though you thought—" I swallowed hard. It was hard enough to think it. I still couldn't make myself say it. "You don't want me on my guard, you want me angry so I'll back you up to Lord Prosper."

"Yes!" Miles had broken into a run now and so, I noticed, had I. "Because that's the only way I can see to get justice for both of us!"

"You don't want justice," I said. The footpath graded up a hill, and Miles started to fall behind. His rugby training wasn't a match for my daily cross-island runs, it seemed. "You want to take Ivo's place."

"That *would* be justice!"

"And what about me?"

I stopped and turned so abruptly that Miles almost ran into me. He stood over me, just a few inches taller. Just the right height. Not like Ivo. Ivo was too tall. Too frightening. Too powerful.

"What do you mean?" he asked, quieter now that our faces were so close. Ivo's breath had smelled like metal, but Miles's smelled like rosé and green onion soup. He knew a spell but wasn't a real magician yet. And the truth was, I was glad of it. I wanted us to learn it together, to become powerful at the same time. Could anyone trust a person who had that kind of power unless they had it, too? I thought of Ivo, forced myself to think of the binding. If Miles hadn't told me this, I might have married Ivo and never known what he had done.

But Miles and I, we were the same. Neither of us belonged, both of us had to prove ourselves. And magic was the best kind of belonging. The best form of proof. No one could deny it, not even Apollonia or Alasdair. Their lives were bought with magic. This island was made of magic. If we had magic, we would have everything else, too.

Miles didn't back away. If he became a magician, he would certainly look the part—tall, dark, gorgeous. Mysterious. Not like Ivo, who was simply confusing, hard to figure out. Miles was the kind of mysterious to make you want to know more. My breath became shallow. He inched closer. I'd had dreams that started just like this.

"What happens to me when Ivo is banished and you get your place at Lord Prosper's right hand?"

Miles tilted his head to the side and studied me. He was too close, and this was no dream. If I weren't so upset, so hot, and so angry, I might have shied away like a nervous horse. But I was all those things, and it made my blood rush and my lips throb. For once I didn't want to make myself smaller or less visible. Let him see it. It was time he knew.

"I don't know, Mae." He said my name differently, like it was a question he was asking for the first time. "What do you want to happen to you?"

"You really don't know?"

"Tell me."

"I shouldn't have to," I said. "You should have seen it by now."

Miles moved his hand toward me, and for a moment I thought he might touch my face. Instead he touched a lock of my singed hair, rubbing it between his fingers until the burnt ends came off as ash. "Tell me what I missed."

He lowered his face another inch toward mine. An invitation or a challenge. I couldn't tell which.

"You weren't the only one who belonged here but didn't." It wasn't necessary to speak above a whisper now. Once, I could have shouted without getting his attention. Now his eyes watched my lips so closely, I hardly needed to make a sound. "You weren't the only one they ignored and slighted. You aren't the only one with ambitions they won't let you rise to. I'm just like you, but you have always been too busy brooding to see me."

"I see you now," he said.

He could kiss me, if he wanted to. Nothing stood in his way but a few inches of empty air. Or I could kiss him. He would kiss me back.

And I knew why.

"Because I'm part of your case against Ivo."

He shook his head. "That's not why."

"Because I was on fire?"

He smiled. It crinkled his eyes and filled his whole face with fondness.

"Yes," he agreed. It didn't matter what he said now. The smile said everything I wanted to hear, and for the moment, I believed it. "Because you were on fire."

I kissed him, and he kissed me back.

CHAPTER ELEVEN

Miles walked me back to the big house. He let go of my hand when we were close enough to the house to be seen, which reminded me that I was still officially engaged to Ivo.

"I should find Ivo and tell him it's off," I said.

Just the thought of it filled me with dread. All I really wanted was a long bath and then a longer nap—or to kiss Miles some more.

"Wait until we talk to Grandfather," said Miles. "Just don't go off alone with him again."

It was midafternoon now. Lord Prosper always slept at this time. Officially this was because he rose in the middle of the night to observe the stars and spheres, but it probably had as much to do with the fact that he was an old man. Miles and I had agreed to meet before the party began and go together to share our case against Ivo.

"I don't like still being engaged to him," I said. The house spirits were setting up tables for the party and gold pennants across the back patio and gardens. They were so blank and docile. I thought of the well spirit blazing into flame and shivered.

"I don't like it, either," said Miles. "But it's better if he doesn't suspect anything yet."

I wondered what Ivo wasn't supposed to suspect. That Miles and I were—whatever we were? Or that I was helping Miles in his quest to prove that Ivo had done—

It took me a moment to remember what it was Miles thought Ivo had done.

And that in itself was proof, if not that Ivo had bound me, then that someone had.

I forced down the nausea, less now than it had been, and turned the idea over and over. It snagged at my mind like a puzzle piece that fit on one side and not the other. Could Ivo have done something so terrible to me, really? If I'd learned it this morning, I would have had no trouble believing. But today Ivo had reminded me of the side of him I had started to see a few months ago. Awkward and difficult, yes, but thoughtful. Sometimes almost sweet. I didn't want to believe this of him now.

On the other side, though, it certainly fit with what he'd said. And it explained other things, too, like why Ivo had been so angry at my attempts to learn magic. If I learned enough, I could throw off the binding. I could take back control of my own mind, remember everything. Whatever it was.

But what was it? What had I seen that he couldn't let me remember?

Miles squeezed my hand as I parted from him and went up the back staircase. I desperately needed a bath. No one saw me steal into Coco's room but the spirits.

Coco's room was beautiful, though nothing like Apollonia's. She didn't have doors opening onto a balcony, and her bed was covered in several brightly colored wool blankets instead of cloudlike comforters. There were film posters on the walls instead of mirrors and oil paintings. Besides the bed, the most notable furniture was a gleaming saddle draped over a pommel, left over from Coco's horse phase. I went into the bathroom, sparkling white and chrome, and turned on the tap in the huge claw-foot tub. Coco wouldn't mind if I took a bath in her room.

I shed Apollonia's ruined dress and slipped into the tub. Then I sank under the water and slowly let out my breath in a stream of tiny bubbles.

My heart was a snarl of emotions, and my thoughts were just as tangled.

I surfaced again and took a slow, deep breath.

There were too many thoughts in my mind, but it was easy to push away the ones I didn't want to think and place the ones I did in the center.

Miles had kissed me. And really, even with all that had happened, how could I think about anything else?

The bedroom door banged open: Coco's usual mode of entering a room.

"I'm in the bath!" I called to her, and then the door to the bathroom banged open as well.

"Oh, good idea, a bath," said Coco, panting. She looked flushed and sweaty. "I certainly need one. Mae—you're not going to believe what I found out!"

"What?" I asked. I reached out through the bubbles for Coco's shampoo, squeezed a dab onto my hands, and lathered it into my burnt hair.

"It's Rex, it's all Rex!" Coco said. "I followed him. After you and Ivo left—I figured I should investigate the real
culprit while you ruled out poor Ivo—who, you know, I just
really don't believe would do anything to the spirits—"

"Hm," I said. Coco rode right past this mild objection,
which wouldn't have been enough to stop her under normal
circumstances, much less now.

"And I was right, Mae! Rex is the one making the spirits
sick!"

"How do you know—"

"I followed him! He took a strange route, around the
south path and then in through a ravine. I didn't realize
where he was going until we were almost there. The wells,
Mae! He went to the aether wells!"

That was strange. Rex wouldn't have been any more
welcome there than I was. Lord Prosper saw to it that each
lesser island-holder received his monthly shipment of raw
aether, which they would then be responsible for processing.
But none of the lesser island-holders had their own wells or
were welcome at Prosper's. And then, of course, there were
the magical protections.

"How did he get past the wards?" I asked.

"Oh. I'm not sure he did. I only saw him just outside the
wells. He had a ship docked there, in a tiny harbor on the
south side. There was some man in it I didn't recognize.
He looked like a mainlander but a dull kind, you know?
The colorless kind who works at a bank or some wretched
thing."

I didn't really know, having never met a banker, but the
picture was clear enough in my mind.

"Rex checked in with the miserable mainlander, then went

right up almost to the wells and came back carrying one of the messed-up well spirits!"

"What?" I sat up, creating a small wave in the tub that splashed over the sides. "You're sure?"

"Of course I'm sure! He put it in the boat in a kind of box, and the miserable mainlander sailed away with it!"

"He stole a well spirit?" I was aghast.

"Yes!" Coco exclaimed. "I couldn't figure out why he'd want a broken well spirit at first, but then I realized. Mae, it's so obvious! He did some sort of magic to the well spirits to make them sick so he could steal one. You could never steal a healthy spirit, right? Because they simply wouldn't go. But if you make it sort of dead like that, then presto! Easy to carry off!"

"Oh," I breathed. I was starting to see.

"So Rex puts a magic plague on the island, then walks off with a well spirit. Why, you ask?"

I had indeed been about to ask why.

"Because he wants his own well!" exclaimed Coco. "Of course he does, right? But Grandfather has never told them how to make one. It's crazy difficult magic, sure, but he figures if he can get some well spirits of his own—" Coco snapped her fingers. "Then, easy! And who knows, maybe he's right!"

"I guess so," I said. I was skeptical that it would be so simple. Magic worked on the lesser islands but not as well as here. But perhaps that was only because the spirits lived here and not there. Perhaps Rex was right that stealing spirits for his own island was the answer. "So you think he can just lift the . . . magic plague, or whatever it is, once he has the stolen well spirit back on his island?"

"Right," said Coco. "And this explains the threat to

Apollonia, too. He must have told her he had the power to do this magic plague and that he could lift it, or not."

"It does make a kind of sense," I said. "Ivo and I went to the wells, too. On the other side. He . . . tried to heal a spirit."

Coco was still nodding with enthusiasm at her own explanation when she asked, "Tried? Did he fail, then?"

"Not exactly," I said. "The spirit woke up, but it turned into flame and attacked us."

"Oh!" Coco looked down at the floor, where the formerly cream-colored dress was crumpled. "So that's what happened to Apollonia's dress! But you're fine, aren't you?"

"Yes," I said. "Ivo drove it off. Do you think Rex could have left some curse on the plagued spirits so that they would attack if anyone but him awakened them?"

"Oh, yes! I bet that is exactly what he did!"

I nodded. I liked this explanation. It loosened the knot of fear I felt at the idea that there might be that much violence hiding under any of the spirits' bindings. They were cursed—magically made to attack. They didn't want to do it. That was better.

"It doesn't explain everything, though." I took a deep breath and swallowed down the faint taste of bile that rose in my throat at the prospect of telling Coco what Miles had said. "Coco, there's something I have to tell you."

"Are you all right?" Coco asked.

"Yes and no," I said. The nausea surged again, and the strange terror with it, but so did my determination. I knew what caused it now. There was something inside me trying to keep me from doing what I wanted. There were enough forces outside me doing that. I would fight whatever part of this binding I could.

"Miles said Ivo put a binding on me, to keep me from doing something or remembering something," I said in a rush. I felt very hot. My stomach seized, and my throat tried to close on the words, but I forced them out. "He recognized the effects of it—said the same thing was done to Imogen. And he's right. There's something there. I can feel it right now."

I leaned forward and dropped my head into my hands.

"It doesn't want me to tell you this," I gasped.

"Mae—" Coco's voice was alarmed. "Are you sick?"

"It's making me sick," I said. "The binding."

"Are you sure that's what it is?" Coco asked.

I was about to vomit. I swallowed down hard and nodded. Pain knifed from the pit of my stomach to the crown of my head.

I couldn't tell her anything more. I took a long, deep breath through my nose and waited for the hot, sick feeling to subside.

"Huh," said Coco. "I don't know, Mae."

"What?" I asked.

"It's just . . ." Coco paused. "You used to be really nosy, you know? And no one is allowed to watch while Grandfather and Ivo do the magic. Maybe you just disobeyed one too many times?"

Slowly, I looked up at her. She chewed her lip, staring at me with conflict in her eyes. My head pounded, and the binding still roiled my stomach, but this filled me with a worse kind of sickness.

"So I deserved it?" I whispered.

"No!" cried Coco. "No, of course not. I know it's bad magic—it's just—it wouldn't be the worst thing, would it? If you'd just been bound from doing something you weren't supposed to do anyway?"

I couldn't argue with her. Even if I could fight past the binding to do it, I didn't think I would have the heart to try to convince my best friend that she should be outraged to find out someone had put a black spot on my mind and my will. I wasn't sure I even had the heart to be outraged myself, if she wasn't. Could it really be as bad as it felt, if this was Coco's reaction? Maybe I was being dramatic. Maybe Coco was right. I slumped into the bath, until the water covered the tip of my chin.

"I know it must be scary, not to know for sure what the binding is," said Coco earnestly. "But I really don't think it's anything terrible. He wouldn't bind you from doing anything you should be allowed to do. Maybe . . . maybe he just didn't want you to get in trouble. And as for Imogen . . ."

"You don't believe Miles at all," I said quietly.

"I believe he believes it," said Coco with a sigh. "Look, if my mother was like his, I'd want some big explanation, too. I'd want someone to blame. But maybe . . ."

I nodded and let out a long breath. Something went out of me with it.

"Maybe there's no one to blame. Maybe it's just who she is," I said dully.

The last traces of the binding's pain and sickness vanished. Almost like accepting Coco's explanation was as good as forgetting about it entirely.

"Or maybe Miles is right, and she was bound. But maybe she was bound from doing something she shouldn't, too." Coco's eyes flicked to me. "I couldn't say that to Miles, though. You know how touchy he is."

The water was starting to feel cold, and the bubbles were thinning. Coco and I had never minded our nakedness around each other, but just now I didn't like feeling so exposed. I asked Coco for a towel, got out of the tub, and put on one of her robes. We went into her bedroom.

"When did Miles tell you all this, anyway?" Coco asked. "I thought you were walking with Ivo."

"Oh." I could feel a blush rising in my cheeks. "He . . . uh . . . he found me. After the walk."

"He found you?" Coco squinted at my burning face. "Why do you look like that? Did something happen?"

I hesitated and flushed more deeply.

"Something happened with Miles!" Coco cried. "Look at you, you're as red as Apollonia's lipstick! Tell me what happened!"

"Calm down!" I exclaimed. "It was just a kiss!"

"A kiss?" screamed Coco. "He kissed you?!"

I laughed awkwardly and sat on the edge of Coco's bed, gripping the side.

"Well, what was it like? No—actually—don't answer that, please." Coco grimaced. "I don't really want to think about my cousin kissing anyone. Not that I blame you! He's very good-looking!" She grimaced again and gagged slightly.

My smile had been real for a moment, but I was already having to force it. The woolen blanket felt rough on the back of my legs, but the rest of me felt blank and numb.

I glanced up at Coco. Her joking grimaces had faded, too.

"You're still engaged to Ivo," she said quietly.

"Not really," I said, though my insides squirmed at the thought.

"He thinks so, even if you don't."

"He said he wouldn't hold me to it. He knows what he did was wrong. Coco—he—" The protest burst out of me like vomit, against my will, against the binding's will, propelled by a last surge of outrage. "He did blood magic on me! I don't owe him anything!"

Coco crossed her arms and chewed her lip. Something swooped low in my stomach, was swallowed by the nausea, then died.

"Do you think I do?" I asked.

"No, I guess not," said Coco after a moment. "I just feel sorry for him."

I looked at her, the blank feeling spreading through me, eating away at the last of my anger, my defiance, until it was small. Small and unimportant, like me.

"Anyway, we can ask Grandfather about it all," said Coco. "I should tell him what I saw Rex do."

I nodded and tried to focus on what Coco wanted me focused on.

"I think we should go now," said Coco.

"Now?" I echoed. I didn't want to do that at all, though I couldn't think of a reason Coco would accept.

"Yes. You should get dressed. Are you still going to wear that purple thing we stole from Apollonia?"

It was burgundy, but I nodded.

"Earlier, Apollonia said I should come by her room and she'd help me get ready," I said.

"Oh," said Coco. A quick emotion flashed on her face and was gone before I could identify it. "You should do that, then, as soon as we talk to Grandfather. You can ask her about Rex."

I nodded. I could never really prefer Apollonia's company

to Coco's, but just now, the promise of getting away from Coco long enough to disperse the resentful feelings gathering in me against her was a relief. And anyway, there was simply no doubt I would look far better after getting ready with Apollonia's help than with Coco's.

"You could come, too," I suggested tentatively. "You'd be much better at getting her to talk about Rex than I would."

"I don't think so." Coco shuddered a little. "I've never willingly subjected myself to the soul-scouring experience that is Apollonia, and I'm not going to start now."

"She's not *so* bad," I said. "She did offer to help me dress."

"Because she has some torture planned for you, you can be sure of that," said Coco. She went to her closet, where we had stored the dress I pilfered from Apollonia's closet, and brought it to me.

I held out the dress with a newly critical eye. I had stolen it because it was several seasons old, torn, and unlikely to be missed. Now that I'd worn a more recent dress of Apollonia's, albeit not one of her more beloved choices, I found this one a little faded in its appeal. It was a beautiful color, at least: deep wine red. I put it on and remembered why I liked it. It might not be the latest in fashion, but it did wonders for my complexion and was tight enough to prove even to Apollonia that my figure didn't need any more lenience than hers did.

"Beautiful," said Coco.

"Thanks." A jolt of anxiety shot through me. "Do you think she'll remember it?"

"Not a chance," said Coco airily. "This was from ages ago, and she has *so* many beautiful clothes."

I nodded. "What are you going to wear?"

"This," said Coco, gesturing to her dust-streaked trousers and sweaty button-down.

"Not really," I said.

"No, not really. I'm going to change later," said Coco with a grin. "You'll see."

I smoothed out my dress and ran a quick comb through my hair. Then Coco and I left her room and started up the stairs.

CHAPTER TWELVE

Coco knocked on the door. I let myself hope that Lord Prosper was still asleep and wouldn't hear us.

"Come in," he said.

Coco opened the door on a wide, circular room, lit by the sun through the glass dome overhead. The walls were lined with shelves, which were filled with leather-bound books, vials, and instruments. There were gleaming wooden tables covered in star charts and shining silver tools. Lord Prosper leaned over one, a pencil in his hand. He looked up at us and smiled.

"Cordelia." His gaze rested fondly on her for a moment before he turned to me. "And Mae. How can I help you, dear girls?"

He straightened, and a shadow passed over his face. He put a hand to his back like it hurt him. Coco hurried to his side. He placed a hand on her shoulder, and she helped him to one of the worn leather chairs along the wall.

I looked up, squinting against the sun. A gold model of the solar system hung suspended above us. If Miles was right, I had seen it before but from above instead of below. I tasted bile and tore my eyes away.

Coco had settled her grandfather into a chair and sat in one across from him. She beckoned to me. I took a few steps toward them.

"You have something to tell me?" Lord Prosper asked.

"I saw something I thought you should know about," said Coco, then launched into her story about Rex and the stolen well spirit. I watched Lord Prosper as she told him. His aged face drew into a concerned frown. I couldn't tell if he was surprised.

"Hmm," he said, when Coco had finished.

"But don't you think that could explain what's happening with the spirits?" Coco asked eagerly.

"It could," he said and let out a long sigh. He leaned back into his chair. His shoulders drooped, and he placed his fingertips on his forehead. He looked completely exhausted. "Rex has been unsatisfied with his place in our order of things for some time. Perhaps I should have done more to . . ."

"It's not your fault that Rex is a toad, Grandfather," said Coco earnestly. "You've been nothing but good to him! What would he have without you? Nothing!"

Lord Prosper smiled at Coco and placed a gnarled hand over hers.

"You are very kind to me, my dear. Very loyal," he said. "I wonder, would you do me a favor?"

Coco's eyes lit up. "Of course, Grandfather!"

"Could you keep an eye on Rex at the party?" he said. "I will have to speak to him soon, but I would rather it not be tonight, when we announce his engagement to your cousin."

"Oh, that's the other thing!" Coco cried. "He threatened

Apollonia! He wanted her to do something, and he said he could hurt her family if she didn't."

Lord Prosper's frown deepened.

"I'll speak to her," he said. "Thank you for letting me know, Cordelia."

His eyes traveled to me. "And you, Mae," he asked. "Is there anything you would like to talk to me about?"

My heart pounded. I swallowed hard against the roiling in my stomach. It had been hard enough to tell Coco about my suspicions. This was much, much worse. I didn't think I could get the words out. I looked at Coco, willing her to tell him for me.

"You seem distressed, my dear," said Lord Prosper, concern in his eyes.

"I—Miles told me something—"

I couldn't. I was going to throw up all over the beautiful white floor of the magic room. I couldn't do it. It was stronger here. Harder. Impossible.

"Coco—" I gasped.

Finally, she jumped in. "Mae thinks . . ." She bit her lip. "Mae thinks there's a binding on her. She thinks . . . well . . . Miles thinks Ivo might have done it."

Lord Prosper's eyebrows shot up.

"What?" His shock was obvious and genuine. "No, surely not! I know he isn't quite—but he would never do something like that!"

"That's what I said!" exclaimed Coco, with relief.

It wasn't quite what she had said. She had said that he might have done it for good reason. But I was as happy to let that go as she was. Lord Prosper's evident horror at the idea was a profound relief. And of course, he was right. Binding me was evil. I would rather Coco refuse to believe Ivo would do such a thing than explain it away.

"But—I don't know who—there's something—"

Lord Prosper rose from his chair and put a hand to my forehead.

"My dear," he said with alarm. "You are very warm. Sit, please."

He stood and offered me his chair, but Coco sprung out of hers and helped me into it before I could take her grandfather's.

"And this . . . this illness happens to you any time you try to speak of the binding?" Lord Prosper asked.

I nodded. It was all I could manage.

He sat back and looked at me for a long, thoughtful moment.

"You do seem to be showing the signs of binding magic. I cannot believe Ivo would . . ." He looked away, and a shadow crossed his face. "Though he has been distant lately. Changed. He is beginning to remind me of his father."

He looked so grieved as he said this that Coco reached out and took his hand.

"But it might not be him," she said. "It could have been Rex, couldn't it? Maybe Mae saw him doing something to the spirits . . . or . . ."

"Yes," said Lord Prosper, a look of profound relief on his face. "Yes, it could have been Rex."

I thought of the way Ivo had looked at me on the trail. So guilty. Sick with it. And what he'd said, about the things he'd done that would be hard to live with.

No, it was Ivo. But that wasn't what either Coco or Lord Prosper wanted to hear.

"Can you remove it?" I asked.

"Not until we know what it is and who cast it. Even then, it is a difficult process." He caught my eye. "Oh, don't be distressed, Mae. I'll free you of it, you can be sure of that. But it won't be tonight. In the meantime . . ."

He fixed me with a long, sorrowful look. I could feel Coco beside me, itching to promise him anything that would make him less sad. But I knew what he was going to ask. This wouldn't be her promise to make.

"I hope you will wait, my dear, before you make any . . . dramatic decisions about your future," said Lord Prosper. "Ivo . . ."

He glanced at the door as though expecting someone to walk through it. He sighed.

"He cares for you," said Lord Prosper. "And I haven't seen him care for anything in some time."

I swallowed.

It wasn't quite what Lady Vivian had said. But it was close enough to remind me of it.

"I don't want to do anything . . . dramatic," I said.

It wasn't a promise. Coco cast me a slightly disapproving look, but Lord Prosper nodded and thanked me. Then he stood and pressed Coco's hand and mine in turn. We left the magic room and went down the stairs with Coco smiling and me trying to.

"I feel a lot better," she said. "It makes so much more sense this way, doesn't it? I mean, we always knew Rex was a bastard. I'll figure out what he did to you tonight, and tomorrow we'll get his binding off you."

I nodded again. It sounded so easy when she said it. I could almost let myself hope it was true.

We stopped on the third floor, and Coco slowed down in front of Apollonia's room. For a moment I couldn't remember why and stared at her blankly.

"You're getting ready with her, remember?" she said.

"Oh," I said. "Right."

I looked at Apollonia's door. It wasn't any less intimidating than Lord Prosper's had been. Coco patted me encouragingly on the shoulder and took off down the hall.

"Have fun with the dragon," said Coco, over her shoulder. "Try not to get burned again."

CHAPTER THIRTEEN

I watched until Coco had disappeared into her own room and then knocked on Apollonia's door, wearing her stolen dress.

"Come in," said Apollonia.

I opened the door but didn't go in. Somehow the first invitation wasn't quite enough.

"What do *you* want?" asked Apollonia. She was draped across her bed, still wearing her blue kimono. Still gorgeous.

"You said I should come," I said. "You said you would help me get ready."

Apollonia's cold green eyes narrowed. She pushed herself languidly to her feet and walked toward me. When she stood directly in front of me, she reached out and took the burgundy fabric of my sleeve between her fingers. She remembered the dress, of course. We'd been foolish to think she wouldn't.

"Looks like I already helped," said Apollonia.

She tilted her head and raised her eyebrows in challenge. I thought about apologizing or offering some explanation. The smart thing to do would be to claim Lady Vivian had given me the dress for the evening—an easily proved lie but one that Apollonia was unlikely to question, at least until later.

But I was tired of apologizing. Tired of pretending and being small. Tired of being Mousy Mae.

So I said nothing and returned Apollonia's gaze. She rewarded me with half a smile.

"You're a bold little minx underneath that meek exterior, aren't you? Mother has no idea what she's really getting with you, poor thing. She thought you'd be so much easier to manage than some rich mainland slut, but she was wrong, wasn't she?"

I didn't answer. There was no way for me to. So many of Apollonia's questions were like that—equally impossible to disagree with as to ignore. Apollonia's hard little smile spread.

"Come in, then." She gestured to the chair before her morning table. "Sit."

I obeyed. The letter that Apollonia had been writing earlier was gone. I tried to remember the name I had seen in the heading. It was the short form of something. Not a common name.

Apollonia stood behind me and ran a brush through my still-damp curls.

"I suppose this means you've finally given up on Miles, have you?"

I blushed. It was becoming acutely obvious to me today that I needed to learn some way not to do that. Perhaps if I thought about very cold things . . .

Like Apollonia's hand on the base of my neck. I shivered at her touch, but the blush didn't recede.

"No?" Apollonia continued. "What, then? Are you hoping

he'll finally take notice of you now that you're engaged to his enemy and wearing my clothes?"

I blushed deeper. I wouldn't have guessed that Apollonia noticed me closely enough to see my obsession with Miles. Shame swooped in my stomach. I must have been very obvious indeed.

"It's not a bad plan, really," said Apollonia. "If I were going to recommend one to you, it might be that. Well?"

Apollonia stared at me in the mirror. This time, I looked away. What could I say? That it hadn't been my plan at all, but even so, it had already worked? Or that it wasn't why Miles had noticed me—that he would have done so without Ivo's presence? But I wasn't sure of that at all. I couldn't say it to Apollonia's face without my paper-thin confidence tearing.

"No? Nothing? How dull." Apollonia pumped some sort of potion from the table into her hands and smoothed it into my wet hair. "If sullen and silent is all you have to offer, perhaps you and Ivo really are meant for each other."

Sullen and silent wasn't any better than mousy and modest. I tried to pull myself together.

"Maybe sullen and silent is all I have to offer to *you*," I said.

Apollonia laughed lightly.

"Do you know why I'm doing your hair and letting you wear my dress?" she asked.

I didn't.

"Because it amuses me to watch you clawing your way up from the steward's cottage," said Apollonia. "Because, in a way, I admire it. I like to think I'd have the boldness to do something similar if I'd been unlucky enough to be born Mae Wilson."

There was just enough praise mixed into this insult that I couldn't immediately work out how I felt about it.

"Though I doubt even I would be willing to go to such an extreme as marrying Ivo," said Apollonia.

"Why not?" I asked. "What's so bad about him?"

Apollonia's fingers went still in my hair. She took them out, wiped them on a cloth, and picked a pot of powder from her table.

"You know what marriage means, don't you?" asked Apollonia. "At some point, someone did tell you about sex, yes?"

I closed my eyes while Apollonia dusted my face with powder. In fact, no one had told me, but I figured out the essentials from books, so I nodded. Apollonia pulled out a dark pencil and began to line my eye.

"And you don't find the thought of doing that with Ivo rather . . . horrifying?"

"I don't know," I said. "How do you find the idea of doing it with Rex?"

Apollonia laughed again, less lightly.

"Rex is very handsome," said Apollonia. "Very well groomed. Cultured. Most women find him attractive."

"Even so, I prefer Ivo." I realized as I said it that, despite everything, it was true.

"Hmm," said Apollonia. "And why is that?"

"I don't like bullies," I said.

"Ah," said Apollonia. "No, I suppose you couldn't call Ivo that. Not in the conventional way."

She finished lining my eyes and opened a pot of rouge.

"So, Ivo." She said it with a thoughtful, just-beginning tone that, combined with Apollonia's rouged finger on my lips, made me feel like a rabbit in a trap. I needed some kind of weapon, something to wield against Apollonia. Rex's threat, perhaps? That was too heavy. I needed something lighter. Like the name on that letter. What was that name?

"But suppose Miles does notice you tonight, what then? Will you marry Ivo anyway? It's not as if Miles would be proposing marriage in his place. Miles doesn't seem at all ready to settle down to me. And you're a practical girl, aren't you? Not the kind who will give up the life she planned on for only the chance of something better."

I remembered the name. Seb.

"I never planned on marrying Ivo," I said. "Not that it wouldn't be nice to have what you have. All the money and luxury, the position. But I want more than that."

I could hardly believe my own nerve. Neither could Apollonia, as was immediately evident from the icy, still silence that followed. Apollonia looked down at me and arched one perfect eyebrow.

"You want more than *I* have?"

Oh, yes, I did. Everything Apollonia had was given to her. She hadn't earned it. She *couldn't* earn it. She was marrying a man she seemed to hate because she had nothing better to do. I would trade my own place for Apollonia's if I could, sure. But no, it wasn't all I'd ever wished for.

Apollonia stared at me as though I had said something unimaginable. After a frozen moment, she laughed. I looked away, and Apollonia went back to dabbing rouge onto my lips.

"What an odd little thing you are," said Apollonia. "You seem so scheming at times that I forget you know nothing of the world. Imagine thinking your position could ever be anything like mine. A little nothing like you."

Apollonia laughed again, and I tensed. She was so smug,

so insufferably sure that she was the pinnacle of my hopes and dreams. And yet for half a moment, I had given her pause. A wild urge seized me to do it again.

"Who is Seb?" I asked.

Apollonia removed her finger from my lip, leaving an unspread lump of rouge behind.

"What?"

I didn't have time to answer. Apollonia drew back her hand and slapped me across the face.

"Get out."

I hardly heard her through the shocked, blank feeling that was starting to turn into stinging pain. Before I had even registered Apollonia's command, she enforced it. She seized me by the arm and dragged me to the door. She threw the door open and marched me out.

"Don't let me see you again tonight, or I'll rip that dress off your thieving back."

She wasn't shouting, but there was something utterly out of control in her eyes. I thanked the planets Apollonia couldn't do magic, or I was quite certain I'd be on fire again.

"Apollonia, what the bloody—"

Alasdair came out of his bedroom and stared at us. He was handsomely dressed for the party and had a cigarette hanging from his fingers. His eyes went first to my stinging cheek and then to Apollonia's vise grip on my arm.

"Let her go, you heartless—"

"Me?" Apollonia demanded. "Heartless?"

Apollonia let me go with a hard little shove and whirled on her brother.

"Do you really think *you* have the right to say *anything* about my heart?"

Alasdair stepped past Apollonia, glaring, and took my arm. He made a show of putting his body between mine and Apollonia's as he escorted me to his room.

"You're welcome, you sneaky little whore!" Apollonia called after us. Her words were so sharp with hatred that just hearing them was like being slashed with a knife. "Looks as if I've given you what you really wanted—the whole set of Prosper men!"

"Bloody hell, Apollonia!"

Alasdair pushed me through his door and slammed it shut behind us. He guided me to the chair at his desk, and I lowered myself into it.

"Spheres—is that blood?" Alasdair asked.

I put a hand to my stinging face and brought it away red. Alasdair stubbed out his cigarette and swore. He pulled a salt-white handkerchief from his pocket and gave it to me.

"I always knew my sister was a tiger, but I've never actually seen her maul anyone before."

"It's not blood," I said. I wiped at it with the kerchief. "It's rouge."

"Well, that's good," he said. He sat on the edge of the desk and pulled a gold filigree cigarette case from his jacket. He snapped it open. "You want one?" he asked.

"I've never smoked before."

"Of course you haven't," said Alasdair. "You're as fresh and innocent as a spring lamb."

He took two cigarettes out of the case and held one out to me with a half smile, and I took it. I put it between my lips, and he leaned down to light it. He flicked the cigarette lighter three times before it caught.

"I keep telling Grandfather he should make one of these

that runs on aether power," he said. "But he isn't keen, some-how."

He sat back upright and lit his own cigarette.

"Right, my spring lamb," he said. "Now breathe the smoke into your lungs—not just your mouth—and then blow it out nice and slowly."

I did as I was told. The smoke swirling into my lungs was thick and choking. I coughed.

He looked me over with a smile that was almost, but not quite, a leer.

"You look nice," he said. "Different."

"Thanks," I said.

"So." Alasdair lit his own cigarette. His lighter was gold, too, and monogrammed. A lovely thing, even if it wasn't aether powered. "What did you do to set her off?"

I thought about lying, but something about the cigarette in my hand, the unfamiliar rush in my head, and Apollonia's slap still ringing in my head made me reckless.

"I asked her who Seb was," I said.

Alasdair took a very long drag on his cigarette.

"And how did you hear about Seb?" he asked in a careful tone.

"I saw his name on a letter she was writing."

Alasdair let out a slow whistle. "You should count your-self lucky she didn't take an eye."

"I do," I said fervently, my cigarette burning down in my fingers. Alasdair took it and tapped off the ashes, then in-serted it between my lips. His hand lingered, and he brushed gently at the cheek Apollonia had hit.

I cleared my throat nervously. "Who is he?" I asked.

Alasdair sat back, though not as far back as he'd been

before. His leg brushed my knee. "Probably Sebastian Wentworth. He's a friend of mine," he said. "Good fellow. Had a disagreement with his parents recently, though, and got cut off without a cent. Had to get a job as a newspaperman, poor man."

"What was the disagreement about?"

"He refused to marry the girl they picked for him," said Alasdair with a shrug. I took a second drag on the cigarette. This time I managed not to cough.

"Nice girl," Alasdair went on. "From a good family. Lots of money. His parents had arranged it a long time ago—something to do with cementing some business merger."

"And?"

"And he wouldn't do it. Said he didn't love her. Poor girl. Sebastian chose to become a penniless newspaperman over her. She found someone else quick enough, of course, but still. Must sting, don't you think?"

I nodded. I took a half puff on the cigarette. My head was starting to spin.

"Speaking of," said Alasdair. "I heard best wishes are in order for you. You're not in the family way, by chance, are you?"

"What?" I was aghast. "No!"

"All right, all right, no offense meant," said Alasdair. "It was just a little sudden, is all. And Ivo would be *such* an easy mark for it."

"Mark for it?" I repeated with horror. "I didn't trap him! It wasn't even my idea!"

"Of course it wasn't, sweetheart, don't know what I was thinking," said Alasdair mildly. "It wouldn't be your idea any more than it was Ivo's, would it?"

I started to rise from the chair, but Alasdair hastily clenched his cigarette between his teeth and pushed me back down, one hand on each of my shoulders.

"Oh, come on now, don't be angry," he mumbled through his cigarette-clenching teeth. "I humbly apologize."

He lowered himself onto his knees in front of me and folded his hands in an absurd posture of repentance. It wasn't especially funny, but it was meant as a joke, so I forced a laugh.

Alasdair grinned at me and put a hand on my knee to steady himself as he sat back against the desk leg. Once he'd settled himself, he left it there. His thumb stroked the indent on my knee, but he was busy with his cigarette and didn't even seem to notice he was doing it. I thought about objecting, but I wasn't sure how when it was so casually done. Surely he would remove his hand on his own in a moment.

"It'll be nice to have you around more, when I'm at home. I suppose you'll like living in the big house instead of off in your little cottage?" Alasdair asked.

He hadn't removed his hand yet. An anxious feeling crawled up my neck. I could have ignored it, probably, if I didn't feel it was a little wrong to let him leave it there. I busied myself with my cigarette and tried to feel as nonchalantly about it as he seemed to.

"Yes," I said. "That will be nice."

"You'll want to do something to Ivo's rooms. Have you been in them? They're—"

He made a face, took another drag of his cigarette. His hand slipped an inch up my leg. It could almost be said that it was on my thigh now, and that *certainly* wasn't appropriate— but on the other hand, could it really be wrong if Alasdair was talking of Ivo the whole time? He must not think it was very inappropriate. Maybe this was how fashionable people behaved on the mainland and the uncomfortable flutters I felt were a normal part of their casual conversation. Probably, if I were more sophisticated, I wouldn't feel them at all. I didn't want to seem like a shy, sheltered little girl. So I tried to take it in stride.

"I'd like to decorate a room," I said. I'd thought about this, about what I would do to Miles's room if it were ever mine. "I'd like to do something a bit more like Apollonia's— let in the light."

Alasdair's hand had reached the hemline of my dress. He was fiddling with it now, his thumb tracing the line of it, first over the top, then just under.

"And you're already on your way to having a wardrobe like Apollonia's," said Alasdair. He took my cigarette out of my hand and reached up to the ashtray to stub it out. "But you'll never really be like her, you know."

"That's fine with me," I said. I was starting to get irritated. I should leave—but how to get Alasdair's hand from my thigh?

"The real difference between you and Apollonia isn't anything that can be bought," said Alasdair. He looked at his hand on my thigh.

"What's the real difference?" I asked.

"Put it this way: you made Apollonia angry. And what did she do?" Alasdair smiled. "She slapped you and threw you out. And a few minutes ago, I made you angry, didn't I?"

I couldn't deny it. "Yes."

"And what did you do about it?"

"I—"

"I'll tell you what you did. Nothing. And then you let me

fondle your knee and slide my hand up your thigh. And in another moment, when I kissed you, you would have let me do that, too."

Much too late, I pushed Alasdair's hand off me.

"My guess is you would have let me go even further than that if I'd pushed, even though you don't really like me, Mae, do you?"

"No," I agreed, cheeks blazing. "I don't."

Alasdair stood, slowly, the smile on his face of a different kind now.

"So why smoke my cigarette and submit to my advances?"

I stood, too. I didn't have an answer for this. I had never been so ashamed not to have an answer. I had wanted to push his hand away. It should have been as simple as that, but it wasn't.

"I know, you don't know why." Alasdair shook his head wryly and smiled. "But I do. It's because despite all that, you still want me to like you. You're desperate for it. You're like a dog looking for its master's approval. You barely even know how to want anything else."

My eyes stung. Shame crawled on my skin every place I had let Alasdair touch me. My arm, my shoulders, my face, my leg. Why had I let him touch me all those places? I shuddered.

"And that's the real difference between you and Apollonia. She doesn't care what anyone thinks, and you always will. She'll never be afraid to do what she wants, and you will always be asking permission. You would never dare just take it."

"I'm going to go," I managed to say. I was amazed at how steady my voice sounded.

"You should," said Alasdair. "But before you do—you aren't feeling a need to mention Seb to anyone, are you? Who Apollonia writes letters to isn't anyone's business but hers, is it? Just like who I woke up next to in my bed this morning is no one's business but yours. Wouldn't you agree?"

I couldn't miss the threat. I nodded, choking back tears, and fled.

CHAPTER FOURTEEN

I bit my lip to keep the sobs from escaping. My tear-filled eyes and flaming cheeks would tell the story clear enough to anyone who happened to venture upon me, but I would at least keep from wailing and drawing every Prosper within earshot to see my humiliation.

I reached the staircase. But where was I going? I needed to find Coco.

No, I needed to find Miles. His bedroom was downstairs. No.

I knew what I needed to do next, and I had let them both talk me out of doing it in their own ways.

I went up the stairs.

The worst of it was that Alasdair was right. I was like a dog looking for approval. It was so obvious that even Alasdair, who barely noticed me at all, had noticed that much. I agreed to marry Ivo because I couldn't bear to say no to Lady Vivian. I agreed to keep on being engaged to him to please Coco and Miles and to keep from having to say no. I agreed

to support Miles's accusations about Ivo to please Miles—
even while I was still engaged to Ivo. And that lunch! I
thought of my murmured agreements and lowered gazes, and
my whole body recoiled in disgust. My small acts of rebel-
lion were pitiful set against my overwhelming need to please
the Prospers. Even my little challenge to Apollonia had been
nothing but a misguided attempt to win her respect. Apollonia had said she admired my boldness, hadn't she? So I had
tried to be bold. Fool.

And Alasdair. I couldn't think about what had happened with Alasdair. I shook my head, forcing the awful
memory out.

Ivo's room was on the fourth floor. It was a smaller floor.
Ivo's bedroom was here, and Lord Prosper's, and the library.
Above them was the glass-domed magic room. The patterned
spells that lined the floors of the grandchildren's bedrooms
lined the hallways here. Their pulse of light was stronger,
and I stepped around the glowing patterns. It felt wrong to
step on them, like stepping on something alive. I stopped before Ivo's door and stared at it. Instead of a starburst, like the
bedrooms downstairs, Ivo's door was stenciled with a pulsat-
ing sun, snaking arms of light representing its beams.

I stared at it.

Whatever they thought of themselves, Alasdair and Apollonia weren't the most important Prosper grandchildren.
They might be the most popular, the most beautiful, the most
admired and outwardly favored. But they were only stars,
and Ivo was the sun. Their job was to twinkle prettily in the
Prosper firmament; Ivo gave the real light, the magic.

Alasdair's voice came back to me.

You would never dare take what you want.

I knocked. Ivo opened the door. He was wearing a midnight-blue evening suit, brand-new for First Night. Lady Vivian ordered him one every year, reasoning that if he couldn't wear it until the party, he couldn't make it shabby. And he hadn't, though Ivo was clearly ill at ease wearing it. He had not washed, apparently, since our outing into the hills. He still smelled like sweat and spirit fire and the smoke of my burned clothes.

Ivo looked at me without surprise, like he'd expected me. He opened the door farther to let me in, and I entered his room.

It was bigger than Apollonia's but darker even than Alasdair's. Once my eyes adjusted to the dim light, I realized this was not for a lack of windows—there were many—but because the curtains were drawn on all of them. The only light came from the pulsing glow of the spelled patterns, which crawled from the floor up the walls and across the ceiling. The patterns were different here than on the floors downstairs and even the hallway outside. Instead of curling and branching, they moved at harder angles, then ended in circles with strange glyphs inside that made them look disturbingly like faces. The patterns were sharper, and the light was whiter, colder. Everything about them was a little harsher, except for the gentleness with which the light faded in and out.

Ivo walked to one of the windows and opened a curtain. Light spilled in, and the glow of the spell work faded. The room was huge but extremely clean and nearly empty—a complete contrast to his shack on the hill. Of course, the spirits cleaned here and not the shack, and yet the difference was more than that. There was nothing in this room that spoke of Ivo at all, except for the spells. The bed didn't look slept in. The leather armchair seemed like something Alasdair might sit in at a club. There was a table with a vase of flowers on it that Ivo had surely not picked and nothing else.

"Do you want something?" Ivo asked.

Yes. I did. Something he had made clear he didn't want me to have.

I stood by the door. Ivo made no move to sit or offer me a chair. His arms were crossed over his chest. His face was closed, and his muscles were tensed, like he was expecting some blow to fall.

"I need to know why there's a blank in my memory," I said. The nausea rose again, and my head started to throb, but I pushed past it. "I need to know what binding was done on me, and why, and who did it. I need—"

I broke off and bent over, gasping. Pain was twisting up my neck again, into my brain. Another moment and I would vomit or collapse.

Ivo was at my side. He took my arm gently and guided me toward the chair.

"It's all right," he said quietly. "You don't have to say anything else. I understand."

I sank into the leather chair but clutched at his arm like he was still the only thing holding me up. He knelt beside me and didn't pull away. I tried to speak.

"Please don't," he said. "Don't make it hurt you. I'll tell you what I can."

I stared at him, startled by the anguish in his voice.

"I never—I never wanted to hurt you," he said. "It's the last thing I wanted. I tried—I tried to protect you."

There was a thin sheen of sweat on his forehead. He was breathing hard, looking down. I followed his gaze to my hand on his arm. I let go and started to draw my hand away, but he took it in both of his and held it.

"I did it," he said, his voice ragged. "I did blood magic on you, bound you from climbing the tree. From remembering what you saw."

He fell silent. I could feel his heart pounding in his palms, pressed against mine. His shoulders heaved.

"What about Imogen?"

He closed his eyes. He shook his head but not in denial. In refusal.

"Something happened to her, didn't it?"

Ivo let go of my hand, still shaking his head. He stood abruptly and walked to the window. He gripped the sill and bent over it, breathing hard.

"Something happened to her," I pressed. "Miles said—"

Ivo flinched and turned his head away.

"What did Miles say?" he asked in a low voice.

"He thinks that whatever happened to her made her the way she is." It was good Ivo wasn't looking at me. Easier to get it out. "That you hurt us the same way."

Ivo turned to me sharply, jerking his hands off the windowsill.

"No." He took a step toward me, his arm half reaching, and then stopped. "No. I did what I said—I can't say I never hurt you—but what happened to Imogen—I would never let that happen to you."

"Then—what happened to her?"

He shook his head again and said nothing.

I pushed myself from the chair and clenched the hand Ivo had been clasping a few moments ago. I should be angry with him, so angry. He'd done magic on me, taken away a piece of my mind. Instead, all I felt was a wild sense of loss, sinking so hard and fast, it felt like falling. He'd told me the truth, but he hadn't made it better. He couldn't. The despair in his eyes made that clear.

"But why bind me?" Tears stung my eyes. "Why do forbidden magic just to keep me from seeing something you would never let me have anyway?"

"What you saw was dangerous," said Ivo.

"Dangerous how?" I asked.

He didn't reply, and the set of his mouth made it clear that he wasn't going to.

"I've wanted to be a magician all my life," I said. "Every day of my life."

"I know," said Ivo quietly.

"You could teach—" I said. My voice broke on the word. I swallowed and tried again. "You could teach me if you wanted to."

"I could teach you," Ivo agreed. "That's why—"

He fell silent and swallowed hard. A bead of sweat slid down his face.

"You won't teach me," I said, to confirm.

"No," gasped Ivo, like it hurt him. "Never."

He looked at me like he had when I first walked in, waiting for me to end it. He wasn't angry, only sad. He'd keep his word. He'd take the blame for our broken engagement, I knew he would. He'd made it so easy.

So why was it still so hard?

"Rex stole one of the broken well spirits," I said.

"I know," said Ivo.

"You—you do?"

"Aeris saw it."

Aeris. Of course. I had always assumed Aeris spied on everything on the island, but I didn't know how much he reported. My heart stuttered at the thought of what else Aeris might have seen today. I thought of the hard way Ivo had said Miles's name.

"Coco thinks the spirits are falling sick because Rex put a spell on them to make it easier to steal one," I said quickly. "So he could examine it and figure out how to make his own aether wells."

Ivo nodded slowly, considering it.

"And you?"

"I don't know," I said. "It seems rather extreme, doesn't it? Endangering the whole archipelago's aether for a chance at more control? And it's not as though he needs his own wells. He has enough money."

"Men like Rex never believe they have enough of anything."

"So you think Coco is right?"

Ivo looked at me again the way he had after the spirit's attack, like he was willing something into my mind.

"You know." I was suddenly sure of it. "You know what's happening to them."

"I didn't," said Ivo. "Not until this afternoon."

"When we went to the wells?"

Ivo fell silent, again with finality.

I turned it over in my memory—the spirit on the ground, Ivo muttering over it, magic between his hands. "Was it . . . some kind of test? You were testing it?"

There was a hissing sound from outside the window, a burst of force, and then the vigorous sound of water gushing. The fountains had burst up into their full party height, like champagne continually exploding from a just-opened bottle. In the distance, I saw pennant-flying boats make their way through the sea in broken lines.

"We'll have to go down soon. It's almost time. Mae." He stepped toward me. "I should have talked to you first. Before she did."

"Vivian?" I asked, and Ivo nodded. "Well . . . she caught me completely off guard. I'm sure she did you as well."

"No," said Ivo. "I had time to think about it."

"Oh." I thought about the sketch Miles had shown me, and my pulse sped up. "Then . . . why didn't you ask me yourself?"

"I was sure you'd say no," he said. "I told her. I'm—I'm too old for you. And you'd never—you'd never think of me that way. She said I was wrong."

I stared at him.

I'd imagined him certain I would say yes, so sure, he hadn't bothered to ask me himself. As sure I would marry him as Apollonia was that her life was everything I dreamed of.

But no. Ivo's imagination had failed him in the other direction. He had thought it would be simple. I would not want him, and I would refuse. He hadn't seen everything that might force my hand.

"Ivo . . ." I said.

He stood in front of me, looking at me with some emotion that made my breath come shallow, waiting for me to end our engagement.

I couldn't marry him. I knew that. Even if I could set aside my feelings for Miles, I wanted more than what Ivo was offering me. I wanted more than to live like Apollonia did—a pampered, glamorous, useless life. It should have been easy to tell him that. To throw his refusal to teach me magic back in his face. He admitted it all. I should be furious.

I wasn't. It was with another emotion entirely that I finally forced myself to say it.

"I can't marry you," I said.

Ivo nodded, not surprised. Not surprised at all.

"I'll tell them," he said quietly. "Tomorrow. Don't worry."

He took a small wooden box from his pocket and held it out to me. I hesitated.

"I made this for you," he said. "I want you to have it. Please."

Something hollowed out inside me at the tender note in his voice. I took the box but didn't open it.

"Please wear it tonight. Don't take it off. Don't give it to anyone," said Ivo. He walked quickly to the door, then stopped and looked back at me. "When the fireworks start— make sure you're near the house, will you?"

"I . . . all right . . . but—"

"It's important," said Ivo. "Promise. Please."

I stared at the box in my hand.

"I promise," I said.

Ivo nodded, a slight exhale of relief escaping his lips. Then he left.

CHAPTER FIFTEEN

I stood numb in Ivo's room. I couldn't leave quite yet, as he had just left, and I would feel awkward catching up with him on the stairs. Instead, I opened the box and gasped despite myself.

It was a ring. The most beautiful ring I had ever seen. It made Apollonia's priceless art-deco platinum and diamond look like a cheap bauble, though this one had neither diamonds nor platinum.

No, this ring was made of magic.

The metal band was a weave of delicate petal-pink gold threads that twisted together in a way that reminded me of the spell patterns on the floor and walls around me. At the top, they branched into a setting for the stone. Not a diamond but an aether-stone. It was smaller but brighter and more alive than any of the stones that had studded Coco's necklace. I knew at a glance that, glorious as those had been, this was of a purer, higher quality.

I put it on my finger without a second thought, until a

cool, prickling feeling came over me, like the lightest patter of rain all over my body.

Magic. Of course it was spelled. Why else would Ivo want so particularly for me to wear it, even after I had broken our engagement? I should have known that. I should have asked him what it did. Panic rose in me while the prickling grew, and then in a shudder that made me cry out, it passed.

I was suddenly dizzy. I reached for Ivo's bedpost and held myself steady.

Then, I remembered.

I was above them, peering down while they did magic. But not the beautiful magic they usually did. Not the music of the air and the spheres. This was something else, I knew it.

Because of the blood.

Blood, in vials. Perhaps Ivo's blood. Perhaps Lord Prosper's. But someone's. Fresh, like it had been taken yesterday. The sight of it had turned my stomach then, and not just because it was blood. I had no fear of simple blood. But they were using this in their elixirs and for their spells. Their faces changed when they did it; their movements and their heads drooped like they became heavy.

Blood magic. They knew it was wrong.

But what was it for?

My normally dry and steady hands had grown damp and shaky while I watched. I slipped, made a noise. They looked up, and the glass I clung to vanished—I started to fall. Something caught me. I tried to get up, but my limbs wouldn't move. I lay on the floor of the magic room staring up at Ivo's anguished face, knowing I was in trouble.

"Don't, Grandfather. She doesn't know what it means. She won't tell anyone."

"Your feelings make you foolish. You know we can't take that risk."

Ivo turned to me, lowered his hand to my forehead. It was hot.

"Ivo . . . please . . ."

His face twisted. He closed his eyes.

And then, pain.

It was agony, the magic Ivo did on me. Like a surgery without anesthetic but on my mind. I screamed and screamed. He cut me open, pried me apart. Everything went black.

I stood, rolling my shoulders. The memory of the pain he had inflicted on me was sharp, like a broken piece of glass slicing deeper with every thought. But I remembered his face, too, as he'd done it. He hadn't wanted to. Lord Prosper had forced him and then pretended to me that he knew nothing of it. Let me think he couldn't believe Ivo would do something like that, when it was only at his command that Ivo had.

Lord Prosper, doing blood magic. Telling Ivo to slice my mind open, to hide it.

I would have refused to believe it if I had any choice. It terrified me to consider what it meant. Lord Prosper was our security, our constant. The man who had made this island a place we could be, made the aether a thing we could use. What did it mean if he would lie to me about this? And why did he lie? What was the blood magic for?

What was the risk they couldn't take? The one that convinced Ivo to bind me, with tears in his eyes and agony on his face?

I willed strength into my trembling arms and legs and held out my hand in front of me. There was power in that ring. Ivo's power. He had given it to me. He wanted to make things right.

An avid desire to use it washed over me, overwhelming everything else. This was magic. I had to try it out, see what it could do.

With my eyes on the brilliant aether-stone, I focused my mind on one word and called it aloud.

"Aeris!"

Something had resonated in me when I said his name, like a bell being rung hard and true. A slow ripple in the air gave him away.

"Hello, Aeris."

"Hello, Mouse," said Aeris sulkily. His bland, corporeal form materialized halfway.

"If I were really a mouse, would you come when I commanded?" I asked.

"Mouse has a new toy," said Aeris. "Master Ivo shouldn't have given it to her. Dangerous. Mouse should take it off now, give it to Aeris."

"I will not take it off," I said. "And I think that as long as I'm wearing it, you have to do what I say."

"No," said Aeris mulishly. "Only some things."

"What do they need blood magic for?" I demanded.

"None of Mouse's concern," said Aeris.

I tried again. "Tell me why the spirits are getting sick."

"Won't," said Aeris. His mouth appeared on his face and formed a smug smile. "Don't have to."

"Tell me who is responsible for it."

The smug smile widened.

I grunted in frustration. "Fine. What about Rex? What can you tell me about him?"

"Oh, Rex," cooed Aeris. "He's a naughty, naughty man. Perhaps that is why Mae asked? Perhaps Mae has learned to enjoy the company of naughty men today?"

"I have not," I snapped. "And don't do anything horrible about it. I don't want to end up being tricked into a compromising situation with Rex, understand? I command you."

Aeris's form dimmed slightly, and I felt confident that command, at least, had hit home. I tried again.

"Does Rex have anything to do with . . . whatever's wrong on the island?"

"Poor Mae," said Aeris. "Poor Ivo. He showed her everything, but she is too dim to see it."

"Showed me . . . do you mean with the ring? Or do you mean the spirit he healed?"

"Poor, dim Mae."

"All right. The spirit Ivo tested, by the wells," I said. "Why did it attack me?"

"Why wouldn't it?" Aeris asked. "Does Mae think the spirits should love her? Mae should know better, now that she knows what it is to be bound."

Dread swooped low in my stomach.

I didn't want to ask this. I didn't want to know.

"They—they feel it?" I asked.

Aeris was quiet. His smile slowly drooped.

"Ask what's going to happen when the fireworks go off," he said quietly.

"What?" I asked, pushing away the horror crawling up my skin. "What's going to happen then?"

"Can't tell," said Aeris. "But Mae should see it."

"See what? The fireworks? I see them every year."

"See the fireworks," quoted Aeris in a mocking singsong.

"See the fireworks? Does Mae think Master Ivo watches the fireworks? Does she think Lord Prosper does?"

"Don't they?" I asked.

"Even the Nosy Mouse doesn't notice anything during the fireworks," said Aeris, clucking. "No one does. No one sees they aren't there or knows what they do at the wells."

"So . . . they're a distraction?"

"They're good fireworks, yes?"

"But a distraction from what?"

A cool wind blew on the back of my neck, raising the hairs there.

"Aeris?"

But he was gone.

CHAPTER SIXTEEN

I walked slowly out of the room and onto the small balcony overlooking the back patio and gardens. The noise of the party was growing. The spirit music was louder and livelier, the hired acrobats and other performers were shouting to one another while they set up. The party preparations were in their final stages. The pool had been glassed over for a dance floor and studded with spells to keep it from cracking under the weight of the dancers. Soft, glowing orbs of fire hovered in the air like lightning bugs, still dim until the sun had fully set. The acrobats were human, but they had been trained over the years to perform spirit-assisted tricks and tumbles. Their skintight suits were an array of shimmery pastel colors, so they looked almost like spirits themselves. A few guests had arrived. Alasdair already sat on a bench by the pool, drinking straight from a bottle of French champagne, smoking a cigarette, and watching the acrobats. The spirits were nearly finished weaving a massive spire out of ice in front of the pool, with tiered ledges to hold the assorted delicacies. Most of the tiers were well out of reach of humans, but spirits stayed on hand to lift the guests to their desired level. They stood there, blank. Lovely and lavender. Part of the scenery. Waiting to be used like furniture.

I never questioned it. The spirits obeyed. They never protested, never made any sound at all. It seemed natural, unquestionable. But, of course, they were bound with magic to be that way. I had never imagined what they would be like unbound. If I had, I would have pictured them like Aeris. Mischievous, irritating, but ultimately harmless.

But then, Aeris was bound, too.

Guilt churned in my stomach. I resented the Prospers for not seeing what it was like for me, for assuming I was as free as they were, for not seeing how many reasons I had for never raising any protest against the life they had given me. And yet I never thought to question the life they gave the spirits. I never looked past their silent obedience and wondered what it felt like to be even less free than me.

And now that I did, I didn't like how it felt to wonder.

The sharp edge of memory turned over again. I had been bound from one thing. It had been agony. The spirits were bound completely. Did that mean . . . ?

No. It couldn't be like that. They must not feel it like humans did. If they did . . .

I shuddered and forced the thought from my mind.

Voices drifted up from the balcony below me.

"What are you doing here?" Miles. Friendly enough.

"Waiting for Mae," said Coco. "Apollonia's doing her hair and makeup. I don't really know how long that takes, but I figure they should be done pretty soon."

"How long did it take you to do that?" There was a smile in his voice.

"About ten minutes," said Coco. "You like it?"

"I do," said Miles with a laugh. "But I don't know if Grand-father will."

There was a pause, during which I could imagine Coco's rebellious shrug. I considered calling to them or going down the stairs. I should at least walk away. It was one thing to listen in on Vivian and Apollonia, but these were my best friends. My only friends.

"So," said Coco. "You and Mae."

I gripped the railing so tight, my knuckles went white.

"She told you?" he said, with a trace of annoyance in his voice. It was faint but still enough to steal what was left of my breath away. I sank slowly to my knees. I had some instinct to make myself smaller, as if somehow that would make me less exposed.

"Mae tells me everything," Coco said airily, instead of what I longed for her to say, which is that I hadn't really told her, I just wasn't able to conceal it. "I'm her best friend."

Something about the way she said it lodged painfully in my mind. Miles heard it, too.

"But she's not yours?"

Another pause. It wasn't really silent. The spirit music sang in my ears like it always did, but for once I couldn't hear it. I couldn't hear anything at all until Coco spoke again.

"Mae's sweet," she said. "Really sweet. And . . . you know . . . I do love her. She's kind of like a sister to me. A little sister."

Miles made a sound of agreement. "A sheltered little sister."

"Right," said Coco. "Though not like a sister to you, of course."

"No, not like a sister," said Miles. But there was no smile in his voice. Nothing pleased, to show he was thinking of our kiss with fondness.

"She tries *so* hard," said Coco. "With the running and the poems. Always looking for something to impress me with. It gets boring."

I pressed my head into the railing. The bars were cold against my face. For a moment it was all I could feel.

"Yes," said Miles. "I can imagine that."

"But you like her, right?" asked Coco, a trace of anxiety in her voice. Realizing, perhaps, that she should be talking me up instead of putting him off me.

"Sure, I like her," said Miles. "But it's like you said. It shows. That she's never been off the island. Not her fault. But still."

"Not like the last girl you were seeing," said Coco, with a knowing tone. Coco had never told me Miles was seeing someone.

"I wouldn't say I'm seeing Mae, exactly," said Miles.

"She certainly thinks you are," said Coco. "She's giving up Ivo for you, you know."

"That's not—" Miles's tone had changed. He sounded irritated. At Coco? Or at me? Most likely it was both. "I didn't propose or anything. There's nothing serious yet."

"No, but you have to understand, Mae's been in love with you forever. She has your rugby pictures tacked to the wall in her little house."

"What?"

I was numb. I couldn't even analyze Miles's voice anymore.

"All I'm saying is it's a big deal to Mae," said Coco. "I just want you to be careful with her."

"I need to go change. I'll see you later."

"Oh, all right," said Coco. "Bye."

A door shut, and I pushed myself up slowly. My muscles resisted, and my joints creaked like I'd aged a thousand years in the last three minutes. It was too late not to hear any of this, but I could pretend I hadn't. I had to pretend. What other choice did I have? I had things to tell Coco. I would tell them quickly and then go somewhere else.

I went back inside the house and took the stairs down. My mind was thick and fuzzy. I opened the balcony door, and Coco jumped up and smiled blindingly at me. If I only had that smile to go off of, I would never have imagined I bored her.

Certainly Coco could never be boring. She was wearing a men's suit, beautifully tailored to her own figure. I stared. She had on bright red lipstick and pearl stud earrings, but otherwise she might have been mistaken for a lovely, androgynous young man.

"You look . . ." I thought for a moment. "Fascinating."

Coco grinned. "I do, don't I? Mother hates it."

"Your mother is here?" I asked automatically. Coco's mother would be a good, safe topic.

"She just arrived," said Coco. Her smile dimmed. "She and father are having a massive row. He stormed off with Uncle Stephen to have some cigars, and she's lying down in her room with a little vial of something or other."

Laudanum, probably. Imogen wasn't the only one in the family who enjoyed it on occasion. Though Coco's mother, Edith, was only a Prosper by marriage. Deep down she was still a mainlander at heart. She hated most of the Prospers, even if she loved their money. Coco's parents fought often and loudly. I grimaced my fake sympathy.

"She says she's going to put in an appearance and take the boat back home as soon as she can," said Coco. "Which is fine, really. She'll be out of my way."

"Out of your way?"

"For watching Rex!"

"Oh," I said. "Right. Of course."

"I spoke to Grandfather again, while you were with Apollonia," said Coco eagerly. "Grandfather expects Rex to try something this evening, during the fireworks."

I stared at her. Her grandfather, who had commanded Ivo to bind me with magic. Who had lied to us both and let us think he knew nothing about it. I had to tell her, but I knew she wouldn't want to hear it.

"During the fireworks," I repeated.

"He asked me to follow him," said Coco. "See who he talks to. Spy on him, basically."

"Yes." I remembered that much, though now it struck me as somewhat strange. "Why would he ask you to do that instead of Aeris?"

Coco's lower lip plumped out in a slight pout. "Aeris can't spy on other island-family magicians, apparently. It's part of his binding. And anyway, I can be helpful, you know."

Coco looked hurt. For the first time I could recall, I didn't really care. But even so, I couldn't stop myself from placating her.

"Of course, of course you are," I agreed. "I'm just . . . a little surprised. You're not much of a spy. I mean, you don't exactly . . . blend in."

I eyed her outfit. Coco grinned and leaned back against the railing, draping her arms languorously behind her.

"Oh, do you think I stand out?" Coco asked, wiggling her eyebrows suggestively.

I forced a laugh.

"I can't imagine a place where you wouldn't stand out."

I tried to imagine what it must be like to feel as Coco did. To feel so secure in your belonging that you could afford to flaunt your difference. Bold enough not to care what reaction she provoked. No one would ever call Coco mousy or modest. Or boring. And if they did, she would simply laugh.

Coco's eyebrows stopped wiggling and went straight and earnest. "But you know, there are such places, Mae. I wish I could convince you to come with me and see them. This island isn't everything."

If I hadn't heard what I'd just overheard, I might have found this touching. Instead it sounded like Coco proposing a remedy for my deficiencies. Go with her, see other places. Then maybe I could stop boring her.

"I know it's not everything," I said dully. I glanced down at my ring. "But it's home."

Coco's gaze followed mine. Her eyes narrowed on the ring. "Is that . . . ?"

I was wearing it on my fourth finger, like an engagement ring. I hadn't thought about how it would look when I put it on, but now I was afraid to take it off, even to switch fingers.

"Ivo gave you a ring?" Coco asked.

I nodded. Coco's eyes widened.

"And you took it?" she asked. "Did you change your mind?"

"No," I said. "I told him I won't marry him, but he still

wanted me to wear this. It's not an engagement ring—or, not *only* an engagement ring."

Coco stared at the aether-stone, transfixed. Coco had sold off an entire necklace of these, but even she wasn't immune to its hypnotic dance.

"Definitely not," agreed Coco. "The stone . . . I've never seen one that looked so . . ."

"Powerful," I supplied. "It is. I felt it the moment I put it on."

"Put what on?" A man's voice came from behind me.

I turned to find Miles coming onto the balcony through the glass-paned double doors. He saw the ring before I could even think of hiding my hand. He tilted his head, lips slightly parted in question.

"Ivo gave it to her," said Coco.

"And you took it," he remarked in a neutral tone.

I forced myself to look him in the eye.

"I broke it off with him," I said. "He wanted me to have this. It's spelled. It made me remember."

Miles's gaze sharpened. He straightened. "And?"

I glanced at Coco then away. This was going to hurt her. Even as angry as I was at her, I didn't want to see the blow land.

"It was both of them." I hesitated, waiting for the nausea that came with talking of the binding, but it didn't come. Whatever spell Ivo had put on the ring had freed me of it. "Ivo and Lord Prosper. I used to spy on them, and I saw something I wasn't supposed to." I sorted through the new memories, still laced with pain. "Blood, in vials. It wasn't just Ivo. They were both using blood. And they didn't want me to know."

"Both of them." Coco drew back. Her eyes narrowed, tightened. "No. That can't be. Grandfather said—"

"He lied to us," I said. "Your grandfather knew exactly what happened. Ivo did the binding on me, but he didn't want to. Lord Prosper insisted."

Coco's arms came down from the railing. She shook her head, pursing her painted red lips. "No," she said. "I don't believe that. You're remembering wrong."

"I'm not," I said. "There was a whole shelf lined with vials of blood, a dozen of them, maybe more."

I risked a glance at Miles, to see if Coco's disbelief was on his face, too. But he looked at me and pressed a thumb onto his lip in thought.

"Blood magic," he said. "But what for?"

"I don't know." The question had been tickling at the back of my mind. It was the center of the mysteries that swirled around the island and its magic.

"Grandfather has always said that blood magic had nothing to do with the magic of the spheres and the elements," said Miles.

"Maybe it doesn't," I said. "But it has something to do with your grandfather."

"Think about what you're saying, Mae," said Coco. She had made an attempt to iron the disbelief out of her face and looked carefully, determinedly calm, not much like her usual self. "You're accusing Grandfather of lying to us, all these years, and doing a kind of magic he always said was evil."

"I know I am." I matched Coco's false calm. "I'm telling you he and Ivo were doing blood magic before I found them, and then they did more on me. I remember it."

"You think you do," said Coco. Her voice was slowly

rising. "Because Ivo put a spelled ring on your finger and it *all* came flooding back."

"Yes," I said.

"Oh, come on, Mae, don't you see?" Coco asked. "If Ivo could do a spell that took your memory away, he could do one that put a false memory back!"

My mind recoiled from this idea. I shook my head silently, trying to find the rational denial to match my instinctual one.

"Shh!" Miles hissed at her. "People are watching!"

The acrobats below them weren't staring, exactly, though their movements had slowed, and their heads were tilted in a way that betrayed their attention.

Coco glanced down at them with angry, narrowed eyes, then started again in a very loud whisper.

"Do you really believe Grandfather could have done something like this?" Coco hissed at Miles. "Isn't it more likely that Ivo is hiding something?"

"He'd want to hide it but not like this," said Miles. "Why give Mae any memories back at all? Especially after she had already broken the engagement. It makes no sense, Coco, you can see that."

Coco crossed her arms in front of herself.

"Maybe he thinks she'll change her mind," she said. "If she doesn't know what he really did."

"Two hours ago you didn't think Ivo had done anything wrong at all!" I exclaimed, fury rising. "You were blaming me for deceiving him! Feeling sorry for him!"

"But then I talked to Grandfather," said Coco. Color started to rise in her cheeks. "You heard him, Mae. All that stuff about how he's changed. He sounded really worried about him."

Miles looked at Coco with a doubtful twist of his mouth that bordered on contempt. I felt Coco's hackles rising, and with them, my own instinct to smooth things over. To please them both.

"Maybe you're both right," I said. "Maybe Lord Prosper has some doubts about Ivo—and maybe he's right to, I guess I don't know for certain—"

"Maybe this, maybe that," Coco broke in sarcastically, twisting her face into a parody of my wiped-clean calm. I drew back, stung. Coco's mocking version of my own conciliating expression bit deep and true. Did I really look so false? So weak? Even when inside, I was furious with her? I knew I did. It was pathetic.

"Don't say things you don't mean," snapped Coco. "How foolish do you think I am?"

"Foolish enough not to see what's staring us in the face," said Miles. "Or at least blind enough."

He'd stepped forward until he was by my side, facing Coco.

"What is staring us in the face, Miles? What's so obvious that I'm a fool not to see what you two see, hm?"

"You think I don't want to keep on thinking about Grandfather the way we always have?" said Miles. "The great, benevolent magician who gives us everything and demands nothing? It's a myth so big, even I believed it, even though—"

He broke off and shook his head. He didn't have to say it.

"None of this is what we thought," he went on in a quieter voice. "Something is wrong on this island, with this family. It isn't just my mother, and it's not just Ivo, either. Whatever is happening, Grandfather is involved."

"He's involved in trying to fix it!" Coco cried. "A couple

hours ago, you were ready to believe the worst possible things about Ivo. But now that you've found a bigger target for your resentment, you're willing to trust the magic memories he planted in Mae?"

Miles went very still. I didn't have to look at him to imagine his face: brown eyes flashing, his face a mask of controlled anger.

"This is not about me," he said.

"Please," spat Coco. "It is *entirely* about you. It's about finding an excuse for your mother and proof that your—" She tripped on this. I hoped for a moment that Coco might have thought better about throwing Miles's uncertain origin in his face, but the venom that dripped from her next words proved that hope wrong. "Your birth—that *you* are someone else's fault."

I exhaled sharply. This was the sort of thing Apollonia or Alasdair would throw at him, but Coco? Beside me, Miles took the blow silently, his body tensed.

"You think *I'm* the embarrassment?" Miles said quietly. "I'm not the one hiding who I am."

Miles aimed a pointed look at Coco's suit, and his lip curled into a sneer that might have been Apollonia's. I took an unconscious step backward. I didn't want to see this battle—my instinct was to flee.

Coco flushed scarlet. She bared her teeth into something like a smile.

"I don't hide who I am." There was the faintest tremor in her voice.

"Is that so?" remarked Miles. "So Grandfather wouldn't get a shock if I told him what they say about your schoolgirl friend?"

I made a low, quiet sound of dismay. Coco had come back from school one Christmas with eyes swollen from constant crying and explained what Apollonia had said to turn the school against her. She'd been despondent for a week. Then she'd been angry. And then, defiant.

"But Apollonia started those rumors, Miles," I said.

"Doesn't mean they aren't true," said Miles. He didn't look at me. His eyes were locked on Coco's, who stared back like the first one to look away admitted defeat.

"Grandfather wouldn't be shocked at all," said Coco. "You think Lady Vivian never told him I like girls? He's heard everything you have, and he hasn't thrown me out of the family."

"Yet," said Miles.

I stared. It took a moment for my brain to understand what Coco had just said.

I looked at Coco. Even with everything else, I wanted to show her it didn't matter to me, but she didn't look back at me. She and Miles glowered at each other like I wasn't there at all.

"He never disowned your poxy whore of a mother," said Coco. "So I'd bet I'm safe."

Miles lunged forward. Coco staggered, but I just had time to grab him and pull him back.

"No." My heart was a drum in my ears. I said it to myself as much as to them. I refused to let this happen. "No."

Miles looked down at me but without recognition. His eyes slid to my hand on his arm, then to his clenched fist. He slowly unclenched it, stretching out the fingers.

Coco was breathing hard.

"He wouldn't have," I said.

"He would," said Coco. "He would have."

I let go of Miles's arm. I shook my head. At Coco's statement. At their fight. At all of this.

"He's using you, Mae," said Coco. The anger in her eyes was mixed with pain. "He doesn't care about you. Do you really not see that?"

Of course I saw it. But after what she'd said to him about me before, her warning didn't sound like real concern. She was just rubbing it in.

I looked up at Miles. If he'd heard that, if he'd heard anything after Coco called his mother a whore, he didn't show it. He stared at Coco with a focused, unmoving hate, like a statue made of frozen fury. He didn't so much as glance down at me.

"Come on, come with me, Mae," said Coco. She wiped the tears from her eyes with the back of her hand and shook her head at them angrily. "I need your help watching Rex."

Miles glanced down at me then. Watching from far away.

I had to choose. I couldn't make them both happy, but I still wanted to.

Why? I knew now what all my efforts to make them happy had won for me. All that trying, all that care for their feelings, steering the conversation to safe waters, pushing down anything of my own I even suspected they wouldn't like—it was for nothing. Instead of pleasing them, I had bored them. And it was never the other way around. Not even for a moment. I had tried to be a confidante, a perfect friend. But even so, Coco hadn't confided in me. Cruel as Apollonia had been in spreading the rumor as she had, it had been true, and Coco had let me think it was a lie.

And Miles.

He wouldn't even look at me. Neither of them cared about me the way I cared about them. They fought with each other like it didn't matter that it hurt me to be between them. Like I didn't matter at all.

"You're selfish." The anger ripped its way out of me in a snarl. "Both of you."

And I left them both on the balcony.

I went back into the house, down the stairs, and across the grand entry, past the shooting fountains, and down to my oak tree.

What I wanted to do was cry. But what I needed to do was think.

CHAPTER SEVENTEEN

I stared out at the sea, wedged tight into a sturdy bend of my oak tree. I was getting dirt and bark on my party dress, but that barely bothered me. Everyone who mattered had already seen me in it, and come to think of it, none of them had seemed particularly impressed except Alasdair.

I had planned so meticulously for this night. It seemed foolish now. The party hadn't even begun, and it was already unimportant. No matter what happened now, I couldn't go to Lord Prosper and ask for magic, with or without Miles standing by my side. Not now that I knew what he had done to keep me from even remembering the magic they had done.

I had left the only two people who really mattered to me. Miles, staring after me with that shuttered expression. Coco with tears in her eyes. Tears I couldn't trust anymore.

He's using you.

My vision blurred, and I hastily dabbed the tears away with my fingers to keep my eye makeup from running. I had risked letting Apollonia near my eyes with pointy instruments for the sake of that expertly applied makeup. I was not going to ruin the results by crying.

Anger stabbed at me, sudden as lightning and fine and sharp as a needle.

None of them were worth crying over. None of them except Coco had ever given me a second thought until today, and now I knew what her thoughts really were.

Boring. I couldn't stop thinking the word.

And if it was pathetic to cry over Miles when he was probably not crying over me, then it was pathetic to have pined for him for so long when he had certainly never pined for me. When he agreed with Coco about my failings. When he didn't even bother to deny that he was using me.

I shook my head to clear him out of it and clenched my fingers into a fist. My aether-stone bit into my palm, and I imagined I felt the wild, trapped movement of it beating in tune with my heart. It stirred something dark and deep in me to hold that much magic in my hand. I closed my eyes and tried to imagine what it would be like not just to hold it but to wield it. To use it.

They wouldn't think I was boring if I could do magic. I wouldn't be boring. I wouldn't be the unsure, inexperienced girl they grew tired of. If I could do magic, Coco would look at me differently. They both would.

A massive wave crashed against the cliff face, and I snapped my eyes open.

There was no point in daydreaming. The Prospers would never let me have it. They barely shared their magic within the family. I had never even dared to ask for it—all I had done was want it—and just for that small bit of boldness, they had carved out a piece of my mind.

But there was one other magician I did know. One I wouldn't have to leave the island to find.

And that was Rex.

Rex, who Lord Prosper thought was behind the attack on his spirits. Who had threatened Apollonia in the garden, claiming the power to hurt her family. Who stole a spirit. Rex, a man who never accepted anything less than the best and the most, yet who had been relegated to third place, kept a second-class magician, away from the true power.

I hated Rex. He was selfish, immoral, probably violent. He had never for a moment in his life thought about pleasing anyone except himself. He had every advantage, every luxury, every privilege that had ever been denied me. And yet, we had this much in common:

We both wanted more than the Prospers offered us.

With a shiver, I realized Coco was exactly right. Of course, Rex was behind the attacks on the spirits. Of course, he was scheming to take the Prosper secrets for himself. The real question wasn't why he would risk everything for this chance to understand what had been hidden from him but how he had waited so long before making his play. I was glad he had, though. Now was the right time for Rex's coup, because I was ready. I had finally learned how little I could wring from the Prospers by trying to please them. If I wanted more, I would have to take it.

I could join Rex. I could help him in exchange for knowledge. For magic and a place to practice it.

I could betray them all.

The thought sent a shiver down my back that was made as much of pleasure as horror. Mousy Mae—the one they scorned, or took for granted, or simply overlooked until they had some use for me—what would they think when I had their secrets and their magic and used it to take everything they had for myself?

It was a delicious, seductive, terrifying thought. I pictured the Prosper faces in my mind. First the ones whose shocked horror would delight me: Lady Vivian, Lord Stephen, Alasdair, Apollonia. Then those whose disappointment I could bear. Ivo. Lord Prosper. I thought of the gentle, caring expression on Lord Prosper's face when he lied to me and pretended he had no idea who had bound me. I ground my teeth together. I had never hated him before. But, oh, I did now.

Last of all, I thought of Coco and Miles.

Whatever they thought of it when they found out, would it really be so much worse than what they thought of me now? A sweet, sad, sheltered little thing. Mousy Mae, even if Coco had told Aeris not to call me that. Even if Miles had kissed me and seemed to enjoy it.

But now I knew the truth, and I was glad of it. I knew I couldn't keep being the girl the cruel Prospers mocked and the kind ones pitied.

No more.

Rex would need proof that I was serious and that I could be of use. I sifted through everything I had gathered from the Prospers. Everything they'd given to me, or I'd taken, that I could use against them.

The things I'd seen, the blood, the fact that they'd kept it hidden. There was what Ivo had shown me, his experiment with the spirit. Rex was a magician—perhaps he would know how to interpret all this better than I did. Then, there was information of another sort. About his fiancée. Information

Apollonia had slapped me and thrown me out of her room for knowing.

Seb,

A slow smile spread across my face until I considered that Rex would likely not be pleased to hear that his fiancée was writing secretive letters to a young man. Especially one who was romantic enough to work a trade rather than marry without love. He might not want to believe it.

For this, I would need proof. I thought of the letter, folded and sealed on Apollonia's desk, and spared an absurd wish that I had somehow managed to secret it out of her room, followed by the even more absurd notion of going back there and stealing it now.

Apollonia wouldn't leave that letter lying untended, especially if it contained anything incriminating.

That brought me to the third thing I had to offer. I turned the ring on my finger and stared into the stone as I had before. I put my mind onto the same word and again called:

"Aeris!"

I felt his presence before his form started to materialize, yards past me on the branch. He sat cross-legged, balanced in a way no real body could. His eyes, when I could see them, were angry slits.

"Minxy Mae calls again," he said in a hiss. "Aeris liked her better before."

"The letter Apollonia wrote to Sebastian earlier today," I said. "Do you know where it is?"

"Yes," said Aeris sulkily.

"Tell me where," I said, focusing all my attention on the command.

Aeris's form rippled.

"Apollonia gave it to a house spirit to deliver."

"Deliver?" I asked. "But house spirits don't leave the island."

"Deliver to a guest," said Aeris.

I looked out to sea, to the broken rows of boats starting to arrive at the dock. The air spirits streaked above them. Faster than usual, perhaps.

"Sebastian is coming, then?"

Aeris's translucent shoulders rose unnaturally high and dropped again: the spirit's attempt at a shrug.

"Does the spirit still have the letter?"

Aeris rippled. "Yes."

"Where is it waiting?" I asked. "At the dock?"

Aeris gave me another comically exaggerated shrug, though with a long enough pause before it that I suspected I had guessed correctly.

"What is Minxy Mac plotting?" Aeris asked.

"One more thing." I wasn't sure the ring gave me the power to make this command, but I had to try. I focused on the stone again. "Tell no one what I asked you or what I am doing. For the rest of the night."

Aeris opened his mouth in protest then rippled again.

"Thank you, Aeris." I smiled at him, and he glowered back. "You may go."

CHAPTER EIGHTEEN

I walked along the water toward the dock. There was a kind of path running along the cliff face. It was not the smooth, paved path the Prospers and their guests took, with their spirit-borne bags floating behind them. The trees and bushes on the cliff's path obscured the view of the house, which Lord Prosper wished his guests to see first when they stepped off their boats and onto the island.

But the path along the cliff's edge, which was really just a somewhat less thorny line through the underbrush, ended in the trees overlooking the dock. It was easy to hide there and watch the boats as they arrived. No one else on the island knew about that spot, as far as I knew. No one but me ever had much cause to hide and spy.

The house spirit had faded itself to a pale green color and stood among the leaves of a fern. It held the letter in front of it, level between its two flattened hands, and stared straight at the boats. It made no response to my approach, whether because it didn't see me or simply didn't care. I crouched beside it. I looked from its blank golden eyes to the letter in its hands. I twisted the ring on my finger. If it could force Aeris to obey me in some things, perhaps it was strong enough to override Apollonia's command as well.

I tried to turn my thoughts to the stone as I had to command Aeris, but something in my mind snagged. The unprotesting stillness of the spirit caught my attention in a way it never had before. I knew, now, from the spirit that attacked me, that total docility was not their natural state. Whatever this spirit was when it wasn't bound, it was different than this. I tried again, concentrating my mind without moving my eyes away. Perhaps the spirit felt my efforts. It moved its gaze slowly to meet mine.

The spirit's eyes were as blank as ever, and yet I found myself staring into them, unable to look away. Surely it knew I was about to bend it to my will. It had felt my ring's power, or why else had it looked at me? There was nothing there that I could see. No pain, no regret, no reproach. And yet . . .

It felt wrong. Wrong to force its hand. Wrong to give it an order.

Giving a spirit an order had never felt wrong before.

But what was different now, really? I'd always known they were bound in some way. It didn't really make sense to object to it simply because I'd been bound, too, did it? It wasn't the same thing to bind a spirit as to bind a human. They couldn't possibly feel it the same way, surely.

Surely.

And anyway, what was the alternative? There was no aether without the spirits. There was no life on this island without them. No, the problem with the spirits was that Rex was making them sick. The best thing I could do for them was join him and convince him to stop doing that. And then, maybe after that I could find out if their binding hurt them. Which it probably didn't. But if it did, I could find some way to fix it. Later.

Right. So I would do that.

"Give me the letter," I said and felt the power go out.

The spirit dropped the letter to the ground. I picked it up and opened the seal, swallowing down the slightly sick feeling in my throat. I looked at the spirit.

"Go back to the house," I said, then turned my back on it as it drifted away.

I read the letter.

Seb,
I heard you are coming tonight. Turn around and go back. I don't know how you got your hands on one of Alasdair's invitations, but you ought to know better. You know what is at stake.

That was all.

It wasn't signed. Apollonia's slanting, careless script must be signature enough for Sebastian.

I read it again, then sat back on my heels, staring at it and chewing my lip.

It wasn't much. No profession of love or admission of guilt. Almost the opposite—she was sending him away in no uncertain terms.

And yet there was something furtive in it. Something that showed a need to hide. Something that Sebastian's presence here tonight would put at risk.

I tried to imagine what I would think if I had a betrothed who wrote such a letter to another woman.

I folded the letter again. Yes, Rex would want to see this.

I pulled apart the shrubs that blocked my view and looked out at the harbor. A boat had just pulled in and was spilling out loud, stylish young men and women who looked like Alasdair's sort. I recognized one or two of them from previous First Nights. There were several opened bottles of champagne among them already, and the merry talk and laughter suggested they weren't the first. Alasdair's set treated parties like a calling and always went prepared.

I don't know how you got your hands on one of Alasdair's invitations . . .

Sebastian was in that group. The spirit had been waiting to deliver it to him.

The glamorous party set was meandering up the pathway now at none too swift a pace. I had plenty of time to observe them, picking out the ones I remembered and the ones who were already drunk. I imagined Sebastian would want to be sober for tonight, at least to start with. Apollonia didn't care for sloppy drunks.

He would be handsome. Tall. Apollonia couldn't bear short men. She said they always tried too hard to make up for their size. And he wouldn't be wearing the very latest fashion, since he'd been cut off by his family.

But the crowd went by without presenting any tall, handsome men who were wearing a good suit from last year and weren't yet drunk.

Maybe he hadn't come after all.

I stood, giving up the cover of the shrubs. The partygoers were ahead of me now and wouldn't notice. I stared down at the letter in my hand. It was time to make my first solid betrayal of the Prospers. The first one I couldn't take back.

There was a burst of sound, glass shattering, and a flash of light.

I startled and stared. A young man holding a camera stood on the path below, grinning up at me.

He was tall. Blond. Very good-looking. His suit was exactly the sort all the fashionable young men had worn to First Night last year.

Sebastian.

"I'll call that one *Girl Making a Plan*," he said.

I hastily stuck the letter into my dress.

"You aren't allowed to take pictures on the island," I called down.

It was one of the Prosper rules. No photographs. No press.

Then I remembered what Alasdair had said: Sebastian had been forced to take a job at a newspaper after his family cut him off. Poor fellow.

"Oh, I know," said Sebastian. "I'm rather hoping you won't give me away, though."

"Your camera won't be easy to hide. Are you going to skulk around all evening and only take pictures when a loud noise goes off?"

"Like a firework, perhaps," said Sebastian. "Good idea. Do you have any more tips? You seem rather experienced in skulking around."

This was true enough that I couldn't muster up much outrage at it. I pushed my way through the shrub and climbed down the cliff face. At the bottom, I brushed off my dress and faced Sebastian.

"You're as good as a mountain goat on that hill." He examined me thoughtfully. "That's Apollonia's dress."

"And you're Apollonia's Sebastian," I said.

Sebastian's eyebrows flew up, but he showed no alarm.

"Are you a friend of hers, then?"

"I know her," I said. "And I can tell you she won't be pleased that you're taking pictures on the island."

"I don't need you to tell me that, whoever you are." He looked at me expectantly. When I said nothing, he added: "That's your cue to tell me who you are."

"Give me the film," I said. "You can hide the camera here and pick it up when the party is over."

"No thank you, little goat," said Sebastian.

"You don't understand what you're doing," I said. Panic started to rise in me. Apollonia could not see that picture. "This won't make her happy."

"I know that," said Sebastian. "Believe me, I've taken the master course in what does and does not make Apollonia happy. I tried flowers and jewelry and poems. I tried moping about, looking desperate and distraught. Now, you know Apollonia, don't you? So how well do you think any of that worked?"

Apollonia had dozens of admirers, many almost as good-looking as Sebastian, who had tried all of those ways to her heart. All had failed.

"Not well," I said.

"No, not well at all," Sebastian said. "Apollonia is a warrior at heart. A Viking. A Hun. She only values strength."

I couldn't help but nod.

"So you see," said Sebastian with a small smile. "I've tried groveling. Didn't work. So I'm trying something else."

"Which is what? Selling her family's secrets?"

"It will be the story of the year," said Sebastian. "It could be the making of me at the newspaper."

"I tried crossing her recently," I said. "It went badly."

"Oh, I know it's a risk," said Sebastian. "But she's in love with me, deep down. She's waiting for me to take a risk."

I considered the camera. He wasn't going to give me the film, that was clear. I twisted the ring on my finger and wondered if it might work on humans.

"Best of luck to you," I said. I put my will into the ring, just to try. "But I need you to give me that film, all the same."

Sebastian grinned as if I'd told the perfect joke and he was proud of me.

"Can't do it, my little goat," he said. "What is it that troubles you so much about the picture I took, anyway? Hiding something?"

"If I am, it's nothing to what you're hiding," I said. "I could tell Lord Prosper that someone from the press is sneaking around the island and have you booted out faster than a spirit does what it's told. And that's if he doesn't decide to punish you first."

"I know you could, love," Sebastian said, unruffled. "But I'm taking the chance that you won't. You know why I took your picture up there on the ledge?"

I frowned. I didn't know.

"I saw you crouching in those bushes with that letter in your hands like it didn't belong to you, looking for someone in the throng of partygoers, and I recognized a kindred soul."

My frown softened, turned quizzical.

"You're a clever, sneaky little thing on the make, just like me," said Sebastian. "So tell me your plan, little goat. I've told you mine, after all. I'd bet you my last monogrammed cuff link that we could help each other."

I shook my head. Sebastian wasn't an ally. Once I threw my lot in with Rex, I didn't gain much by making friends with the man trying to steal his fiancée.

"I don't have a plan," I lied.

Sebastian snorted.

"All right, then," he said. "How about this—I won't print the photo of you holding the letter that isn't yours so long as you don't mention to anyone what I'm up to. Fair?"

"Fair," I said.

Sebastian stuck out his hand, and after a moment's hesitation, I took it. He had a firm, manor-house handshake. He smiled at me with genuine warmth, and I tried hard not to like him. Then he tipped his hat to me and strode away whistling softly.

"Wait," I called after him.

He turned and gave me another expectant smile.

"Are you sure you really want her?" I asked. He kept smiling, but I couldn't help wanting to warn him. "Like you said, she's a warrior. A predator. She eats men whole and spits out their bones. Even if she chose you—" I shook my head. I couldn't imagine it. "She'll make your life hell, you know."

"I do know," said Sebastian. His grin dimmed a little. "But I love her. Who was it that said, 'The mind is its own place, and in itself, can make a Heaven of Hell, a Hell of Heaven?'"

"I think you know," I said, judging from the perfect fluency of the quote. "That's Satan's line."

He grinned again. "And you read, too!"

"Apollonia doesn't read," I said. "She wouldn't recognize a Milton quote if Satan himself appeared before her and said it."

"Right again," he said. "But nobody's perfect, not even me. There are plenty of people who would say Apollonia and I deserve each other."

"Nobody deserves Apollonia," I said.

Sebastian cocked his head.

"You know, I'm not actually sure which way you mean that."

I chewed my lip. It should have been easy for me to say which way I meant it. What did Apollonia really have but beauty, money, an ice-cold heart, and the style to pull it all off like a damn queen? Nothing. But there was no way to say that without sounding twice as envious as I really was.

"I'm getting the sense that you're not exactly cheering for our grand romance, little goat," said Sebastian.

"It's nothing to me," I said with a shrug. I reminded myself that I had my own purpose and more to think about than Apollonia's love affairs.

"Good luck to you, Sebastian," I said with finality. I climbed back up the hill, leaving Sebastian peering quizzically after me.

"Good luck to you, too, little goat!" he called.

Little goat. I liked it better than Mousy Mae, at least. Goats weren't the loveliest creatures, and I was sure no one would ever dare to call Apollonia anything so unflattering. But Sebastian had chosen the name for something he'd seen me do well and said it with something like affection. I wouldn't mind having friends who called me *little goat*.

For now, though, the only friend I planned to make was Rex. And I doubted he would call me anything affectionately, no matter how successful I was.

I sighed, and straightened, and turned back toward the house to find him.

CHAPTER NINETEEN

The problem, I realized, was getting Rex alone. Coco had promised Lord Prosper to watch him, and she kept her promises. I could hardly make a deal with Rex without Coco noticing something was going on.

The party was in full swing. The spirit music had swelled and sped. It didn't soothe and calm anymore. It did everything good party music did, and more. It set the guests' blood moving. It made them want to dance, to tell secrets, to fall in love. To live a whole life in one night. It was as intoxicating as the champagne, which the house spirits poured freely into wide-rimmed crystal glasses. It was richer than the food.

I went through the house, smiling at the guests, trying not to let the atmosphere turn me from my purpose. I stepped out onto the back patio, and it all hit me. Lord Prosper cast this party like he cast his spells. I couldn't help but feel at least some of what he wanted his guests to feel.

The sun had set, throwing purple light onto the wisps of cloud painted across the sky. The little orbs of light that bobbed like fireflies over the party glowed brighter and brighter as the sunlight faded. The acrobats tumbled and swung on the edges of the crowd like a living tapestry. All the colors were soft and blurred. Guests were dancing already on the glassed-over pool. There was food, there was drink. The air itself had a flavor, and it settled onto the skin like the most delicate perfume. A few admiring glances turned toward me. At First Night, everyone was disposed to like everything they saw. I spotted Rex, standing a little apart, watching the dancing. Coco couldn't be far away, but I didn't see her. A blandly good-looking young man came up to me and held out his hand. I took it. Dancing was as good a way as any to cross the floor, survey the crowd.

He put his other hand on my waist and swung me into motion. He was a very good dancer, the kind who could cover a partner's inadequacies. I followed his lead, spun, dipped, and stepped my way into the heart of the party. Soft light swirled under the glass, in the pool's water. My partner, the night, and the music made it easy, so easy, to dance. I could have let my plans slip off me like a silk dress. I could keep dancing, dissolve into the party and the night like sugar on the tongue.

When the song was done, the young man led me to the side and placed a glass of bright, bubbling champagne in my hand, then went off to find another partner. I made my way to the ice tower and sampled the food on the bottom row—oysters, abalone, spot prawns poached in butter, fragrant meats wrapped in pastry—before I took a sip of champagne. I couldn't afford to let the wine affect me. Not tonight.

Still, it was very good champagne. I took another small drink and looked around.

I found Miles first. He was on the second-story balcony,

arms folded on the railing, staring down at me. He was surrounded by guests—they had even started dancing on the
stairs, which couldn't have been very safe—but not speaking
to any of them. There was an intensity to his gaze that told
me he'd been watching me for some time. The other guests,
the dance floor, all of it blurred into a pleasant background,
framing him alone. For a moment that seemed like its own
age, he was the only clear, definite thing.

He was so beautiful: black hair falling in his eyes and
wearing the hell out of his perfectly tailored suit. Women
glanced at him as they moved past, some hoping to catch
his eye, some just unable to stop themselves. His eyes on me
made for a temptation like none I'd ever experienced. Miles
looking at me, Miles *seeing* me, was its own kind of magic,
one I had longed for almost as much as the real thing. And
now here it was. It was enough to make me forget everything
else. All his indifference, the things he'd said, everything I
had planned—suddenly it didn't seem important, compared
to the chance to have Miles tonight. Even if all he wanted
was my memories and my help proving his mother had been
wronged, maybe it would be worth it. First Night was its
own kind of eternity. Under its spell, I didn't fully believe in
tomorrow, so what did it matter if he broke my heart then?

Then his eyes flicked behind me, and his expression
changed.

"Mae," said Coco.

I turned. Coco came toward me, both her hands sheep-
ishly tucked into her pant pockets. She had wiped off the red
lipstick, for some reason, but even without it she drew a few
scattered glances. None that lingered, as she wasn't the only
partygoer in some sort of costume, and First Night cast an

aura of acceptance over everyone. The glow of anticipation was gone from her face, and her shoulders were uncharacteristically slumped.

Still, she was beautiful. All these wretched Prospers were so wretchedly beautiful. No wonder they found a little thing like me dull. I had a sudden urge to leave the island forever, go somewhere where I wouldn't always be the plainest, smallest, least interesting person anyone around would meet.

"Hi, Coco." I swallowed down a bitter taste, and the magic of the night flattened to a dull buzz in my ears.

"You left," said Coco. "I didn't think you would just leave like that. After what Miles said."

"I wish he hadn't spoken to you like that," I said. "But you said some horrible things to him, too."

I couldn't meet her eyes, and I didn't want to look at Miles anymore, either. The things they had said about me rang in my ears. I scanned the crowd for Rex. My way out of being who they thought I was. Rex was still standing off to the side, his back to the hedgerows of the gardens.

"You can't even look at me," said Coco.

There was a note in Coco's voice that startled me back to attention. It matched the look on her face. Vulnerable, like she expected whatever I said next to hurt. I stared at her in shock.

"What?"

"That's why I didn't tell you before," said Coco. "I didn't know . . . if it would change things between us."

"What, that you like girls?" I asked, incredulous. "That doesn't make a difference to me! That's not why—"

I broke off. I did not want to have this conversation.

Something tight was swelling inside me. It was going to
burst if I kept talking.

"Why what?" Coco prompted. "Why you won't look at me?
Because I can tell, Mae. You're not as good at hiding your
feelings as you think you are. I can always tell what you're
thinking."

"Right," I said bitterly. "Because you're my best friend."

Coco's eyes widened slightly. I saw it there, a flicker of
uncertainty. The flare of guilt at the possibility that I might
have heard something she hadn't meant me to.

"I . . . yes," she said. "I am. Aren't I?"

"Oh, yes," I said. "Not that I've had many choices."

"Mae," she said. "What's going on?"

Her eyes were wide and earnest, genuinely worried. They
did nothing to melt the sheet of ice around my feelings for
her. I knew, dimly, that underneath that frigid layer, I did
care about our friendship, and didn't want to say anything to
hurt it or her. Even more, I knew I needed to stay focused on
my plan, and fighting with Coco wasn't part of it.

"I heard you, Coco," I said. "I heard everything you said
about me to Miles."

Coco let out a breath just a little too shallow to be a gasp.
She stepped toward me, reached out her hand.

"Mae," she said. "I don't know what you heard—"

"I heard all of it," I said. "You can spare me the explanations."

Coco was shaking her head, like she could change what
she had said with the force of her own vehemence.

"No, Mae . . . it doesn't mean what you think—"

"I know I'm awfully sheltered, but I still don't think *boring* means anything different to you than to me." I turned away, and my eyes went to the balcony against my will. Miles wasn't there anymore.

"Mae, wait." Coco grabbed my arm. "If you heard everything, then you heard me say I love you."

"Like you'd love an annoying little sister who tries too hard and bores you."

"No! I mean—you are sheltered, and—"

Shame and anger crawled up my neck.

"I heard it already," I said. "I don't need you to remind me."

"It was Miles who said you were sheltered," Coco said desperately.

"And you agreed," I said. "Were you trying to talk him out of liking me? Because you certainly seemed to do a good job."

"I wouldn't do that!" Coco exclaimed. "You know I wouldn't!"

"I know what I heard," I said flatly. "You made me look pathetic. Like I ran right from kissing him to you and told you everything."

"I didn't mean to . . ." Coco looked around desperately, like the way to fix this would surely appear somewhere in her peripheral vision. "I didn't think . . ."

I closed my eyes and took a breath. I had a plan to execute and Coco to get out of the way.

"I didn't just tell you, you got it out of me, remember? You should have told him that," I said.

Coco's wide eyes lit with hope. She seized this suggestion, as I'd thought she would.

"I will tell him!" she cried. "I'll tell him right now."

She looked back up at the balcony where he'd been standing.

"I think he went into the house," I said.

"I'll find him," said Coco. "I'll fix this, Mae. And then—then can we talk about what Miles said?"

"Yes," I said. A thin sliver of guilt wriggled in my stomach. She should have told me before. At any other time in my life, I would have wanted nothing more than to talk with her for hours about who she was, what she wanted, what it meant and didn't mean. Last year's First Night, if Coco had told me, I would have grabbed two glasses and a bottle of champagne and gone off with her to talk until everything that could be said about love and friendship had been said and any cracks between us were sealed forever.

But now I knew better. The cracks between us were chasms, and it wasn't Coco who caused them. Because the real problem wasn't what she said about me, or what Miles did, or even Alasdair.

The real problem was that everything they said about me was true.

Coco was off, running up the stairs. Leaving behind her mission from her grandfather for me.

I turned away and put Coco out of my mind. I squared my shoulders and went to Rex.

CHAPTER TWENTY

Rex appeared to be the only person at the party who wasn't enjoying anything about it. He wasn't drinking, smoking, or eating. He certainly wasn't dancing—or even speaking to anyone. The expression on his face was more than enough to keep a reasonable person with no particular agenda from attempting to make conversation with him.

But I, of course, had an agenda.

Rex narrowed his eyes at me as I approached.

"What do you want?" he asked.

"I'd like to talk to you," I said.

"Not bloody likely," said Rex.

I pursed my lips and shrugged.

"Maybe not," I said. "And yet here I am."

"What about?" Rex asked.

"Could we speak somewhere more private?" I asked.

I didn't mean it to sound suggestive, but the immediate change on his face told me that it had. He took my hand. I looked around but didn't see either Coco or Miles on the balcony. Ivo hadn't emerged yet, that I had seen, nor had Apollonia.

I didn't pull my hand away, and Rex led me behind the hedge, through the bougainvillea vines, and into the thickest part of the garden. We passed several couples on our way who clearly shared Rex's intentions.

"I heard Apollonia gave you a good smack earlier," said Rex. "Is this about that, then? Want to get a bit of revenge?"

"Actually, yes," I said.

Rex snorted and stepped toward me.

"Happy to oblige. I'm getting engaged to that bitch in an hour, and she hasn't even bothered to show up yet. Any time you want to punish her for pushing you around, you come tell me."

He reached for me, lowering his mouth toward mine. For a half second, I froze under the spell of the same inability to displease that had paralyzed me with Alasdair and all my life.

Until now.

I stepped back. I put out a hand and pushed Rex away.

"What?" he said, anger and confusion flashing on his face. "This was your idea."

"I want a bit of revenge, yes," I said. My hand on Rex's chest trembled, but my voice was steady. "But not this kind. I had something else in mind."

Rex straightened up, towering over me. A grimace tore across his face.

I'd had a speech prepared, though I hadn't expected to start it like this, with Rex seething at my rejection.

"There's something we both want, more than just revenge," I said.

"And what is that?"

"Magic," I said.

"I have magic."

"More than you have," I said. "All of it."

"How."

It was not a question. It was a command.

"I know what you've been doing," I said.

Rex pushed my hand down and seized my shoulder, this time with fear, not desire. I saw it in his face, looming above mine. I saw it in the rapid contraction of his pupils, the flare of his nostrils, the seizing of his jaw. Then his expression closed.

"And what is that?" he said coldly.

"I know you've been hexing the spirits, and I know you stole one. And I know why."

"Is that right." Rex released my shoulder. He pulled himself together and away from me.

"They've kept you down, haven't they?" I said. "They hoard the real magic for themselves and give you what's left over. All you get on your island are the vapors of magic, what's left over when they're done. They treat you like a glorified servant—"

Rex folded his arms across his broad chest.

"I want magic, too," I said. "I used to spy on them. I learned quite a bit, until they found me and burned it from my memory. I've only just recovered it. I've learned—well, I've learned a lot. Enough to know they will never share. Not with you, and not with me."

"What's that to me?" Rex asked.

"I want to help you do what you're doing," I said. "I can be your spy. We can join our knowledge and our power. And we can make our own aether wells. All I ask is a share in the magic."

Rex stared at me with an intensity that could have been hatred, or lust, or fear. For a moment, I thought he was going to turn and stride away, rejecting my offer. Refusing my betrayal.

"How do I know this isn't a trap?" said Rex. "How do I know you aren't going to take everything I say back to your fiancé?" He nodded at my ring.

"I have something for you," I said. "To prove I mean it. And that I can be useful."

I pulled the letter from my dress and handed it to him. It seemed a small thing, now. A proof of Apollonia's infidelity, when a second before Rex had been swooping down to kiss me.

He took it, glowering. He read it in half a moment, his glower deepening.

"So?" he asked. "What's this supposed to mean?"

"Only you and Apollonia know that," I said. "But she gave it to a house spirit to deliver. And I got it from the house spirit."

Rex rolled his head to one side, thinking.

"That's powerful magic," he said. "Getting a spirit to disobey its binding."

I nodded, relieved.

"How did you do it?" he asked.

I couldn't afford to tell him the truth. It would be too easy for him to take the ring from my finger and leave me with nothing.

"I've learned a few things," I said. "I told you, I watched them."

It was a dangerous lie. He'd certainly find the truth before long, but now was the time to convince him. Once we were deep into this together, he would have to accept a few admissions.

"What about Ivo?" he asked.

"What about him?"

"You're going to marry him."

"Am I?" I asked.

"He thinks so. And the rest of them."

"So they won't suspect I have any reason to turn against them," I said. "They're giving me their prize son, after all."

The bitterness in my voice surprised even me.

"You're a cold one, aren't you?" Rex asked. "A proper little villainess."

"They did blood magic on me," I said. "They cut out a part of my mind, just because I wanted to learn their magic. Then they tried to marry me off to the one who'd done the cutting. They're the cold ones."

"They are at that," muttered Rex. "Let's say I want to take your deal—where would you start?"

I had thought about this.

"Do you know what Ivo and Lord Prosper do at midnight?"

"The fireworks," said Rex.

I shook my head. "No. What they do during the fireworks. At the wells. While everyone else watches the fireworks."

Rex narrowed his eyes. "What."

"I'm not sure," I said. "But I think we should find out."

CHAPTER TWENTY-ONE

We came back out of the garden apart, passing a few other couples in the shadows.

My senses sparked like they were under their own spell. Even in the darkness, every softly glowing orb looked like the sun. The stars looked closer, brighter, like they had dropped from the sky to be closer to us for First Night. The smells were thick enough to be almost solid, something I could stick out my tongue and taste.

I'd done it. I had said no to Rex and won him to my plan. I had refused something I didn't want and demanded something I did. And now I would get it.

Exhilaration buoyed me up. I felt taller, stronger, and certain I would have everything I wanted. Alasdair was wrong about me. I knew what I wanted, and I dared to take it. The magic, the island, and . . .

Miles. I scanned the crowd for him instinctively. My skin prickled at the thought of finding him, summoning him. But for what? I'd always wanted Miles with a vague, unformed longing. But now with the magic of First Night and my newfound power thrilling through me, the details began to take shape. I wanted to take his hand and go into the garden, push him against a tree. I wanted to feel his hands on the places I hadn't let Rex touch. Show Miles he was wrong about me. That I didn't have to be an experienced mainland girl to be exciting.

I didn't see him. Instead, my eye snagged on Ivo, standing on the outskirts of the party, in the shadow. Watching the dancing without seeming to see it. Strikingly alone, even in the middle of this crowd.

It was strange. This was his party, if it was anyone's. He was the only one of them, other than Lord Prosper, who could do the magic we were gathered to celebrate. The rest of the grandchildren drew eyes and admirers everywhere they went. Alasdair, Apollonia, Coco, even Miles, as much as he sometimes tried to discourage it. But somehow Ivo succeeded in avoiding attention entirely. No one was looking at him but me.

It came to me, for the first time, that this was entirely his choice. He could enjoy the perks and privileges of being a Prosper if he wanted. He didn't have to stay on the island all the time, solitary and austere. He could have anything that magic or the mainland had to offer. He was twenty-five. He had access to his money in full. If he didn't want the parties, clothes, or adulation Apollonia enjoyed, or the food, alcohol, cigarettes, gambling, and women that Alasdair preferred, then he could do what Coco did. Buy a plane and the lessons to fly it. Horses, fast cars, safaris. Collect rare, first-edition books. Pursue whatever eccentric hobby or expensive interest happened to seize him.

But Ivo never bought anything. He never went anywhere,

except the few times Lady Vivian forced him to make social calls on the other islands. He never seemed to want anyone's attention, except possibly mine. And even when Lady Vivian had tried to make a present of me to him, he'd been quick enough to set me free again.

I peered more closely at him. There was a resolute set to his shoulders and a deep sadness on his face.

His sadness had always seemed an inseparable part of him. People talked of it in different ways. He was grumpy. Unsociable. Strange. But I was certain, suddenly, that he might not have been any of those things if he hadn't always been so sad. Burdened.

There was an ache in my chest I didn't want to feel. Not now. Not for Ivo. I told myself it wasn't my job to make him happy. And it wasn't. It couldn't possibly be, after all that had happened.

And then he looked at me.

I stepped back with a start, inside the shadow of a hedge, and then back again until I was certain he couldn't see me any longer. Still, he stared in my direction for a long moment, until Lord Prosper's voice cut across the music, and every eye turned to him.

"Thank you all for coming," said Lord Prosper. His voice carried through the air to every ear, like he was speaking beside them. A few of the guests twitched or patted at their ears. There were those every year—first-timers who knew of magic in the abstract but startled at every fresh instance of it. Lord Prosper stood on the balcony, a little stooped but still impressive. He wore a shimmering cape of the deepest blue that would look like a silly costume on anyone else, but on Lord Prosper, it completed the magic aura of the evening. He held up a hand, and the spirit music stopped, followed closely by everything else. The guests quieted, turned, and the spirits moved silently through the crowd distributing glasses to anyone who didn't have one in their hand and filling every glass with champagne.

"Every First Night is a special one," said Lord Prosper, and cheers and whoops of agreement went up from the assembled throng. Lord Prosper nodded and smiled and let them finish.

"Yes, indeed. Every year, we commemorate the original First Night, when my family and I learned the secrets of this island, so long uninhabited, secrets that made it possible for us to bring aether into the world."

Uninhabited. My mind snagged on the word. I glanced to the edges of the crowd where the spirits hovered, ready to do whatever they were ordered. This had been their island, before the original First Night. I'd never stopped to think about what that had been like. They said everyone had been afraid to come here until Lord Prosper tamed the spirits. I'd always thought that was simply because they were strange—eerie. But perhaps it was more than that. Perhaps they had fought their conquest.

A shiver ran over me. I thought again of the spirit at the wells bursting into flame and attacking me. It might have been like that. Lord Prosper's magic against theirs. A war he had won.

I stared at a spirit holding a tray and swallowed down a sick feeling of guilt. I thought again of the agony when Ivo had sliced into my mind with magic.

I jerked my head away from the spirit, back to Lord Prosper and his kind, grandfatherly smile.

No. No. It couldn't be like that. Lord Prosper wasn't a monster. He'd bound me, yes, and I wasn't ready to forgive him for it. But that was only once, and worse than binding them. I reminded myself again that they weren't human. They probably didn't feel the way we did. And maybe—maybe if they were violent underneath—maybe it was better this way. Better that they were bound and under control.

The thought landed edgewise in my mind. Not comfortable. Not quite right. But I didn't have time to examine it now. I told myself I would come back to it later and turned my attention back to the speech.

"But tonight we celebrate more than that," he continued. "Tonight we celebrate the love of two of our islands' most beloved young people. Apollonia, come here my dear."

Apollonia stepped toward him from Rex's side. Lord Prosper took her hand between his own and bowed his snow-white head over it. I searched a bitter memory and confirmed that it was indeed the hand Apollonia had used to slap me that Lord Prosper was bent over in blessing now.

"The world is full of darkness," said Prosper. "There are things in it no man wishes his children and grandchildren to know. But it is full of light as well, and for you, Apollonia—"

He placed one of his gnarled hands on Apollonia's head. I doubted anyone else noticed the slight twitch backward of Apollonia's posture. She wouldn't want even her grandfather's hands mussing her perfect hair.

"For you, all the blessings that my labors on these islands can bestow, and none of their burdens. All the privileges I have earned for my family, and none of their responsibilities. My Apollonia, may you know only the good, light, beautiful things of this world, just as you are good, light, and beautiful."

I almost laughed out loud but stifled it at the last minute into a derisive snort.

"Careful now, Mae," said a cold, quiet voice behind my shoulder. I whipped around and saw Alasdair leaning against a tree only a few feet away, deep in the shadows. "Tonight everyone agrees Apollonia is good, light, and beautiful. Even if they were kissing her fiancé in the garden a few moments ago."

Alasdair took a swig out of a bottle of champagne and set it down beside him.

"Especially then."

I forced down the panic that rose in me and watched with feigned calm as Alasdair fished out his gold cigarette case. His fingers, I noticed, trembled slightly. Lord Prosper's words still rang in my ears; I tuned them out.

"I wasn't kissing anyone," I shot back. "So why should I pretend to think anything I don't?"

Alasdair raised his eyebrows.

"I should think the answer to that is perfectly obvious." He took out two cigarettes and held one out to me.

"It's not," I said.

I wanted that cigarette. I held out my hand, palm up. Alasdair hesitated a moment and then walked toward me and placed the cigarette in my palm. He reached out to light it for me, but I took the lighter from his hand as well.

I didn't really know how to light the thing or get the cigarette burning properly, and I took rather a long time of it while Alasdair offered lightly amused suggestions. When it was finally lit, I took a puff and immediately choked.

"Should I spell it out for you, then?" Alasdair said. "We're both going to act as though what I saw in the garden didn't happen, and everything will go as planned. Apollonia's engagement won't be tarnished, nor will yours."

I laughed at this, coughing and wheezing as I did.

"Oh, good," I gasped, when I managed to draw enough breath to do so. "Celestial spheres forbid my engagement should be *tarnished*." I broke into laughter again, all the more delighted for the look of confusion on Alasdair's face.

"That's funny to you." His light tone turned heavier, harder. "Would it still be funny if Apollonia found out you tried to seduce her fiancé and told Grandfather and Ivo? Your engagement would be over. Your life here, over."

I took another puff on my cigarette and coughed again. I didn't care. I could rattle Alasdair without looking smooth and cold like he did while doing it.

"How's she going to find out?" I asked. "Are you going to tell her?"

His smile was gone now. His false friendliness was as thoroughly dropped as when he'd turned on me in his room. Good. I hated that smile. It was a thrill to wipe it from his face.

"I might," he said.

I shook my head. I threw my cigarette on the ground and stepped on it. Somehow Alasdair made them look fun, but they weren't really. Not at all.

"You won't," I said. "You want Apollonia to marry Rex."

Alasdair's eyes emptied. A small muscle pulled around his mouth, and I knew I was right.

"You do!" I exclaimed and laughed again. "Why? He's a terrible man—maybe even worse than you!"

I couldn't stop laughing, despite the rapid darkening of Alasdair's expression. He looked like he might actually hit

224 ᔓ SAMANTHA COHOE

me, but even that hardly bothered me. This new freedom was too delightful. If I'd only known what it would feel like to defy Prospers, I would have started doing it long ago.

"It's been nice talking to you, Alasdair," I said. "But I have things to do."

I had turned away from him when he seized my arm.

"Wait," he said.

"I don't want to," I said, raising my voice almost loud enough that those on the edge of the crowd might hear me.

Alasdair hushed me angrily, and leaned close to my ear.

"What are you going to do?" he hissed.

"I'm going to take what I want," I said. Alasdair's fingers bit into my arm, but I didn't care. My head spun but not from anxiety. The sharpness of the evening had turned to a blur that made it easier to believe I could do what I was about to do. I jerked away, but he gripped me tighter and yanked me back.

"Let go of her."

Ivo's voice, low and furious. Alasdair's hand flew off me. He staggered back.

"Ow!" he yelped. "What the hell, Ivo! That hurt!"

"If you touch her again, it will hurt worse," Ivo said. He stepped in front of me, facing Alasdair so he was between us.

"I wasn't trying to molest your precious fiancée, you creep!" Alasdair said. "Get control of yourself!"

"I'm under control," said Ivo. "You aren't."

And when he said that, I noticed it. Alasdair's slightly bloodshot eyes, the slight tremble of his hands, his desperation to know my plans. Something had him terrified.

"If I'm not, then neither is she," said Alasdair, stabbing the air violently in my direction. "You need to get control of

your woman, Ivo." He took a step toward us, but Ivo sliced
the air with his hand, and Alasdair stumbled back again.

"I know what I need to do," said Ivo. He turned and
stalked away, barely glancing at me. I watched him go for a
moment and then started toward the house.

"Mae, wait—wait. You don't know what you're doing,"
said Alasdair from behind me, a note of panic in his voice.
"You could ruin everything."

"I'm not going to ruin everything," I said.

I was going to take it.

I left without a backward glance.

CHAPTER TWENTY-TWO

The luminous clock that hung from the ceiling in the grand hall said nine thirty.

Two and a half hours until midnight and whatever it was Ivo and his grandfather did that made the island's magic work.

"Mae!"

Coco ran toward me, down the grand, curving stairway. She elbowed her way past several older people congregated at the bottom, drawing an outraged retort, which she ignored.

"I couldn't find him!" Coco said breathlessly. Her eyes were wide. "I looked everywhere! He wasn't anywhere in the party or in the house. I even looked down by the dock. I couldn't find him."

"That's strange." My mind came around to Coco's words slowly.

"I did try, Mae. I swear I did," Coco said earnestly. "I know you're probably thinking it's convenient that I couldn't find him—"

"Oh, no." The sliver of guilt wriggled again as I remembered sending Coco off to fix things with Miles so I could talk to Rex unobserved. "No, of course not. There are dozens of places he could be."

Though once I thought of it, I wasn't sure what they were. From the way he had been staring at me from the balcony, I had assumed he'd seek me out soon. I had sent Coco to distract him as much as to distract her.

"You said he wasn't at the party?" I asked. "Maybe he went to his room?"

Coco shook her head. "I checked his room. I checked all the bedrooms."

"Even Ivo's?"

"Well, no," said Coco. "Not Ivo's."

"Or the fifth floor."

"No." Coco's eyebrows shot up. "You don't think—"

"I don't know," I said. "You heard him earlier. He's sure your grandfather did something terrible to his mother. He might have decided to find out for himself."

"He'd never get past the wards," said Coco. "On Grandfather's room or on Ivo's."

I looked past Coco, up the stairs. He didn't have to get past the wards if he had decided to confront them in person. I remembered his gun.

"Listen, Mae," Coco said. She had that wide, earnest look on her face again. "I'm sorry about what I said, and not just because you heard it . . ."

"It's all right," I said. And it was almost true. "I already knew all that stuff. It hurt to hear it, but I needed to."

"But it's not true—not like you're thinking—"

"You don't know what I'm thinking, Coco," I said.

The music changed, speeding up from the slow, romantic

beat it had played for Rex and Apollonia to dance together as newly betrothed. Through the tall glass doors, I looked at the crowd moving, pairing up, spreading onto the dance floor.

"I guess I don't," said Coco. "And I guess you're not going to tell me."

I didn't answer. There would be time, later, to make this right. But it wouldn't be tonight.

"You should go," I said. "You're supposed to be keeping an eye on Rex, remember?"

"Yeah," said Coco. "Are you going to look for Miles? I'm a little worried he might be doing something . . . you know . . . Miles-ish."

"I'll find him," I said. "Don't worry."

❖　❖　❖

I climbed the inside stairs, pushing through the crowds until they thinned to nothing.

I stopped in front of Ivo's room. I put my hand on the sunburst; voices came from inside.

"How do you know this?" Ivo's voice, low and sad.

"Mae told me. Some of it I already knew," Miles said. A few moments of silence, then: "I think you feel guilty over it. Over all of it. Why else would you show her that? She's not going to marry you now."

"She never was going to."

"She might have," said Miles. "You were offering her a lot. She might have taken it."

I closed my eyes and let out a slow breath. Miles had seen me better than I thought, if he knew that.

"But your conscience wouldn't let you marry her with

that secret between you. Which means, at least, that you do have a conscience."

"Of course I have a conscience." Ivo's voice was flat.

"I didn't think you did," said Miles. "Not until Mae told me you gave her that memory back."

"What do you want from me?"

"I want the truth," said Miles. "The rest of it. I want to know what you and Lord Prosper did to my mother. I want to know what the blood magic is for. I want to know why you keep it all hidden."

"No," said Ivo. "You don't."

"Don't tell me what I want." Miles's voice grew louder, sharper.

"You could have figured it out by now," said Ivo. "If you really wanted to. If either of you did."

The door opened. Ivo looked at me sadly, without surprise.

I jerked away and then froze.

"Oh," I said. "H-Hello."

"Come in," said Ivo.

Miles stood by the table, staring at me. He held out his hand, palm up. "Wait—"

"She wants to hear this, too," said Ivo. "Come in, Mae."

I did, ignoring the warning in Miles's eyes. I wanted the truth. I would have been happy to hear it standing outside the door, but I wouldn't get it that way now. The spells snaking up the walls and across the ceiling were throbbing harder than earlier. Ivo went to the window and closed the curtains. The room fell into darkness, with only the light from the spells to see by.

Ivo turned toward us but stared at the floor in front of his feet.

"You think you want magic," he said in a low voice. "You all do. You think I'm lucky."

"Aren't you?" I asked. "You have what everyone wants."

"Alasdair didn't want it," said Ivo.

"Because he was no good at it," I said. "He couldn't do it. And he was lazy."

Ivo shook his head. "As soon as he understood what it really was, he went to his mother, and she stepped in. Then it was just me. All of it, on me."

"All of what?" asked Miles.

Ivo looked at Miles, not meeting his eyes but scanning the rest of him as if taking an inventory of unfamiliar features.

"You wouldn't exist if it weren't for all this," said Ivo.

Beside me, Miles tensed.

"What does that mean?" he asked.

Ivo's eyes flicked to me. "You'd exist, Mae. But you would be someone else. Who knows what you would be like, or what kind of life you could have?"

"What do you mean, I wouldn't exist without this?" Miles asked again, louder. "What does that mean?"

"Your mother," said Ivo. "Grandfather didn't want to let her leave the island, but she told my father she would kill herself if she had to stay all year. He convinced Grandfather to let her go. You would never have been born if he hadn't."

"Too bad it's too late to thank him," Miles said bitterly.

Ivo ignored this. "I took the binding off her last year. I thought—if she remembered—if she understood—" He broke off, shaking his head. "Stupid."

"My mother isn't stupid," said Miles.

"No," said Ivo. "She isn't. I am. Imogen found a way not

to come back. I didn't think she could do that unless she was dead. Maybe she is."

"She isn't dead," said Miles.

"I hope not," said Ivo. "And I hope she never comes back. But she knows what it means."

"What?" Miles demanded. "What does it mean?"

Ivo stared at the ground. His mouth moved, but nothing came out.

"What?" Miles was almost shouting now. "What is going on, Ivo? What happened to my mother?"

Ivo shook his head. He held his hands out in front of him, facing each other.

"Magic," I said. "He's doing magic! Miles!"

Ivo raised his hands. Something sparked between them. Miles lunged for him, but Ivo turned his hands outward. Threads of glowing light like the ones on the walls spooled from Ivo's hands and wrapped around Miles.

"Run! Mae, R—" One of the threads whipped across Miles's mouth, stopping the words. I stared in horror. There was no point in running for the door. Ivo stood in front of it, his hands extended to Miles, but his eyes on me. I backed toward the opposite wall.

"Don't hurt him," I begged Ivo. "Please don't hurt him."

"I don't want to," said Ivo. "I never wanted to hurt anyone."

"Then don't," I said. "Please, Ivo, whatever it is—I can help you."

Ivo's eyes shone in the light of his spell work. Prosper green. The way the light hit them, I saw the color from across the room. The ends of the glowing spell threads emerged from his outstretched hands and wrapped around Miles. Ivo turned to me.

"No." I shook my head. "Don't. Ivo—Please—"

"You don't understand," he said. His voice was thick.

"Then tell me!"

"I can't," he said. Ivo raised a hand.

I flinched.

He raised it away from me, toward the window. The threads that worked their way from the floor and up the walls crawled over the closed curtains of the window, too, like the bars of a prison. Ivo backed toward the door.

"I should have found some way to take you away from here a long time ago," said Ivo. "Before the binding—before it came to this. But it would have crushed you, and I couldn't—"

His voice broke. He swallowed hard, and his shadowed eyes met mine.

"It will be over soon," he said. "I'm sorry, Mae. For all of it."

He opened the door, stepped out of the room, and shut it behind him.

I ran toward the door, but before I got there, the glowing threads snaked across it. I reached for the doorknob, but my hand jerked back before I could even touch it. I tried again, to the same effect. I tried to bang on the door, but my fists didn't reach it.

I turned back to Miles, standing bound and silent in the middle of the room.

We were trapped.

CHAPTER TWENTY-THREE

I tried using the ring, but without much hope. Sure enough, it did nothing against the wards Ivo had left to keep us in his room. I tried using it on Miles's magic chains. Nothing. I tried every window, tried to pound on every inch of the wall. It was as though every surface was covered in invisible rubber. My fists bounced right off.

"Mae," said Miles.

I ran to him from the wall I'd been fruitlessly trying to punch. The glowing thread had pulled back from his mouth and was slowly retracting into itself.

"Are you hurt?" I asked. I touched his cheek where the thread had slapped across it. It hadn't left a mark.

"I don't think so," said Miles. "Look at my hands, the magic is pulling back there, too."

I stepped back and looked. Sure enough, the threads were retracting, slowly leaving more and more of Miles free.

"The magic you tried, with your ring. It must have worked," said Miles.

I shook my head. I knew what it felt like when the ring

worked and what it felt like when nothing had happened at all.

"It wasn't me," I said. "Ivo must have meant it to fade. He didn't need you chained up for long, just long enough to trap us in here."

"Oh." Miles frowned. "That makes sense."

"But the rest of it doesn't," I said. "What was he talking about, Miles?"

"I'm not sure," said Miles. "I was right, though. About my mother. He admitted it."

"He admitted something. Something bad happened to her—but what?"

"It was something to do with the magic. Unless—do you think he was lying?"

"No," I said. "I don't know. About which part?"

"He said my mother could have told me," said Miles. His hands and lower arms were free now. He bent his arms at the elbows and flexed the muscles. "That he took the binding off a year ago."

"I don't know," I said. "It would explain . . ."

"Why she left."

Though not why she didn't explain anything to Miles. I didn't have to say this out loud. I saw the thought moving across his face, tightening the muscles, drawing his mouth down. I changed the subject.

"Do you think what he said about Alasdair is true? Because if it is—"

"Then Alasdair knows something. Maybe all of it," said Miles. The last of the magic threads faded off him. He rolled his shoulders.

"We could ask him about it. If we could get out of here."

I sighed. All the quick, heady energy of the evening had gone out of me, and I was limp with exhaustion. I sat on the edge of Ivo's bed and gripped the heavy oak frame with both hands.

"It will be over soon," quoted Miles. "He's going to do something. He locked us in here so we couldn't interfere."

Miles paced the room, frustration rolling off him in waves, but I couldn't even muster the energy to watch him. My wild plans were in ruins now. If I couldn't get out of this room, I couldn't spy on their midnight magic. It had been so easy for Ivo to stop me. A bitter taste rose in my throat.

Miles walked toward me and lowered himself onto the bed. His arm brushed mine, hard muscles flexing as he gripped the bed frame. I wanted that arm around me. I wanted to forget that he didn't really want me and lean into his chest. Rest my head on his strong shoulder. My chest ached with wanting it, but I stayed where I was. He would hold me, probably, if I made the first move. But it wouldn't mean anything more than our kiss had. I wasn't going to change how he felt about me by wanting his comfort.

Should I tell him about my plan? It would surprise him, at least, and I did want to surprise him. But it seemed so stupid now. Such a weak, foolish scheme. If we were stuck here, it was thwarted, and I was more ashamed of how easily that had been done than of the betrayal it involved.

Miles looked down at me, a tight, expectant frown on his face—like he knew, somehow, and was waiting for me to confess. My pulse sped. I took a long, shallow breath. Preparing.

But then Miles ducked his head and sighed.

"I'm sorry," he said.

I stared at him, and my fears began to change.

"What for?"

"For the way we treat you," he said.

And although I'd been brooding all day about the apologies the Prospers owed me, this wasn't the one I wanted.

"You don't have to apologize for your family," I said. "You aren't like the rest of them."

"I am in some ways," he said. "I've been thinking about what you said—that I wasn't the only one who belonged and didn't belong. I've spent a lot of time feeling sorry for myself—"

"I didn't mean that," I interrupted. "They don't treat you fairly. You have every right—"

"I know, Mae. I know," Miles said. He moved his hand over mine, the first bit of affection he'd shown me since our kiss. My breath caught, but I tried to hide it. The last girl he'd gone with, whoever she was, surely hadn't stopped breathing every time he touched her. "I mean, I thought about how unfair it was for me all the time, but I never thought about what it was like for you."

"I didn't really expect you to," I said.

"I know," said Miles. "But that doesn't make it right."

Miles took a breath, like he was about to say something, and then didn't.

I waited. He did it again.

"What is it?" I asked.

"I need to say sorry," he said.

"You already did," I said. The hairs on my arms pricked with foreboding.

"I do like you, Mae," said Miles.

"Thanks," I said. My heartbeat slowed to a dull thud. He said it just like Coco. *I do love her.* If they cared about me the way I wanted them to, they wouldn't need the unspoken qualification.

"I shouldn't have encouraged you to stay engaged to Ivo to spy for me. I shouldn't have . . . What Coco said . . ."

He trailed off. Coco said a lot of things, but I knew exactly which one he meant.

"That you were using me," I said. My voice sounded strangely loud, slightly off pitch.

"She wasn't wrong." Miles exhaled sharply and took another deep breath. "I was using you. And anyway . . . well . . . I think you know that. And I'm sorry."

I did know, of course. But I didn't want to know it. I wanted to ignore it, make him see me differently, and then kiss him again. At least, I wanted to have my fantasy for a few more hours. This wasn't what I wanted at all.

"I hope you can forgive me," said Miles. "I hope we can be friends."

Friends.

"Of course we can be friends." My throat was tight, but I did my very best to sound unworried. "It was just a kiss. It's not like I thought we were going to . . . going to . . ."

My voice was on the verge of cracking, so I fell silent and shrugged. He was still close enough that he would hear it if my breathing went ragged and feel it if my hands trembled.

"Maybe I was wrong," said Miles carefully. "But I thought I might have led you on. Because I'm not . . . you know . . . I'm not looking for a wife, like Ivo . . ."

This was just not getting any better. I swallowed and tried again.

"No, of course not," I said and was pleased with how steady my voice sounded. "And I'm not looking for a husband."

"You're not?" Miles asked. He sounded incredulous, as well he might.

"Well, not . . . not exactly." I moved my hand out from under Miles's and knotted it together with the other, then twisted the ring around on my finger. "I'm looking for something. Some way to belong here, I suppose."

Miles nodded. We were silent a moment. It felt easier to sit beside him now. My hopes had made me edgy, but this disappointment was familiar. My insides were hollowed out but calm.

"Have you ever thought that it might not be such a good thing?" Miles asked. "Belonging here?"

"No," I said. I stared down at the ring, shining and dancing on my finger. It was entrancing. Like a little piece of the island, set in gold. It made everything else look dim and dull. "No, I never have."

And then I remembered. I stood, eyes widening.

"What?" Miles asked.

"I forgot," I said and didn't bother to explain further. I focused and called: "Aeris!"

A ripple of light. He came.

Miles jumped to his feet as well.

"Can you get us out of here, Aeris?" I asked. "I command you to tell me truthfully."

"No," Aeris answered sulkily. "Can't undo Ivo's magic."

My heart sank. Then, another idea: "Can you summon someone for us? Tell me the truth."

A ripple went through him. "Yes."

"Good." My pulse started to race again. "Get Rex. Tell him I am trapped in Ivo's room and I need him to come get me out."

"Why would Rex get Mousy Mae out of any place?"

"Go, Aeris!"

And he went, leaving Miles staring at me with his mouth open.

All he could muster was: "Rex?"

"He's the only other magician on this island besides Ivo and your grandfather," I said. "Do you think I should send for them?"

Miles shook his head.

"But—I don't want to sound like Aeris, but—why would he come?"

I had been a few breaths from telling Miles everything before his own confession, but his painful honesty had somehow stripped me of all desire to make my own. I turned toward the door, away from his gaze.

"He might not," I said. "I thought it was worth a shot."

I didn't have to look up at him to imagine Miles's perplexed look. The suspicious, narrowed eyes. Those eyes had been narrowed often enough at me today. The image was fresh.

"Mae." His voice was gentler than I expected. "Is there something you aren't telling me?"

I stared down at the doorknob. My stomach was a bitter pool of regret. Maybe I should have stuck to my original plan. I should have gone to Miles when he stood on the balcony looking at me instead of going after Rex. I should have seized that moment when I could, instead of leaving it for the future.

"There are a lot of things I'm not telling you," I said.

"Like what?"

He sounded so genuinely perplexed. I turned toward the

door and tried the handle again, and again my hand didn't reach it.

"Mae," Miles said. "Did I say something wrong?"

I shook my head. "No. You did the right thing to tell me." I held my hand over the doorknob again, moving around in a circle, my fingers less than a half inch away from the cool brass. So close, and nothing visible in between. But I couldn't touch it.

"And you're right that I knew, anyway," I said. "But still. I wish you hadn't said it."

"Said I was sorry?"

"Yes," I said. "I wish you hadn't said you were sorry. I could keep pretending until you did that."

"Oh," said Miles. He let out a long, slow breath. "Mae, I think you might have misunderstood . . ."

Footsteps came pounding up the stairs. Heavy ones.

Rex. I willed him to trip on the landing and give us another moment.

"What did I misunderstand?" I asked Miles.

"I didn't mean that none of it was real," he said.

I looked up at him again.

"Who's in there?" Rex demanded from behind the door.

He hadn't tripped.

"Mae and Miles," I called.

"He came," said Miles, with a questioning frown.

I ignored it and waited for Rex. There was silence then a grunt and a curse.

"Did you hear me?" I asked.

"Yes, yes, I heard you." Rex grunted again, and something slammed into the door. "Shut up and let me focus. These wards are strong."

I had never seen Rex do magic, but now that it was happening just out of sight, it was hard to imagine that he was actually up to the job of undoing Ivo's spells.

He swore again.

"Aeris," I whispered.

He didn't appear, but a cool breeze circled my neck.

"Can you tell him how to do it?" I whispered to the spirit. "Give him a hint, maybe?"

Light laughter chimed in my ears like obnoxious little bells.

"Rex needs more than a hint to undo any spell of Ivo's."

I twisted the ring on my finger. I was afraid of that.

"Um . . . Rex?" I asked.

There was a pause in the frustrated muttering from outside the door.

"What."

"Is there . . . anything we could do to help?"

"I know some telekinetic spells," said Miles. "Well. One. Could that help?"

"*You* know magic? Is the old man giving it away to everyone now?"

"I learned it from a book, so I only know a little," said Miles. "What's your excuse?"

Another bang on the door. Probably a fist.

"Remind me why I'm helping you, Mae?" growled Rex.

"Because I'm going to help you!" I called back and shot Miles a stern look. "And because Miles is going to stop talking."

"That I'd like to see," said Rex. "Right. I'm trying an unbinding spell, but it isn't getting through."

Aeris chortled in my ear.

"I'm going to try a bigger one—you try to join me. The spell is stronger with two magicians."

"That's Lord Rex," giggled Aeris into my ear. "Try a bigger one. Try it harder. Master Ivo has more magic in a fingernail than Lord Rex has in his whole—"

"Confringenda vincula!" shouted Rex.

When Ivo had chanted spells, his voice had gone deep and somewhat rough. Rex's voice sounded no different than usual, simply louder. It was not the sort of voice that sounded natural chanting magical incantations. My skepticism increased.

Miles squeezed his eyes shut and started to chant along with Rex. I looked from him to the door. Nothing was happening. I felt it—or rather the absence of it. I had seen Ivo do powerful magic enough times now that I knew how to recognize it, how the air thickened and every bare inch of skin tingled and the hairs on it stood in warning.

I looked down at my ring. Without thinking, I caught its power with my mind and felt it there, ready.

"Oh, I wouldn't do that," whispered Aeris.

I stared at Miles until he looked up and caught my gaze. I sent the power to him.

White light. Deafening noise.

Then nothing.

CHAPTER TWENTY-FOUR

"Mae. Mae!"

I was asleep, and I didn't want to wake up. But someone wanted me to, very much. He was shouting.

"Mae!"

A sharp sting. My eyes flew open just as the open palm smacked my cheek again.

"Ow!" I protested.

Miles sat back on his heels and exhaled in relief.

"I thought you were dead," he said.

I lifted my head and didn't understand what I saw. Dust filled the air, swirling around the empty space where the door and walls had been a moment ago.

I tried to push myself up. Miles helped.

"What happened?" I asked.

"I don't know. I didn't think the spell was working, and then, all the sudden—"

"Oh, no," I moaned. "It's my fault. I used the ring."

"That explains it," said Miles. "We should get out of here. Ivo must have heard that."

Miles stood and helped me to my feet. We picked our way through the debris toward what used to be the doorway.

"Where's Rex?"

We found him halfway down the hallway, thrown there, apparently, by the force of the blast. His massive body was still. His face was turned away. Beside him knelt a figure, covered in dust.

Coco.

Of course. Coco had been following Rex. She wouldn't have been far when it happened. Coco looked up at me, her eyes wide and blank with shock.

"He isn't . . . ?" I asked. Coco stared and didn't reply.

Miles dropped to his knees on Rex's other side and felt for a pulse for what seemed like a very long time.

"Mae," Miles said quietly.

"Oh, no," I breathed.

Miles sat back and looked up at me. He stood.

"He's not—"

"He's dead," said Miles.

My breath caught. I wanted to deny it again, but all I could do was gasp for air.

Aeris had warned me, and I'd done it anyway.

Rex was dead. He was dead because he had tried to help me.

It was too heavy. I shook my head against it. A man couldn't be dead because of me. Not even that man.

"Don't, Mae," Miles said. "It's not your fault."

"Are you sure about that?" asked Coco.

She stood slowly, staring at me with wide eyes.

"There was something between you and Rex, wasn't there?" Coco asked. "I heard him say your name to that mainland suit not half an hour ago. And then he came here, when you told him to. What's going on, Mae?"

I closed my eyes and shook my head. I couldn't defend myself now. Even if I had a defense, I couldn't keep it straight. My mind was shocked still.

"What mainland suit?" Miles asked.

"The one who helped him steal the spirit. He was from the oil company. Rex was selling him information on the aether and the spirits. He was a traitor."

"He was . . . what?" asked Miles.

This was certainly news, but I could hardly take it in. Had I been wrong about Rex? If he was spying on the island for the oil company, that would explain why he'd stolen the spirit. Why he'd acted guilty when I said I knew what he was up to.

I said, "So . . . so that's why he was making the spirits sick?"

"Don't play innocent," Coco snapped. "I know it wasn't him doing that, I heard him say so. But you must have known that. And you just let me believe it."

I stared down at Rex's lifeless body. If he wasn't the one making the spirits sick, then maybe he hadn't been trying to steal the magic at all. He probably hadn't known how.

My plan lay there with him, dead as he was. Dead even before he died, if Coco was right.

"We have to get out of here," said Miles.

"Aren't you listening to me, Miles?" Coco demanded.

"We'll talk somewhere else," said Miles, glancing at me. "Ivo will be back any moment."

"Rex was a traitor!" Coco cried. "And Mae—you were in on it, weren't you?"

"No, no," I said, shaking my head. "I didn't know he was selling secrets to the oil companies."

"There's no time to talk about this here!" exclaimed Miles.

Coco stared at him then, eyes even wider.

"Holy spheres, I am so stupid," she muttered. "You were in on it, too."

"What? No!" said Miles.

"You were!" she exclaimed. "Of course you were! You were only too ready to be angry at Grandfather! Mae must have snooped around and found out what the oil man and Rex were doing. And then she got you in on it. The perfect revenge for never really being accepted. Did you even care what would happen to the rest of us if we can't make aether anymore? How much did Superior Oil offer you for betraying your family?"

Miles took my arm and pulled me past Rex's corpse and Coco's accusing glare.

"You're insane," said Miles. "We're going now."

"You make me sick," said Coco. She pushed past us and started down the stairs.

"Coco," I said. My voice shook.

Coco didn't look back, which was just as well. I didn't have any other words. Coco practically flew down the stairs. Miles pulled me after him but cut down the side stairway and out of the house through the servants' exit. Outside, and down the footpath that led into the hills, we started to run.

I followed without thinking, grateful to have this decision made for me. Grateful to have something to do that blunted the growing scream of protest in my mind. Running was perfect. I followed Miles, pumping my arms and legs, taking deep and regular gasps of air. The tears streaming down my face could have been from the sting of the cool night air. The burning in my lungs could have been from the exertion.

It wasn't until we cut up the last hill that I finally realized where we had been going. Miles took my hand at the top and led me toward Ivo's shack, where we had met that morning.

"Why here?" I asked.

"It's out of the way. And he won't think to look for us here."

I glanced over my shoulder. A full moon hung over the sea as if Lord Prosper had set it there to cast sparkling light over the water. The dancing and laughter floated up from the party, undisturbed by the magical blast that had occurred a few floors above it. Maybe no one even knew, except us.

And Coco.

"I should have explained," I said. "I shouldn't have let her go believing that."

"She wasn't listening," said Miles. "And you were in shock."

I looked up at him. Even in the soft moonlight, even through the tears that blurred my vision, Miles's face was clear, bright, and beautiful. And kind, suddenly. When I least deserved him to be kind.

"And . . . you didn't," said Miles. "You didn't help Rex sell secrets to the oil company, did you?"

"No!" I said it with all the vehemence that I felt and pushed away the nagging fact that what I had intended to do with Rex wasn't so very different in spirit. "I didn't, I swear I didn't."

Miles raised his free hand to my face. He brushed the tears away with his thumb.

"All right," he said. "I believe you."

He pulled me into his chest. My breath came faster. I put

my palm against the hard muscles under his collarbone and traced them through his shirt with my fingers. He wrapped his arms around me; his hands were warm against the small of my back.

I closed my eyes and drew in a deep breath.

I knew why he was holding me, just as I'd known why he kissed me on the hill. He'd wanted to use me then, and now he felt guilty for it and wanted to comfort me. But knowing that didn't stop it from feeling like everything I wanted. Longing welled up from deep inside me, strong enough to drown the rest.

No more regrets. No more waiting. I was going to take my chance.

I turned up my face, my lips slightly parted, and Miles leaned down.

The kiss started softly at first. The warmth and the slight tremor in his lips as they moved against mine were enough. Then his mouth was open, and his hands were pressing me closer to him, and our lips were hot instead of warm. Our breath came faster, and there were other sounds, little gasps and moans and something from my own mouth that was like a sob. Miles let me go and pulled me into the shack, slamming the door shut behind him.

He shrugged off his jacket and let it fall to the floor. He tugged at his necktie, but it caught. I grabbed his hands off and wound my own fingers into it, untying it with ease and flinging it aside. I flew at the buttons, undoing them as quickly as if I had trained for it. Something animal had awoken in me, and I had never wanted anything in my life as much as I wanted Miles's shirt off him and my hands on the bare, tanned skin of his arms and chest and stomach. I undid the last button and threw his shirt open. I ran my hands up his body to his shoulders.

He leaned into me, wrapped his arms around me again. He lifted me a little off the ground and kissed me.

There was nothing soft about it now. His hands moved down, and the animal that had woken in me was ravenous now. I kissed him harder and deeper. I needed to kiss him more than I needed air. He groaned, and his teeth came down on my lip, and the sharp thrill of it sent me somewhere else. Good. I wanted to go away, far away. To forget everything. I reached up, ran my hand up Miles's cheek and knotted my fingers in his hair.

And then. Miles pulled back.

I opened my eyes. My mouth reached for his again, but he shook his head. My heart plunged. So soon. Already he'd had enough.

"What is it?"

"Your wrist," said Miles. There was an odd look on his face. "Why does it smell like Rex?"

I let go of him like he'd suddenly caught fire.

Instinctively, I put my wrist to my nose. It smelled like Rex's unmistakably horrible cologne. I knew why at once. Rex had pulled me into the garden by my wrist, when he had thought I wanted a tryst. I looked up at Miles and saw him drawing the same conclusion.

"You weren't helping him sell secrets to the oil company," said Miles.

"No! I wasn't!"

"I believe you," said Miles slowly. "So why did he come when you sent Aeris for him? Why did Coco overhear him saying your name?"

"It's not what you think," I said.

"What do I think, Mae?" Miles asked. "Because I'm trying not to think it."

Miles let go of my waist.

"I'm not . . ." I stammered. "I wasn't . . ."

"Weren't what?" Miles's voice twisted with disgust.

"I wasn't having an affair with Rex!" I cried. "And I wasn't selling secrets with him, either. I was—I was—"

There was nothing for it now.

"I'd made a plan with him. I thought he was the one poisoning the spirits so he could take one and learn to make the aether himself. I thought he was staging a coup against your grandfather, and I wanted in." I looked away, out the window. The floating orbs of flame that lit the party looked like tiny pinpricks of light from here. Almost an illusion.

"Why would he include you?" asked Miles.

"I made him think I had more magic than I do," I said flatly. "I told him I could help gather information. I guess I would have been helping him sell secrets to Superior Oil if the plan had gone ahead. But I didn't know that."

"And this is better?" Miles demanded. "Stealing well spirits? Making more wells, more aether?"

"Not much better, no," I said. "It's still a betrayal of your family, I know that—"

"Betrayal of my family? You think I care about that?" Miles demanded.

"Don't you?" I asked.

"No! You know I came here with a gun, and you know what I planned to do with it and why! I don't care about family loyalty, and anyway, you don't owe us a damn thing."

"Then what are you so angry about?"

"Mae, have you not paid attention to anything that's happened today? Didn't you hear what Ivo said?"

"I heard him," I said. "But I don't know what he meant."

"Some of it was clear enough," said Miles, his eyes wide and incredulous. "He's tortured by what they do. The magic is a burden to him."

I snorted. "I've heard Lady Vivian say the same thing about having so much money. I'd take that burden, and whatever Ivo is complaining about, I'd take that, too."

"What about my mother?" Miles asked.

"What about her?"

Miles squinted at me in disbelief.

"Did you not hear what Ivo said about her?"

I stared up at him defiantly, stung by his tone.

"I don't know what Ivo said about her, and neither do you. Something happened to her, yes, and then they bound her from talking about it or remembering it—just like they did to me, remember?—but I don't know what they did or why, and neither do you."

"We know it was something bad!" said Miles. "And it was something to do with the magic! I don't want you having anything to do with that!"

"So, what? I should just give up? The magic they do is wicked somehow, so we should leave them to it, not interfere?"

"No, of course not!" Miles snapped. "I'm here to interfere, you know that. I came here for justice."

"And revenge," I said. "Against Ivo."

"All right. Yes. But now I know it's bigger than Ivo," said Miles. "I don't know how exactly. But it's not—it's not what I thought."

"So you don't want to take his place anymore?" I said.

Miles hesitated, longer than I would have expected given the way he had been talking a moment ago. He opened his mouth to reply then didn't. My eyes dropped from his tortured expression to his bare torso. The dark hairs had risen on his perfect arms. A shiver of cold rippled across his shoulders.

I picked up his shirt, crumpled by my feet, and handed it to him.

"I don't want you to be cold," I muttered.

"Thanks," said Miles.

Miles shrugged on his shirt. He tucked it in, ran a hand through his hair. He looked so beautiful, it made my chest tighten. A small sound almost escaped my mouth. I looked away.

He sighed.

"I don't know, Mae," he said. "I guess there's a part of me that's still hoping it will be possible. Maybe I can fix what's wrong, help Grandfather move past it. But I don't know what's wrong. I don't really know what any of this means."

"No," I said. "Aeris keeps saying I'm dim for not understanding, but I can't put all the pieces together. There's too much, and I don't see what it all means."

I looked around the shack. We already knew there were no answers here, but I did see Miles's thermos of alcohol from the morning on Ivo's table, and it seemed an answer of a certain kind. I picked it up and took a swig then choked on the unexpectedly sweet, thick liquid.

"This is—this is—chocolate?" I sputtered.

Miles looked at me with a bemused smile. "I don't like coffee."

"I thought that meant it was alcohol!"

"At eight in the morning?" He looked mildly offended. "Is that what you think of me?"

My mouth opened helplessly. It was exactly what I thought of him, but apparently I was wrong.

"You did show up this morning with a gun," I said.

Miles looked away, shamefaced.

"I wasn't going to use it," he said.

I glanced to the door. When I'd opened it this morning, he'd been standing there with the gun pointed at me.

"It seemed like you were," I said.

Miles sighed.

"I didn't want to kill anyone," he said. "I just wanted the truth."

The moonlight streamed through the window on him like a spotlight. He turned away from it.

"And I never drink," he said. His eyes met mine in the darkness. They weren't narrowed in suspicion. This time, he didn't look away. Maybe it was easier in the shadows. "I've seen too many drinkers to want anything to do with alcohol."

"Too many?" I repeated. "Not just your mother?"

Miles let out a breath.

"Alcohol has never been my mother's drug of choice," he said. "It's too slow. But her friends . . ."

I nodded. I knew from his tone what kind of friends he meant.

"They're why I bought the gun in the first place, years ago," said Miles. "Not for Ivo. For them."

Years ago. I wanted to ask how many, but I didn't want to picture twelve- or thirteen-year-old Miles finding someone who would sell him a deadly weapon or what had happened to drive him to it.

"To protect yourself from them?" I asked quietly.

Miles shook his head.

"If I wanted to protect myself, I could have just left," he said. "I didn't have to stay with her. Grandfather always made that clear. I wanted to protect her."

Even in shadows, his sadness was as vivid as the moon. I wished I knew some way to comfort him. I took a hesitant step toward him.

"But I could never protect her. It didn't matter if I stopped them. She didn't care what they did to her, because the real enemy was always in her own mind."

"Miles . . ." I started to reach for him, but he turned away. He went to the front window of the shack—simply a square gap in the wall—and looked out toward the party and the sea beyond it.

"I thought I had figured it out," said Miles. "I was so sure it was Ivo. But it wasn't just him, was it?"

"No," I said. "I don't think it was."

"So what, then?" Miles asked, his voice almost breaking. "What happened to her here? What did they do to her?"

I took a deep, slow breath.

"I don't know," I said. "But I think I might know how to find out. There's something they do with the magic. They do it during the fireworks so no one will know. Aeris told me. At the wells."

"The wells," Miles repeated, a trace of hope lifting his features. "That explains why Ivo tried to trap us in his room. During the fireworks . . . that's . . . that's soon. I should go."

It was the obvious conclusion, but I couldn't suppress a

shudder. It was one thing to go with Rex, who at least was a real magician. But his death had left a sharp ache in my heart where my reckless courage had been before.

And yet I couldn't let this night go by without taking my last chance to see the magic at the heart of the island. One last chance, however slight, to take it. No. I wouldn't go back to the house, with Miles or without him. I wasn't going to let the rest of this night slip away from me and allow the morning to come and leave me with nothing. I couldn't give up yet.

"I'll come with you," I said.

Miles tucked his hands into the pockets of his jacket and tilted his head at me.

Then, from outside, came an unexpected voice. Colder than the night air. Sharp as a knife.

"If you think I'm going to roll around on the floor with you inside Ivo's little shack, you're madder than I even thought."

CHAPTER TWENTY-FIVE

Miles stepped back from the window abruptly, deeper into the shack's shadows.

"I'm more than happy to roll about anywhere with you, my love." Sebastian's voice. "I was merely trying to be considerate of your desire for privacy. But here—this patch of grass looks especially soft."

There was a rustle of clothes and the sound of a slap—much gentler than the one I had received from the same hand.

"Get your hands off me," said Apollonia. "I said I wanted privacy because you wouldn't leave me alone, and I preferred you not to make whatever scene you're about to make in front of everyone."

"Everyone," said Sebastian scornfully. "Who's that? Why pretend you care what any of those people think, Apollonia? We both know you don't."

"I can't believe you came here with a camera," she muttered. "If Grandfather found out, he'd destroy you."

"Still, you didn't have to throw it into the ocean," said

Sebastian. "I took some beautiful pictures. Some of them might even interest you."

Another light slap, the sound of one hand smacking another away perhaps.

"Stop it, Seb," said Apollonia.

I could hardly believe the tone of Apollonia's voice. The words were as harsh as ever, but there was a sadness underneath it that blunted the edge.

"You can't marry him," said Sebastian. "I can't believe you'll do it. I won't believe it."

"Believe what you want," she said.

Miles and I exchanged a look. Was it possible that no one had discovered Rex after we fled? There had been no pause in the party that we could discern from up here. Coco had run to find her grandfather, but perhaps she hadn't found him. If she had, it seemed he had chosen not to share the news, even with Rex's fiancée.

"You're Apollonia Prosper. You don't have to do a damn thing you don't want to do," said Seb. "Especially not this."

There was a soft, rustling quiet. A small wet noise and a sigh. He'd kissed her, and she hadn't slapped him away. Miles and I exchanged another uncomfortable glance. What if Apollonia and Sebastian did decide to "roll" around in the grass? There was no way to sneak past them.

"Let's leave," said Sebastian. "Let's go, right now. We can get married tonight, if we want."

"It's not that simple," said Apollonia.

"Why not?" Sebastian demanded. "It's exactly that simple if we want it to be. And you do want it, don't you?"

A small silence followed. Enough, it seemed, for Sebastian to hear what he'd hoped.

"Then marry me, Apollonia!" Sebastian cried. "You know I love you. I gave up everything I had for you, and I haven't regretted it for one moment. Marry me, my love. It's what you want. I know it is."

"Isn't this charming," came another voice.

"Alasdair." The icy chill returned to Apollonia's voice. "Put that ridiculous thing down."

"Let's make a deal," said Alasdair. "I'll put this ridiculous thing down if you tell your ridiculous thing to get up off his knee."

"What are you going to do with that?" Sebastian asked. "Kill me?"

I startled and stared at Miles.

"She told you it wasn't so simple," said Alasdair. "You need to learn to listen, my friend."

"Put the gun down, Alasdair," snapped Apollonia. "I'm not going to do what you're afraid of."

"I don't believe you, my dear sister," said Alasdair. "I saw your cold heart leap when he dropped to his knee."

"If my heart is so cold, then what are you worried about?"

"Cold toward me, Apollonia," said Alasdair. "Cold toward your loving and deserving brother."

"What do you care if she marries me?" Sebastian asked. "They're not going to cut her off."

"They might," said Alasdair.

"Even if they did, so what? More Prosper money for you."

"Ah, if only it were that simple," said Alasdair. "But you know, even Prosper money runs out if you spend it certain ways. And my allowance ran out quite a while ago."

There was a click, the sound of a gun cocking.

"Listen to me, Alasdair," said Apollonia, her voice rising.

"If you hurt him, I won't marry Rex. He'll leave you to the wolves, and they'll tear you apart. He will, too. You know he will."

"What are you talking about?" Sebastian asked.

"You're a liar," said Alasdair. "If I kill him, you'll cry and rage and then marry Rex anyway. You want the life he can give you. You don't want to be a newspaperman's wife, living in some wretched mainland flat. You'll remember that a few moments after I pull this trigger."

"Maybe I will." Apollonia's voice was cold enough to shatter glass. "But before I do, I'll tear you apart with my bare hands. Put it down, Alasdair!"

"I will," said Alasdair. "Just as soon as you go back down to the house, find Rex, and spend the rest of the night at his side. He'll pay off the rest of my debts, you'll marry the right man, and you can keep seeing Seb on your shopping trips to the mainland. If you time it right, you won't even have to have Rex's children. Everyone will get what they want."

"Put down the gun, or I'll go to him right now and tell him not to pay your debts," said Apollonia. "I'll tell him I don't care if those gangsters rip out your spine through your teeth. I'll tell him I want them to."

"Is that what this is about?" Sebastian demanded. "Rex paid off your gambling debts so you want to sell your sister to him?"

"He didn't pay them off," said Alasdair. "He paid an installment. And as long as he keeps paying them, my legs stay unbroken."

"Oh," I breathed. *You know what I can do to your family.* Rex had been talking about Alasdair.

"All I want is for Apollonia not to blow up our lives in a

fit of temporary madness," said Alasdair. "I don't even want to kill you. I'd rather you come right now and get on the next boat."

"Not unless she wants me to," Sebastian said. "And not with a gun pointed at me."

"Get out of the way, Apollonia," said Alasdair.

"Put down the gun!" There was a shrill note to Apollonia's cry.

I stepped forward. Miles grabbed for my arm, but I slipped past. I threw open the door, blocking Miles out of sight behind it.

"She isn't going to marry Rex," I said.

Alasdair turned the gun on me with a jerk that made me flinch.

He swore. "Sneaky little slut," Alasdair muttered. "Is he hiding in there with his pants off? I suppose you think you're going to marry Rex instead, is that it?"

Apollonia's mouth dropped open. She peered past me, into the shack.

"No," I said. "No one is going to marry Rex. He's dead."

"Is that supposed to be a joke?" snapped Apollonia.

"No," I said. "I'm sorry. It's not a joke."

Alasdair stepped toward me, gun still raised. His hand was shaking.

"What is this?" he asked. "You think you'll stop me from shooting him if you make me think Rex is dead?"

"It's the truth." My voice was barely trembling.

"How do you know he's dead?" Sebastian asked.

"I saw him," I said. "I . . . I was there. It was on the fourth floor, outside Ivo's room. His body is there still."

"Ivo's room?" Alasdair asked. "Are you saying Ivo killed him?"

I shook my head.

"It was an accident."

"You're a lying little sneak," said Alasdair. "You want Apollonia to run off with Seb and leave you to console Rex. That's it, isn't it? You planned some seedy little tryst up here with him, and now you're trying to clear us out before he arrives."

"No," I said.

"What are you talking about, Alasdair?" Apollonia said.

"I'm talking about this little vixen's attempts to steal your man. He had her against a tree in the garden a few hours ago. Do what she says if you want her to end up in your place, with your house and money and—"

"Rex is dead, Alasdair," I interrupted. "Killing Sebastian will get you nothing but a murder charge and two witnesses to attest to it."

"Assuming I don't kill you, too," said Alasdair. "You were next on my list to deal with, in fact."

"Alasdair—" Apollonia stared back and forth between her stone-faced brother and me. "What in the heavens are you saying?"

"Mae knows enough to ruin everything." Alasdair's hard features split into a cruel leer. "And little enough that she might even do it by accident."

His grin froze then faltered. Alasdair raised his other hand and gripped the trigger of the gun. I hadn't really believed Alasdair would fire it until this moment. Terror shot through me.

"No," I said. "Please."

"All I want is for everyone to do what they are meant to do." Alasdair's breath came heavier. "I want Apollonia to marry Rex and Ivo to do what needs to be done. And *you*," he hissed. "I want you to do the one thing we need you for. Keep him happy. Give him a reason to stay the course, and mind your own damn business. But there's no chance of that, is there? No chance at all."

"Alasdair." The careful note in Apollonia's voice sent another bolt of terror down my spine. Apollonia was never careful. "You aren't making sense. Put the gun down. You don't want to do something foolish."

"No, I don't," said Alasdair. "But Mae does."

"No, she doesn't," said Apollonia. "You're talking about Mae. The steward's daughter. She's not a threat."

"You only think that because you're as much an idiot as a snob." Alasdair kept the gun trained on me but glared at Apollonia. "You've never paid a moment's attention to what really goes on here. As long as you have your nice things and your parties, you don't care to know how you get it."

"You are raving," said Apollonia.

Alasdair turned his attention back to me.

"It's too bad you're not as stupid as my sister," said Alasdair.

"Don't."

"If there were another way . . ." said Alasdair. His hand was shaking, yet his mouth was set. "But we all have our part to play. And this is mine."

I held my hands out, as though that could stop the bullet. I shut my eyes.

Nothing happened. I opened them again.

Alasdair's hands flew into the air. The gun sailed out of them, toward me, then over my head.

I flinched and let out a small, belated scream. I spun.

Miles stood in the doorway of the shack. He caught the gun and pointed it at Alasdair.

"I always knew you were a disgusting bully." His voice was tight with rage. "But I didn't think you were a murderer."

Alasdair swore.

"When the hell did you learn magic?" he said.

"Your name is Sebastian?" Miles said without turning his eyes from Alasdair.

"Wha—yes," Sebastian said.

"There's some rope in the shack, Sebastian," said Miles. "Please get it."

Sebastian stared for a moment then obeyed.

"That's fine," said Alasdair. "Tie me up. Put me out of the way for the evening. Then go back to the party and have a good time. Go back to the party and watch the fireworks with Mae."

Sebastian came out of the shack with two coils of rope.

"Do you know how to tie a good knot?" Miles asked him.

"Yes," said Sebastian. "I used to sail."

Miles nodded, and Sebastian went to work on Alasdair's hands.

"You know what they do during the fireworks," Miles said to Alasdair. "Ivo said you started to learn the magic and then ran to your mother when you learned what it was."

"I know enough," said Alasdair.

"Then tell me," said Miles.

"No," said Alasdair. "You don't want to know."

"I do want to know," said Miles. "So much that I'm going to go right from here to the aether wells and find out what they do during the fireworks unless you tell me why I shouldn't."

Alasdair's lips curled up, baring his teeth like a dog's.

"Do you want to end up like your mother?" he snarled.

Miles strode toward him, and Alasdair reared back from the gun, knocking into Sebastian. I jumped forward and seized Miles's arm.

"Miles," I said. "He's tied up."

Miles took a long breath through his clenched teeth. "Tell me what you meant."

Alasdair shook his head, turning a spiteful grin up at Miles. "I've changed my mind," he said. "You should go to the wells. Go and see for yourself. And take your little slut with you."

Miles moved so fast that my scream of protest only came once it was over. He spun the gun in his hand and slammed the butt of it onto Alasdair's temple.

Alasdair crumpled.

There was a tense, silent moment. Sebastian moved first, to check Alasdair's pulse.

"Is he dead?" Apollonia asked coolly.

"No," said Sebastian, equally cool.

"I suppose that's good," Apollonia replied.

"Tie up his feet," said Miles. "He can spend the night in the shack."

"That seems fair," said Sebastian.

I went up to Miles and put a hand on his arm.

"This is my gun," Miles said, looking down at it. "If he'd shot you with my gun . . ."

"He didn't," I said. "You stopped him."

"I wasn't sure it would work," said Miles. "It's simple magic, but still . . ."

"It worked." I ran my hand down his arm, lowering it. He was shaking. "You saved us."

"Yes." Sebastian stood and brushed off the knees of his pants. "Thanks for that."

He held out his hand to Miles, who stared at it a moment before he took it.

"I suppose you heard everything," said Apollonia.

I nodded.

"Oh, Mae already knew it all," grunted Sebastian. He dragged Alasdair by his tied arms into the shack and slammed the door behind him. "She knows everything that goes on around here."

"Not everything," I said.

Apollonia stared meditatively after her unconscious brother.

"Is Rex really dead?" she asked.

"Yes," I said. "I'm sorry."

"I'm not," said Apollonia.

Sebastian turned a look full of painful hope to her.

"I don't know what's going on," said Apollonia. "And I don't think I want to know. Perhaps Alasdair was right about some things."

"He was desperate enough to keep us from discovering the truth to kill me for it," I said.

"That doesn't mean he was wrong," said Apollonia. She held her hand out to Sebastian, who took it in both of his. "We're leaving. Now. I really think you ought to do the same."

Miles shook his head. "I can't just leave," he said. "I have to know."

Apollonia looked at me. "You could come with us."

"Really?" I was genuinely shocked.

"Just on the boat," said Apollonia. "I'm not inviting you to live with us."

"No, I know," I said.

"Maybe you should," said Miles in a low voice. "Whatever's happening—it won't be safe."

"I know that," I said. "But I'm coming with you anyway."

"You don't have to leave the island," said Miles. His brow furrowed with worry. "You could just go back to the party."

"No," I said.

There was a crack and a high whistling sound. We looked into the sky, and a shower of sparkling pink light exploded above us.

"The fireworks," breathed Miles. "It's time."

"We'll be off now," said Sebastian. "Thank you again for saving my life! And Mae, love—"

Apollonia frowned at the epithet.

"If you ever find yourself in the city looking for a job, come by the *Daily Sun*."

"Why?" I asked.

"Yes, why?" Apollonia snapped.

"I told you, you've got the makings of a star reporter," said Sebastian with a grin. "I don't do the hiring, but I'd put in a good word for you. I expect my own star will be on the rise after the story I'm going to write about tonight."

"Oh." I thought about this strange new prospect for a moment before it occurred to me that it was quite a nice offer. Apollonia had already started down the hill, pulling Sebastian behind her.

"Thanks!" I called after him.

"You're welcome, little goat!" Sebastian laughed over his shoulder. "Stay nimble tonight!"

When they were gone, Miles looked at me.

"Are you sure about this?" Miles asked.

"Miles," I said. "You've learned a little about me today. Do you really think I'm going to stay behind?"

Miles smiled ruefully and shook his head. Then he looked down at the gun in his hand again. He had held it differently this morning, without seeming to think about it. Now he looked at it as if every violent possibility it represented were flashing before his eyes.

"I guess I should bring this," he said.

"I don't know," I said. Just looking at it filled me with dread.

Miles looked back at the shack. "I can't leave it here. What if he wakes up and gets free? I'm not letting it fall into his hands again."

We stared at it together for a moment.

Then Miles flicked the safety on and put it in his jacket pocket. He reached for my hand, and I let him take it.

"Let's go."

CHAPTER TWENTY-SIX

The fireworks were exploding faster and louder, sending bolts of colored light across our path. We ran toward the wells, dread and excitement growing with every footfall.

We slowed as we approached the gates of the aether wells.

"I don't feel the wards," said Miles. "Do you?"

I stopped walking and searched myself for the prickling unease that meant a magical boundary. It wasn't there. I took another step toward the gate, and another, and still felt nothing. We approached, slowly at first, then with more certainty. Miles put his hand on the gate.

"The wards are down," he said. "Why?"

"Maybe they have to be?" I said. "Maybe they'd interfere with whatever magic they're doing."

"Or maybe it's a trap."

We stood outside the gate, staring. Without the magic shrouding it in dread, it wasn't much to look at. Just a wrought iron gate stretching between the canyon walls, only high enough that it would be difficult but not impossible to climb over. I had never been this close to it before.

"Why would they trap us?" I asked. "They want us to stay away—the fireworks—Alasdair—and Ivo locked us in his room to keep us from following him."

"You're right," said Miles. "I'm being paranoid."

Even so, we both stared at the handle on the gate for a long moment before Miles reached for it.

It wasn't locked.

Miles pulled back the gate far enough for us to peer in.

There wasn't much to see. The canyon continued beyond it, the high natural walls blocking the view on one side and dry shrubs doing so on the other. Low voices came from the direction of the shrubs. There was a blur of glowing lavender above them. The air spirits were here, circling.

I had never been inside the aether wells before. They were up ahead, past the shrubs, where the voices were locked in some kind of low argument. The source of everything I had known, my whole life, was in front of me. Nothing was in the way.

I took the first step past the gate. Nothing happened, and Miles went after me. The path wound downward, deeper into the canyon. We walked quietly, listening to the voices that grew louder as they came closer. Ivo's voice, and Lord Prosper's.

Miles seized my arm and pointed to something on our path, faintly glowing in the darkness.

A spirit, puddled on the ground as the first one had been and the one Ivo had cured outside the gate. Golden, pulsing slightly. And leaking.

"Don't step on it," I whispered. "Ivo said I shouldn't touch them."

We walked carefully around it, only to find another two

around the next bend. And beyond that, even more. Miles and I crouched behind a boulder and peered out into the clearing. Piles of them. Like a battle had been fought and the spirits had all been slaughtered.

"Spheres," whispered Miles. "Are they all like that?"

Amid the spirits, just out of sight, someone was weeping.

"I can't," said Ivo, between sobs. "Not again. Not all over again."

"I know." Lord Prosper's voice was infinitely weary. "I know, my son. It gives me more pain than you can know to ask it of you. But it takes us both. You know that."

"I can't," wept Ivo. "We can't. Grandfather, we have to stop this."

"You know what happens if you don't," said Lord Prosper. "And you know why it came to this."

"I didn't want this!"

"You knew what could happen when you took the binding off her," said Lord Prosper. "You put everything at risk. Do you think I wanted this? Do you think I wanted to bind another life? Another of my family?"

There was a noisy burst, and a gust of air blew leaves and twigs into my view.

When Lord Prosper's voice came, it was deeper than I had heard it. Stronger. It was no longer the voice of a weary old man. It was the voice of magic.

"You dare oppose me? You think your magic is any match for mine?"

Miles put a hand on my arm and then crept forward, peeking around the rock that hid us. His eyes widened. He went entirely still.

"What?" I whispered.

He jerked back behind the rock and stared at me in horror. He shook his head.

"What?"

I pulled him out of the way and looked out past the rock.

Ivo was on his feet, his hands out, facing Lord Prosper. They stood in a circular clearing, magic sparking between them. In the center was a sharp chasm, about the length of a tall person and twice as wide. Glowing threads of magic wound up out of it into a dense, intricate column that arced into the air and then spread out like the branches of a tree but unending, thinning across hundreds of feet into invisibility. And in the middle of this column of glowing threads, suspended over the chasm, arms flung out, eyes wide, blank, and staring:

Coco.

I started to cry out, but Miles put a hand over my mouth and pulled me back.

"It destroyed her," said Ivo. "It will destroy Coco."

"It will not," said Lord Prosper. "Cordelia is like me. She is stronger than Imogen ever was."

"It isn't about strength," said Ivo. "She felt what they felt. All their pain and their cries in her mind, all the time. She told me."

"You think I do not know?" Lord Prosper asked. "I hear them, too. I have learned to live with it. Cordelia will as well."

"And if she doesn't . . ." Ivo's sobs had dried into a harsh rattle. "Then no one will be surprised if she goes the way Imogen did. She was already wild. There were already rumors. No loss."

"Be careful what you say, my son," said Lord Prosper. "You have made this magic as surely as I have. You and your father before you. Everything you have comes from me and from this."

"My father didn't want any of it, and neither do I."

Another gust of air, a rush of wind, and then a ringing silence. I knew the kind it was—the silence of magic unfurling.

"I don't want to hurt you, Grandfather." Ivo's voice was ragged with pain.

"You will do this," said Lord Prosper. "We will rebind the spirits with her blood, blood that comes from me. You will survive it, and she will survive it, and we will go on."

"The spirits won't survive it," said Ivo. "They're dying."

"They aren't dying," said Lord Prosper with scorn. "They're rebelling, the only way they can. And they can only do that much because you loosed Imogen's bond and the magic has faded."

"This is how they rebel," said Ivo. "By becoming as close to dead as they can make themselves. We make their lives a torment."

"We make them work, that is all," said Lord Prosper. "Their lives have meaning this way. They had none before."

"You don't know that."

"I do know," said Lord Prosper. "When I first came to this island, I saw all this power, all this potential, and they did nothing with it. Nothing at all."

Ivo didn't reply.

"Ask Aeris, if you don't believe me. He knew we could make more of this place. It was why he helped me. It is better this way. Better for everyone."

"Better for Aeris," said Ivo. "He's the only one of them you let keep any part of himself."

"Ivo," said Lord Prosper. "Do you want to deprive the

world of aether? Deprive your family of all we have? This is how we have lived since you were an infant. It is too late for you to change your mind."

"No," said Ivo. "It's not."

Ivo cried out in words I couldn't understand, and a sharp crack followed. Lord Prosper roared, and a sound like thunder broke over us, so loud and long that we covered out ears and cowered.

When it was over, all I could hear was the sound of Ivo gasping.

"You can't do it without my help," he said, his voice raw.

"No indeed," said Lord Prosper, also out of breath. "But you aren't my only grandson."

Miles rose to his feet, unnaturally fast. He stared down at me in helpless horror.

"What are you doing?" I hissed.

Miles took a step past the cover of the rock. I reached for him but too late. He took another step then walked forward, out of my sight.

"Miles," groaned Ivo. "Why didn't you stay away?"

"Hello, Miles," said Lord Prosper. "I'm glad you've come. And you, Mae dear. You might as well come out also."

My breath caught. Miles had been right. It was a trap after all, one Ivo had tried to keep us from walking into.

"Run, Mae!" cried Miles.

I scrambled backward, pushing myself to my feet. I tried to obey, to run back in the direction of the gate. But the nausea of magic I hadn't felt at the entrance suddenly returned but in the opposite direction, keeping me in instead of out. I gasped against it, tried to fight through. I dropped to my knees and tried to crawl. I started to retch.

"My dear girl," said Lord Prosper, weary again. "Do not torment yourself. You should know by now, the magic will win."

I dragged myself back toward the clearing, and the nausea subsided. I pulled myself to my feet and walked out from behind the rock, my whole body trembling.

Miles stood a few yards ahead with his back to me, rigid and still. Ivo had been shunted to the side. He was on his knees, and his hands were bound behind his back with the same glowing cords of magic that bound Coco, suspended over the chasm.

Stupid. Stupid, stupid, stupid.

Why had we thought we could hide from Lord Prosper? Here at the wells or anywhere else on his island? He had seen it all. He had known we would come. Ivo had known. He had tried to protect us. But I had blown up his room and killed a man while refusing his protection.

"I'm sorry," I said to Ivo. He met my eyes for one moment, then lowered them to the ground.

"Let Mae go, Grandfather." He was pleading, broken. "You don't need her for this. She doesn't need to see . . ."

"She has already seen too much," said Lord Prosper. "And you showed it to her. When this is over, you will help me put it right."

"I won't," said Ivo.

Lord Prosper ignored him. "Mae, dear, you may sit if you like. This will take a little while."

"What are you going to do to Coco?" I tried, in vain, to make my quavering voice hard.

"Cordelia is going to help us bind the spirits," said Lord

Prosper. "It takes powerful blood magic to hold them to my will. All these years, since she was a small child, it was Imogen's blood we used. But she is not here."

"Why Coco?" I asked. "She defends you. She won't hear a word against you. She loves you the most of all of them . . . don't you know that?"

"I do," said Lord Prosper.

"Why use someone from your own family at all?" I asked. "I've been here all along. You don't care about me. Why not use me?"

Lord Prosper leaned forward on his walking stick, peering at me with curiosity.

"Are you volunteering?" he asked. "'Take me, not her?' I didn't think you were so loyal a friend."

I wasn't so loyal. I glanced at Coco's suspended, wide-eyed form. I hadn't meant to offer myself. It wasn't loyalty or self-sacrifice that made me ask that question, just curiosity. But now that I thought of it . . .

I swallowed hard.

"I—"

I wanted to volunteer. I wanted to be the kind of friend who didn't think twice, who threw herself in front of danger to protect the one she loved. Even when I knew I mattered so much less to Coco than she did to me.

I couldn't finish the sentence.

"It was a nice thought," sighed Lord Prosper. "And in truth, I would have used your blood if I could. But no, to bind the spirits to my will requires the blood of my own descendants. Perhaps one of your own children, one day . . ."

Lord Prosper looked meditatively at Ivo, who stared back

at him in misery. Lord Prosper shook his head and turned his gaze to Miles. He made a movement with his hand, and Miles spoke.

"I'm not going to help you hurt Coco," said Miles.

"You weren't so concerned about her well-being earlier this evening," said Lord Prosper.

Miles was very still.

"I was angry," he said. "I didn't mean it."

"You were right to be angry," said Lord Prosper. "Your cousin showed you what she really thinks of you, and it was what you always suspected, wasn't it?"

"No," said Miles. "She was angry. She didn't mean it, either."

"Do you think you care about her more than I do?" said Lord Prosper. "Do you think you are in a better position to see what must and must not be done? This magic gives us everything we have. Without it, the spirits will not produce the aether. They will declare war on us, and this island will no longer be fit for human habitation. Do you see?"

"We'd lose everything," said Miles.

"We would," said Lord Prosper. "All of us. Coco as well. Do you think she would thank you for protecting her when that was the result?"

"My mother hated coming back here," Miles said slowly. "What the magic did to her—it cost her this island, too. It cost her everything."

"Not everything," said Lord Prosper. "She still has her allowance. She can live as she wishes. Destroy the aether, and you take that from her as well."

Miles shook his head again.

"Miles, I am offering you what Ivo has thrown aside," said Lord Prosper patiently. "His place. His powers. His bride, if you want."

"She isn't yours to give," said Miles.

"The rest of it, then," said Lord Prosper. "Do you understand?"

I didn't have to see Miles's face to know he understood. This morning he had arrived at the island longing for this— Ivo condemned, cast down; Lord Prosper offering Miles Ivo's place.

Today had been a day of dreams coming true, as nightmares.

"You always—" Miles's voice caught. "You always said blood magic had nothing to do with the magic of the spheres."

"It doesn't," said Lord Prosper. "With the knowledge of the planets and stars, I can weave the music of the spheres. I can guide the winds and tides and calm the storms. But binding magic is blood magic. It gives us control of the spirits, who distill their magic into aether. It is the reason we have what we have."

"Then maybe we shouldn't have it," said Miles quietly.

Lord Prosper's smile faltered. He drew a long breath and released it in a meditative sigh.

"Three sons, all fools, and three grandsons," said Lord Prosper. "All too weak to do what needs to be done."

Lord Prosper turned to me.

"Perhaps it has been a mistake to look only to my own offspring."

Magic trickled over me like sweat down my back. My fingers, balled into fists, went slack. My mouth fell open.

"That's right, my dear," said Lord Prosper. "You think I haven't seen you, don't you? You think I don't know what you want."

My eyes flicked to Miles and back, but Lord Prosper shook his head.

"No, not him. What you *really* want," he said.

I stared, first at Lord Prosper, then at the glowing column of binding threads rising out of the chasm behind him.

Longing twisted in my stomach. Here it was—the thing I wanted. The magic I had planned and schemed and betrayed in hopes of stealing some part of it.

Lord Prosper was offering it to me.

"Do you mean—"

"The blood we use must be from one of my offspring. But all the magician who assists me needs is the will to do it. Do you have the will?"

I tried not to picture it.

But I couldn't stop myself. My own place—not on some other island of the archipelago but on this one, on my island. My own place. Not because I had married one of its sons or schemed my way into some portion of its magic, but because I was a magician. Lord Prosper's second-in-command.

"Mae—" Lord Prosper made a short movement with his hand, and Miles fell silent. Miles couldn't turn his head toward me. I knew what he wanted to say. Think of Coco. Think of Imogen. Think of everything before you make this choice. This choice to accept everything you ever wanted.

"You can have him, too," said Lord Prosper. "Take whichever of my grandsons you like best."

I didn't bother to protest, as Miles had, that none of us were his to give.

We weren't, but still, I probably could have them. Whichever one I wanted. All it would take was the simple sort of binding they had done to me, cutting away the memory of what I had done to earn my new place. It would have to be done anyway, wouldn't it? I had no doubt that Lord Prosper intended to fix the problem of his rebellious, too-noble grandsons.

Miles would look at me differently when I was Lord Prosper's chosen successor, I was sure of it. I wouldn't be Mousy Mae anymore, or even Minxy Mae. I would be powerful. Desirable.

I looked at the magical column again, trying, for a moment, not to see Coco bound there.

Miles had said no to this very same offer. And Coco wasn't *his* best friend.

But then, she might be my best friend, but I wasn't hers.

I took a deep breath. I wanted it.

Lord Prosper smiled.

"I'll do it."

Ivo started to cry out, but Lord Prosper silenced him with another sharp gesture.

"Good," said Lord Prosper. "She would want you to, you know. She would do the same in your place."

I stepped forward, heart thundering and blood screaming in my ears.

Maybe it was true. It could be true.

"Give me your hands, my dear," said Lord Prosper.

I held them out. They trembled.

"You will need to be strong," said Lord Prosper. He took my hands in his and closed his eyes, murmuring over them. My hands began to tingle. When Lord Prosper released them, sparks jumped from my palms.

"I have put magic into your hands," said Lord Prosper. "When this night is over, we will begin your training. Until then, you will use the magic I have given you."

I nodded, staring at my hands. The power rushed to my head like the cigarette had but a hundred times stronger. A longing for more shot through me, sharp and sweet and ravenous. How could I ever have said no? Impossible.

Lord Prosper and I walked toward the chasm. I looked at the magic sparking between my fingers. No need to look at Coco. No need to look behind me, at Ivo and Miles. They were watching now, but they wouldn't remember, afterward. Their horror, their disapproval—it would be gone as if it had never happened.

Lord Prosper told me the words to say, the way to hold my hands, to focus the magic he had placed in them. I followed all his instructions, one obedient step after another. My head swam with elation. The power felt like soaring, like tumbling and vaulting through the air, through something higher and rarer than the air. How was it possible for magic to feel even better than I had imagined?

Lord Prosper took the knife and cut into Coco's arm.

He drew a circle underneath it, and a shimmering, gold bowl appeared. The blood dripped down into it. Lord Prosper murmured over it, and drops of blood began to rise into the twisting tree of glowing cords. They attached to the cords like beads of dew on branches.

Lord Prosper signaled to me, and I began to say the words he had taught me. The magic Lord Prosper gave me twisted inside me, changed. Instead of soaring, I was falling.

"Be strong, Mae," said Lord Prosper.

I didn't stop chanting, didn't let my legs buckle under me,

even as the magic tilted and dizzied me. I kept my balance by staring at the glowing cords, the blood clinging to them.

Lord Prosper said a word I didn't know, and the drops of blood faded to the color of the cords and vanished into them, absorbed.

Coco's eyes flew open.

I saw them, full of silent agony. I looked away. But there was something else, something louder and stronger in my own mind. Something I couldn't look away from.

Screams. Agony. Deafening, piercing, screams. I pressed my hands to my ears, but it didn't stop them.

"Be strong, Mae!" Lord Prosper's voice thundered over the screams of the spirits.

I knew what they were. Those screams. They were the searing misery of the spirits, keening against the binding that took their will, their freedom. Made them into things, into tools.

We make their lives a torment. Ivo had known. I had, too. If I had let myself.

I had tried so hard not to know this, to hide from it. I'd told myself I would figure it out later when what I truly meant was never. Well, it was really damn late now, and there was no more hiding from it. I lowered my hands from my ears, and still the screaming continued.

"We are almost finished," said Lord Prosper. "Mae. The last spell. Just one more."

I met Coco's eyes again, wide with the same terror that consumed me. This was what Coco would hear, for the rest of her life. Coco would be bound to this horror.

Ivo was right. Miles was right. This would destroy her.

And the spirits.

For the first time, I felt how many of them there were. Not just the house spirits, not just the well spirits, but the air spirits, too. The ones who carried the beautiful music I loved. They were here. I looked up, unwillingly. The air spirits circled above us, faster and faster. The music had changed, become something higher, fiercer. Almost like the screams I heard in my mind. It was the sound of souls bound into something worse than death. They had tried to die, to escape it. With one last spell, I would take even that from them.

I couldn't do it. I couldn't live with it.

I stepped back.

Lord Prosper turned to me, his eyes flashing with fury.

"Have you considered what use you are to me, if you refuse?" he asked, raising a hand.

His magic was still in my hands. I could raise it against him, but it would not hold him back for long. Instead I turned to Ivo.

"Confrigenda vincula!" I screamed, throwing all the magic I held with the spell.

The golden chains that held Ivo fell off, and he leapt to his feet. His hands sparked into flame. Lord Prosper whirled on Ivo with a scream, but the fire seized the old man, winding around him and bearing him up. There was a gust of wind, and Lord Prosper was thrown to the side of the clearing.

"Coco!" Ivo cried, pointing.

The glowing threads around Coco had rapidly begun to unravel. I stood on the edge of the chasm—deep, so deep—and reached for Coco. I seized her hand. Coco dipped lower as the cords snapped. I staggered and nearly fell in. Far beneath me, bright, molten aether bubbled like silver lava. Panic seized me. If Coco was released, we would both fall.

Then there was an arm around my waist and another reaching for Coco. Miles seized her flailing hand and lurched backward, pulling us all from the chasm.

Lord Prosper let out a feral scream.

I looked up, struggling to my feet. The air spirits were circling lower, faster around the threads of magic that weaved into the glowing column. One of the threads snapped with a furious hiss.

"Their bindings are too loose!" screamed Lord Prosper. "Mae, we must finish the magic!"

I scrambled to my feet and turned back to Ivo. His hands were out, his magic pouring toward his grandfather, but his eyes were on the column, full of hatred and desperate resolve. I understood now. That column was the source of the binding.

The air spirits were so close now, closer than I had ever seen them. They were the color of the house spirits but fluid and moving. Molten, like the aether. They circled the cords, a mere inch away. One of them grazed the glowing column and then skittered away out of formation, like it had been shocked. It plummeted then vanished. But the threads it had touched snapped, sparking.

They could do it, I was certain. It might kill them, but they could break the cords, if we didn't finish strengthening the magic that bound them.

Lord Prosper screamed again and threw a wall of flame at Ivo, who staggered backward and fell under it. He could only press it back far enough to keep from burning. With his grandson dealt with, Lord Prosper whirled on the air spirits, hands twisting as a ball of flame grew between them.

"Mae," gasped Ivo. "He'll destroy them!"

I stared at Lord Prosper, the source of everything I'd ever known to want, as he formed an attack, vicious hatred pouring from his face. Behind him, another spirit threw itself into the cords, and then another. Lord Prosper raised his hands.

I didn't know what else to do. I charged. I seized Lord Prosper around the middle and threw him to the ground. His frail, old body went down without protest, and the magic in his hands went out like the air from his lungs.

The air spirits dove.

Straight through the cords. They snapped in two like they'd been cut with a knife. The music grew to a scream and then went out. The bottom threads dropped into the chasm, and the ones above dissolved into the air like salt into water.

Beneath me, Lord Prosper let out a voiceless gasp of horror.

There was a moment of silence. I scrambled to my feet.

And then, the well spirits started to wake.

CHAPTER TWENTY-SEVEN

They stirred, at first. There were so many of them, strewn around, piled up, pressed against the canyon walls. Small movements duplicated across so many bodies made an eerie impression. As though we were on a battlefield and the dead soldiers all started to rise at once. Lord Prosper pushed himself to his knees and screamed, "Aeris!"

The memory came back with terrifying urgency: Ivo calling for Aeris after he'd woken the well spirit outside the gate. After the well spirit had set me on fire.

Aeris appeared in the sky above Lord Prosper.

"Your will?" he asked, then stared about him. "What . . . ?"

"Quickly now," said Lord Prosper. "We have to redo the bindings before they awaken."

"Before . . ." Aeris's voice trailed off in horror. "But—they were tricked the first time—they won't be tricked again."

"There has to be a way," said Lord Prosper. "You found one before. Find one now!"

Aeris's translucent form started to turn around, looking at the different piles of stirring well spirits.

"Can't . . . can't . . ." the spirit stammered. "It's too late."

"Too late . . ." murmured Lord Prosper. He turned on his heel, to me. "Then you've killed us. You've killed us all."

A well spirit rose, slowly, to its golden, translucent feet. It turned its face to Aeris, hovering above it. Aeris stared at it, his mouth slightly open.

Lord Prosper ran, faster than I would have thought such an old man could, back up the path to the gate.

The spirit raised its hand toward Aeris. Aeris screamed and thrashed his arms. Slowly, he sank toward the ground, struggling against some invisible restraint. Other spirits rose.

The spirit with its arm out regarded Aeris with something I had never seen on the face of a spirit.

Vengeance.

The spirit spoke in the same rasping language the one outside the gate had used when Ivo woke it. It sounded like the language Ivo muttered when he said spells. Like magic.

"He forced me!" cried Aeris. "He forced me!" His eyes darted around his head, seeing the spirits rising around him, facing him, hating him. He screamed, as though he could already feel them ripping the threads of his being apart.

And maybe he could.

The spirits let out a collective shriek that raised every hair on my body, and their bodies burst into flame.

They advanced on Aeris, who lifted off the ground, a wind whirling around him. The wind turned, beating back the fiery bodies of the well spirits. Flames whipped back, igniting bushes and spreading beyond the spirits. But still they pressed toward Aeris. The heat of the fire grew, and I stumbled backward, still gripping Coco's arm. Ivo turned and ran toward us.

"Run!" he hissed.

"Run where?" Miles demanded. "The gate is that way!"

He pointed to the path that led out of the canyon and to the swarm of furious spirits that lay directly in the way. Ivo swatted Miles's arm down as he ran past.

"There's a back gate," he cried over his shoulder.

We ran after him, around a bend and down a tree-lined path. I didn't look back, even when Aeris's screams turned from fear and anger into something else, something worse.

"They're spirits," Miles panted as they ran. "We can't outrun them forever, can we? Can't they disappear and appear like Aeris . . . once they're unbound?"

"No," Ivo panted back. "Only the air spirits can do that. The well spirits only have one form. They can fly . . . or glide . . . but they can't vanish."

"Still," I gasped. "There are hundreds of them. What will they do when they're done with Aeris?"

"Go for Grandfather," said Ivo. "Come for us. Or the house."

"Kill us all, basically," said Coco.

"There are wards on the house," Ivo said. "They shouldn't be able to hurt anyone inside."

"Will the wards hold now that the binding magic is broken?" Miles asked.

"They should," said Ivo. Then, "You need to get off the island."

"Sounds like we all need to get off the island," said Miles.

"I have to get back to the house," panted Ivo. "I have to help everyone inside get to the boats."

The narrow path began to broaden, and the trees thinned out in the sandier soil. Coco stopped and bent over, gasping for air.

"Wait," she called out.

I crossed the few paces back to her.

"We have to keep moving."

Coco held up one finger.

I looked around. I couldn't see any spirits coming for us, but something still felt horribly wrong.

Then I realized.

The spirit music had stopped. I couldn't hear anything except, not too far away, the rumble of the ocean.

"Oh," I breathed. Miles put his hand on my arm. I looked up and saw the same recognition tightening his face.

"Do you think it killed them?" I asked Ivo. "Cutting those cords?"

Ivo's miserable expression said enough.

"What happens after we get off the island?" Coco asked. "How do we ever come back?"

Ivo looked back at her, grief lining his face and shadowing his eyes. He was older than Lord Prosper in that moment. He was older than the island.

"We don't," he said.

Miles's hand tightened on my arm. Coco straightened, her face sweaty but bloodless.

"You knew this would happen," she said to Ivo. "You meant for it to happen."

Ivo met her eyes and nodded.

"People are going to die because of you," she whispered, harsh.

And if I'd thought he'd looked sad before, it was only because I hadn't seen him in this moment, with the weight of everything he'd done pressing down on him at once.

"I know," Ivo said. "But no one will ever be enslaved because of me again."

Coco stared at him, fury and anguish battling on her face. She'd heard the spirits, same as I had. She knew what Lord Prosper told us was a lie.

She nodded.

"We have to keep going," Miles said, then looked at Ivo. "Where are we going?"

"To my plane," said Coco, pushing herself upright. "The beach I parked it on is just down there."

Ivo nodded confirmation, and we ran.

Coco was right—the cliff overlooking the beach was only a couple hundred yards away.

"Can it fit four?" I asked.

"It's built for two," said Coco. "But we can squeeze."

Coco scrambled up to the cockpit and pushed the glass dome on top farther open.

"Do you have the fuel to get across?" Ivo asked.

Coco thought a moment as she pulled me aboard. She bit her lip and shook her head.

"It's all right," said Ivo. "Get us to the docks. You can take a boat."

"There's nowhere to land at the docks!" Coco said.

"There's the lawn in front of the house," said Miles. He clambered over the side and pressed into the rear seat with me.

"It's not really long enough. And what if they're there already?" Coco asked.

"I'll protect you," said Ivo.

"Can you?" I asked. I remembered the spirit by the gate.

It had pushed past Ivo's magic like it was nothing. And that was only one.

Ivo wedged himself into the plane next to Coco. "I think so."

"Great," Coco said. "Just great." She turned the engine. It roared to life. She began to turn the plane around in a wide circle. She brought it around, facing the beach. Our runway.

Miles shouted an expletive, followed by, "Look!"

Above us, well spirits lined the cliffside. Smoke and flame billowed up behind them. They had left a roaring wildfire in their wake.

"Oh, holy spheres," breathed Coco. "Let's hope we can take off."

"What do you mean?" I cried.

Coco gunned the engine, and the plane lurched forward, faster and faster down the beach. Coco pushed the throttle as far as it would go. The front wheels of the plane lifted, barely.

"Come on, come on, come on," she muttered.

"Coco!" I cried. "They're coming!"

The spirits on the cliffside burst into flames, just like the one by the gate. Just like Aeris, before they fell on him. They started dropping down the cliff. The ones behind us were too far away to catch us. The ones ahead charged, closing in.

"Coco!" I screamed.

Coco was desperately pulling on the throttle. The plane lifted a little farther.

"We're too heavy," Miles said in despair.

"I shouldn't have gotten in," groaned Ivo.

The back wheels of the plane lifted right as the first spirit reached them. It flew at the cockpit window. Flames spread across the glass, and spidery cracks formed on the windshield.

The glass window shattered, but Ivo's hands pushed outward, sparking, and all the glass fell away from us. The spirit was pushed back and suddenly dropped out of sight.

Coco tugged left hard, and the plane jerked away, skimming so close over the waves that we all coughed and spluttered on the cold sea mist. Behind us on the beach was a mass of flaming spirits. The plane cut straight out into the ocean, leaving them behind.

"Okay," said Coco. Her voice was shaking. "Change of plans. We're not landing anywhere near those things. We're going straight to the mainland."

"No," said Ivo. "There are a hundred people back at the house. And our family. I have to help them escape."

"And you said we don't have enough fuel," said Miles.

Coco gripped the wheel, her arms rigid, and shook her head.

"Coco," I said. "We'll get on the boat. We'll get out of there. Ivo will protect us. You saw what he did to that spirit."

Coco shook her head again. Her mouth trembled.

"We can't just leave them, Coco!" Miles shouted.

"Fine! Fine! You're all so much braver and better than I am, are you?" Coco cried. "None of you are worried about the spirits murdering us the moment we land?"

"We'll beat the well spirits there," said Miles.

"And the house spirits?" Coco asked.

We looked at Ivo. The well spirits were one thing. We knew they were there but rarely saw them. There was something particularly chilling about the idea of the docile, ever-present house spirits turning against us.

I thought, again, of their screams.

"They can't turn to fire like that, can they?" I asked.

"No," said Ivo. "They're air spirits. Like the ones that make the music, bound further."

"And like Aeris?"

"Yes."

"Then they could vanish like him? Appear anywhere? Change the wind?" I asked, panic rising.

"I'll deal with the house spirits," Ivo said.

"Sure. Great," said Coco. "Perfect."

"The ocean can kill us as sure as those spirits if we crash in it," said Miles.

"Fine," Coco snapped. "Fine."

She jerked the throttle to the right, and the plane veered back toward the coast and the house.

"Oh, no," Miles muttered.

Deep, black plumes of smoke streaked the sky above the other side of the island.

The big house was on fire.

"What were you saying about the wards?" said Miles.

"They guard against magic," muttered Ivo with quiet despair. "Fire isn't magic."

"The lighting orbs," muttered Miles.

Coco cursed but didn't change course. Beside her, Ivo spread his hands again and muttered to himself, readying more magic.

"When we land," said Ivo, looking over at me. "Use the ring to amplify my magic."

I twisted the ring on my finger. All this chaos. The house, on fire. The spirits attacking. We could have stopped it. Ivo and I.

In the distance, we could see the fires in the house and the people streaming out of the doors and down the path to the docks. Some boats had already set out and were speeding toward the mainland.

Miles grabbed my hand and made a sound like he'd been punched. I followed his gaze. A house spirit ran through the thrown-open back doors and hurled one of the fiery orbs of light at a fleeing partygoer. The man's suit lit up like a torch, and he threw himself into the pool as flames engulfed him.

The plane started to lose height.

"We're going to pass low over the house," said Coco grimly. "I'll give the lawn one pass to give people a warning to get out of the way."

Ivo pushed himself to a standing position and leaned forward out of the shattered glass window.

"Careful!" cried Coco.

More house spirits emerged from the house, winds swirling around them. Some had their hands extended toward the house, whipping the flames into frenzy. Others were lifting guests into the air and hurling them away. Ivo held out both his hands over the side of the plane. Below, water rose from the pool in a shimmering blanket.

"Mae!" he shouted.

I focused on the ring, and the water rose faster, following below us from the pool onto the burning house as we flew over it. The fire on the balconies and outside steps sputtered out, but smoke kept pouring from the windows. On the other side of the house, Ivo turned his hands toward the fountain that flanked the entrance steps. The tall champagne spouts of water turned until they streamed directly at the house like fire hoses, some hitting the roof, some going into the wide-open

294 ~ SAMANTHA COHOE

front doors. One turned the other way, toward a spirit toss-
ing guests down the stairs. The water hit it with a blast of
force, and the spirit veered away.

Coco flew the plane low over the fleeing guests. They
scattered. She circled, out over the water again in a tight
turn, then back low along the grass.

"It's not as long as the beach," said Coco. "I'm not sure . . ."

The wheels touched down hard, throwing us up. Miles's
head hit the glass above him, and Ivo was nearly thrown
from the plane.

"Hold on," said Coco.

"A little late!" I snapped.

"No, I mean—" Coco pointed. The lawn was rapidly running out, and ahead of us was the oak tree and the cliff face
beside it.

"We're going to crash!" Miles exclaimed.

"Or go into the water," said Coco. "You can all swim, right?"

"If the plane goes over that cliff, it'll be dashed to pieces
on the rocks!" I cried. "The waves are huge there—we won't
get the chance to swim!"

"Aim for the tree," said Ivo.

Coco shook her head. "It's too fast."

Ivo turned out his hands. "Do it."

I tightened my grip on Miles's hand. We barreled toward
the tree. We were going to be thrown from the plane. The
impact was going to kill us.

I closed my eyes.

Then, unexpectedly, wind roared in my ears and pushed
me back. The wind was so strong, it was like blunt force. It
lifted the skin on my bones. It pinned me against the back of
the cockpit.

And it stopped the plane.

Then, as suddenly as it had started, it died.

I opened my eyes to the oak tree looming over us. The plane had stopped a foot away. Ivo had already vaulted out of the plane and was running back toward the house. Coco unharnessed herself and jumped out as well.

"Let's go!" she shouted. "We have to get a boat before they take them all!"

Miles climbed over and held out his hands to me. I took them, and we locked eyes as he lowered me down.

"Miles," I said quietly. Dread pooled in my stomach. "Alasdair."

Miles nodded. "I know."

He looked up toward the hill where we had left him tied up in Ivo's shack.

"He might not even be conscious," I said. "And he's bound."

"And no one on the island knows he's there but us," said Miles.

We looked at Coco, sprinting toward the docks. She looked over her shoulder and noticed us standing there.

"What are you waiting for?" she called.

I ran toward her, and Miles came after. Bloodcurdling screams from the house cut the sound of the waves.

"We left Alasdair in Ivo's shack on the hill," I called to her.

"You—what?"

"Unconscious and tied up. We have to get him," said Miles.

"No," said Coco, shaking her head violently. "No way! Mae, you can't go back there! Come on."

Coco held out her hand. I was halfway toward taking it when I looked down at my own hand and remembered.

"I can help Ivo," I said. "The ring. I can make his spells stronger."

"They're going to take all the boats." Coco's wide eyes fixed on me. "You don't want to die here, Mae. You haven't even been off this island yet!"

"Get a boat, Coco," I said. "Wait for us as long as you can, okay?"

Coco heaved a frustrated sigh and shook her head.

"I can't wait in the dock," said Coco. "Didn't you see those people? They're panicking. I'll never be able to keep a boat there. And anyway, the house spirits already started whipping up the waves . . ."

Coco peered up at the hill.

"I'll wait for you offshore of the east beach," she said. "It's the closest to the shack."

"Thank you, Coco," I said.

"Hurry!" she said and ran.

We ran, too, in the opposite direction, toward the house. Despite Ivo's airborne water attack, the smoke billowing off it was even thicker and darker than when we flew over it.

"I hope everyone got out," I said.

We crossed the lawn, weaving through more terrified fugitives. A man pulled along a sobbing woman with singed and smoking hair, his coat flung around her like a firebreak. Behind them, Ivo stood at the top of the tiered steps, between the fountains, his feet planted wide, his hands out, and his back to the fleeing guests.

He faced a group of spirits. Winds gathered around their feet, picking up rocks and burning embers from the house.

I seized my ring as I ran and turned my mind to Ivo's spell. The spirits attacked, hurling the winds with all they

had gathered at Ivo. Ivo threw up his hands, and the spirits'
winds met a barrier and blew back toward them. The air
spirits were thrown back toward the house then vanished.
Ivo whirled toward us.

"Mae! No!" he cried. "Go to the docks! Go!"

I shook my head as I sprinted toward him.

"It's . . . Alasdair . . ." I gasped, taking the steps two at
a time. "He's tied up . . . in your shack. We left him there."

Ivo's eyes widened.

"That's toward the wells," he said. "The well spirits . . ."

"We can't just leave him," I gasped. "He's there because
of me!"

"Because of us," Miles corrected.

And it was true, we had both tied Alasdair up. Miles had
knocked him out. Apollonia and Sebastian had been the reason Alasdair was on that hill to begin with. And it was both
Ivo and I who had cut the binding.

And now there were people on fire, people screaming and
fleeing. People dead. Rex. Maybe more.

There couldn't be more. I couldn't take it.

"Please, Ivo," I said.

He met my eyes. He understood.

He turned back to the house and closed his eyes.

"There's no one still in there," he said, turning back to us.
"No one alive, anyway. Let's go."

We ran, taking a wide arc around the house and up the
footpath. The rippling sounds of fire and the groaning of the
house followed us.

I allowed myself one last glance over my shoulder before
we passed around a bend out of sight. I stopped, and Miles
stopped, too.

The spirits were clustered outside the house, glowing with a natural light I'd never seen before.

Then the fifth floor collapsed in a deafening roar. The flames rose up, licking the trees I had climbed to spy on the magic room. The spirits threw up their hands and let out a sound.

It started as a cry of triumph—almost a scream. But slowly, their voices wove together from a scream into something more melodic, though no more gentle.

Music. Spirit music.

"Do you hear that?" I asked.

"Yes," said Miles.

"It's so . . ."

I didn't know how to finish. I wanted to say *wild*, but that wasn't right. It was more complex than the music from before. It was harsher. No calming lullaby. The notes traveled suddenly across a surprising, wide range. It made no sense to me. And yet . . .

"It sounds right," said Miles.

"It does." I wiped tears out of my eyes.

Because if this was right, the gentle, subdued, *human* spirit music I had loved all my life was wrong.

All of it had been wrong.

CHAPTER TWENTY-EIGHT

We ran. Up the footpath, the light of the burning house flickering behind us against the black night. The spirit song urged us on.

Then, at the base of the hill with the shack, Ivo stopped abruptly. We caught up and stopped by his side, taking in the scene that froze him on the footpath.

Above, his back to us, Lord Prosper stood motionless, his hands trained on a spirit at his feet. A pack of well spirits stood behind him. They weren't blazing in attack. They were still as I was used to seeing them, though they glowed like the ones by the burning house.

A standoff.

"Ivo," said Lord Prosper. "I have this one. It seems to be the leader. I think I can destroy it. These others have agreed to lower their defenses as they did before. If you will help me, we can bind them again. A temporary binding. Long enough to return to the wells and—"

"No," said Ivo. "We're here to get Alasdair from my house, and then we're going to leave."

"Leave?" Lord Prosper said. "We can't leave. If we leave them alone, they'll build their strength. They'll destroy everything. If we leave now, we can never come back at all!"

"We're going to leave," repeated Ivo. "And you should come with us."

"Mae?" Lord Prosper asked, with a flick of his eyes. "Help me. Use that ring he gave you."

I looked down at the ring again.

"You regret it now, don't you? Now that you see what you have done? " said Lord Prosper. "You didn't want to end our life here. To make exiles of us. Was that what you wanted?"

It wasn't. At all.

The well spirits looked at me. Their eyes weren't blank now. Their wide, golden, pupil-less eyes didn't look any more human than before. But they were alive, so alive with expression and feeling, it was agony to meet them. They had tasted freedom, but they were willing to submit again, to spare their leader.

"They don't deserve to be slaves," I said. "Let him go."

"Him? Him? You think this is a him?" Lord Prosper hissed. His voice started to rise. "They aren't people, you foolish girl! You can't reason with them! All you can do is defeat them!"

With that, he swung both his arms down in a violent gesture, and the captured spirit flickered black. Then a shot rang out.

Lord Prosper crumpled, and the spirit collapsed with him. The other spirits stood frozen.

Beside me, Miles held the gun. He stared at it then back at his grandfather. He dropped it, like the gun had turned to fire as well.

"Run," said Ivo. "Run!"

I didn't hesitate. I seized Miles's hand and pushed past Ivo on our way up the hill. Ivo shouted some spell that cast a shimmering, purple wall behind us and followed.

I reached the shack first and threw open the door. Inside, Alasdair was awake and struggling with the ropes.

"What's happening out there?" he cried as I ran in. "What's that light? Did someone fire a gun? Is it—?"

"Fire," I said. I dropped to my knees beside Alasdair and struggled with the knots at his feet. Miles stood in the doorway, glassy-eyed.

"Get out of the way," Ivo panted from the doorway. I lurched aside, and Ivo cut through the ropes with a quick burst of magic.

"What's happening?" Alasdair exclaimed again.

"We have to go." Ivo pulled Alasdair to his feet.

"We have to *run*," I said. "If you fall behind, we won't be waiting for you."

We ran back out and down the other side of the hill. There wasn't a cleared path on this side. We vaulted over low brambles and shrubs, half running, half falling to the bottom. Fire lit up the ridge behind us, spreading out from the wells. Winds had picked up, unnaturally strong, and whipped the fire from hill to hill. The spirits were going to burn all trace of humans off their island.

I tripped and rolled and was immediately heaved up by Miles. Behind us, the well spirits had sent up a keening cry that wove into the rest of the spirit music and set my heart pounding even faster. I wondered, sick at heart, if whatever Lord Prosper had done to their leader had killed him. If that cry was their mourning.

Alasdair was falling behind. A life of dissolute gambling, drinking, and smoking had left him considerably less fit than the rest of us.

"What's that sound?" he cried desperately.

"Keep running!" I shouted back.

Alasdair tripped and tumbled down the hill and past us instead. He picked himself up, groaning and swearing, just as I reached him.

"Oh, bloody hell," said Alasdair, looking past us, back up the hill.

I glanced behind me. The spirits stood at the top, a row of blazing flame swirling around them. Hot wind picked up, whipping at my face, and the flames raced down the hill toward us.

"What did you do?" Alasdair screamed. "I warned you!"

"And I warned you to run!"

We reached the east beach coughing and choking on smoke. The fire was practically on our heels. Ivo shrugged off his jacket and ran straight across the rocky outcropping of beach and into the water up to his waist. Then he turned back to the beach, hands out. A wall of water rose up from the ocean and rushed straight at us. I held my breath as it pushed past me, coating me in cold seawater, and didn't turn to watch it fall onto the burning landscape behind us.

I staggered into the ocean after Ivo, Miles close behind.

"I don't see the boat!" I cried in panic.

"It's there," Ivo called back. "She's far out, though. It'll be a swim."

I plunged into the water, gasping at the cold. The waves were long and not very high at this beach. I tried to keep running into them, but my body fought against the icy chill.

Beside me, Miles cried out involuntarily. We were just past Ivo. Miles dove under the wave and took off swimming with long, strong strokes.

"They're coming!" Ivo cried. "Hurry!"

I looked back. Ivo's water attack had pushed the fire back a few yards, and Alasdair emerged from a cloud of smoke, singed and coughing. The spirits were close behind. Alasdair tripped and plunged forward, facedown in the smoldering brush. Ivo ran toward him, out of the water. I stood, frozen with cold and horror, watching the flaming spirits bear down on Alasdair. Just before they descended on him, Ivo threw up a shimmering lavender barrier, and they threw themselves against it. With one hand up, Ivo seized Alasdair by the back of his shirt and threw him toward the water.

"Go!" he screamed.

The magical barrier was crumbling at the edges. Ivo's arms trembled, using all his strength to hold it up. Alasdair scrambled to his feet and staggered toward me. He was slow. So slow.

"Ivo!" I screamed.

He turned to me, horror on his face.

"Mae, go! Go!" he cried desperately.

"Let me help with the ring!" I called to him. He was right behind the barrier. If it came down, he wouldn't have time to get away. I tried to focus the energy of the ring on him, but Ivo pushed his hand at me, and I staggered back into the waves instead. The surge of magic he'd thrown at me cost him. He dropped to his knees.

"Let me help you, Ivo!" I screamed. The edges of the barrier were coming down fast, winking out in purple bursts of light, flame curling around the edges.

"No, Mae!" Ivo cried. "Go!"

Alasdair finally reached the water. He staggered into the waves, hacking and splashing.

I looked over my shoulder, out into the sea. A light flicked on in the darkness.

The boat. An aether-fueled engine hummed to life and started to move slowly toward us.

"Ivo, please, come!" I called. "I'll swim if you come!"

Ivo staggered to his feet, his hands still up.

"I'm coming, Mae," he called. "I'll follow. Now go! Please!"

I stared at him a half second longer. His hands were out, holding up the barrier. Keeping them from us while we escaped. A fierce desire to charge back at the beach clutched at me. But he would push me back again, and that could take all that was left of his strength. I took one last look at his face and dove into the waves as hard as I could. The dark cold of the water was almost as painful as death.

Almost.

I surfaced with a gasp and took long, swift strokes, squinting ahead of me toward the light of the boat every so often to make sure I was on course.

When I was near the boat, I treaded water, and Miles called out.

"Mae, what took you so long?" he cried. "I thought you were right behind me!"

"The rope's here!" Coco's voice.

A rope splashed down into the water, and I clutched it. I pulled myself up the side of the boat, and a pair of hands grabbed my arms and pulled. I scrambled over the railing.

As soon as I was over the top, Miles pulled me into his arms, and we both collapsed to our knees. I started to sob.

"That's quite enough of that!" snapped Lady Vivian. "We're not done here! You can embrace and weep when Alasdair and Ivo are aboard!"

"Where are they?" Coco cried. "All I can see is fire!"

I squinted back toward the shore, where the spirits lit up the beach. I couldn't make out Ivo's figure or the lavender barrier.

"He said he would come," I said. "He said if I went, he would follow."

Miles put one hand on the railing and pulled us both back up. I clung to him, trembling, and stared out into the water and back to the shore. There was one set of swimming arms, splashing about with poor form and a lot of wasted effort.

"Alasdair!" cried Lady Vivian.

"But where's Ivo?" muttered Miles.

As soon as he was close enough, Lady Vivian hurled out the rope, and Alasdair clutched it as though he'd been a second away from drowning. I scanned the water behind him. No more splashes. No more arms.

Alasdair couldn't climb the rope. He said his arms were frozen solid. He looped it under his arms, and the three of us hauled him up while he dangled from it like a fat, unwieldy fish.

"Ivo," I said the minute Alasdair was over the railing. "Where is he?"

Alasdair looked up at me. He shook his head.

"He got away, didn't he?" I demanded. "He's coming?"

But I knew. I knew he wasn't.

Alasdair coughed wetly into his arm and didn't look back up when he was done.

"He isn't," said Miles, quietly.

I stared up at him, then back out at the burning figures on the beach. The water lapped against the side of the boat. Across the expanse of dark water, there was no break in the surface of the water until the waves rolled onto shore.

Coco brought up the engine and turned the boat.

"No!" I cried. "You don't know—he might still be coming—"

"He's gone, Mae," Alasdair said. "I'm sorry. But he's gone."

That was enough for Coco. She drove the boat straight away from the island at top speed. I clutched the railing, my tears freezing on my face.

I watched the fires burning on the beach until they finally faded into nothing.

CHAPTER TWENTY-NINE

It was a long, dark boat ride to the mainland.

Miles eventually coaxed me inside the cabin, where Alasdair sat shaking his head and shivering under a blanket while his mother rubbed his shoulder and murmured comforts. The cabin was all cream-colored leather and chrome, a mirrored wall, and soft, dove-gray carpet. There was an empty bottle of champagne in an ice bucket that was now full of water. All the luxury of a pleasure craft that had been on its way to the most exclusive party of the year.

I huddled under a blanket beside Miles on a leather-covered bench.

"I killed him," Miles said. "I killed Grandfather."

"You were trying to stop him from murdering that spirit," I said.

"Yes," agreed Miles quietly. "But that wasn't why I did it."

We passed other boats as we went, most as quiet as our own, populated with still, shocked figures. From one came wild, broken sobbing.

"I warned you," Alasdair said. He held a wet rag to the

swelling knot on his forehead and glared at me. "You couldn't just leave it alone. You couldn't just make Ivo happy and let things be as they were."

"Ivo would never have been happy," I said. "He couldn't live with it."

No more than I could have.

"He lived with it his whole life," said Alasdair.

"Until the end," said Miles. "He couldn't bear it anymore in the end."

"How many people had to die so he could ease his conscience?" snapped Alasdair.

I stood. Hatred welled in me, so fierce and buoyant, I could almost rise off the ground on its power.

"Not you," I spat. "Though you knew it all, didn't you? You knew what the magic was and who suffered for it, and you wanted nothing more than for it to go on, just without you having to dirty your hands."

"Mae!" said Lady Vivian. "Now is not the time!"

"And you knew as well, didn't you?" I turned on her. "Did you know before he ran to you and begged not to be taught? Or after?"

"After," said Lady Vivian quietly.

"And that was how you knew one of Lord Prosper's grandchildren was at risk when Miles told you his mother wasn't coming back. It's why you told Apollonia to keep her engagement to Rex though you knew she hated him. Secure her status as the favored, important granddaughter. Offer up Coco in her place."

Lady Vivian looked down.

"I didn't tell him to use Cordelia," she said. I had never

heard her voice so small, so lacking in command. But that was good. None of the Prospers should ever have had anything to command. And now they didn't.

"Of course," I said. "It could have been Miles, I suppose. No need to step in to save anyone from Imogen's fate as long as the magic went on and your own children were spared. No need to worry that the spirits were in torment and slavery every moment."

"Torment?" asked Lady Vivian. "I didn't know they were in torment!"

Even in her denial, Lady Vivian's eyes flickered with guilt. I understood all too well.

"No, of course you didn't. Just like I didn't," I said, with as much disgust at myself as at her. "There were so many things it was easier not to know."

"And what was the alternative?" she demanded.

"This," said Alasdair. "This was the alternative. Ivo knew that, and he wrecked it all anyway."

"You shut your mouth about Ivo! We went back for you," I said, every word dripping with furious sorrow at the waste of it. "We didn't have to. He saved you from the spirits on the beach when you were too slow and lazy to get away in time. He didn't have to."

I broke off, choking on a sob. Tears filled my eyes and escaped down my face.

"He spent his whole life giving you all what you wanted, knowing it was wrong. Knowing the evil he was doing. Hating himself for it. Even his death was for you. For *you!*"

Alasdair jumped to his feet as well, and Miles did the same.

"Ivo wasn't the one who left me tied up in the hills!" Alasdair said. "He didn't know I was there unless you told him! So whose fault is it that he came back for me?"

I had thought I knew hatred before, but the thing that uncoiled in me now was a different kind of monster. It rippled and snarled. It had fangs. It wanted to kill.

"My fault," I hissed. "It's my fault you're alive and he's dead. Mine. You worthless, selfish, arrogant—"

"It's no one's fault," Miles broke in. "No one's but Grandfather's. He bound us up in this, and Ivo helped him, but Ivo ended it. He set us all free."

"Free," laughed Alasdair bitterly. "I'm a fortune in debt to the mob, and Ivo just freed us of our fortune."

"Good," I spat. "I hope they break every bone in your body. I hope they rip out your poisonous tongue."

I stomped up the hold steps and to the deck.

Coco was alone at the wheel. She faced into the wind, back straight. As I approached, she let go of the wheel and wiped away a tear. I stood by her side and let my own tears fall.

Light was just beginning to silver the edges of the horizon. I saw an outline of land in the distance. The mainland.

"Most people got away, I think," said Coco.

I let out a long, shuddering sigh. It was hard to be relieved about anything, even that.

"I saw my father at the docks," said Coco. "With Uncle Stephen. And my mother left hours ago. He was drunk."

"Lord Stephen?"

"No," said Coco. "My father. I keep wondering if he knew. My mother didn't, I'm sure. But my father—do you think he knew what Lord Prosper was going to use me for?"

I thought about it.

"I don't know," I said. "Probably not, but—"

"But maybe," said Coco.

I didn't deny it.

"I should be grateful," said Coco. "I know that."

"You don't have to be grateful for any of this," I said.

Coco nodded. "I keep thinking, would I have chosen this? If it had been up to me?"

"What do you mean?" I asked.

"I mean, Grandfather tricked me, yes. But if I'd known everything, what it meant for him to use me to bind the spirits . . . what binding the spirits really meant. And what the alternative was. That we would lose everything."

She went quiet for a moment.

"I keep thinking I might have let him," Coco said quietly. "Even though it would have hurt me like it hurt Imogen. Even though it tortured the spirits. Even though it was wrong."

"No," I said. "You wouldn't have."

Coco shook her head.

"I might have," she whispered.

A low foghorn groaned out across the water. Not far away, a beam of light from a lighthouse scanned the moving surface of the sea. Guilt churned in my stomach.

"Could you hear us, when you were bound over the aether well?" I asked Coco.

"Yes," said Coco. She shuddered. "I heard everything."

"Then you know," I said dully. "What I almost did."

"Yes."

A small sound escaped Coco, like the stifled beginning of a sob or a hiccup.

"I'm sorry, Coco," I said wretchedly. "You were right about me. I'm a traitor."

"Are you even listening?" Coco wiped her nose with the back of her hand. "Part of me wanted you to do it. I know it was horrible and wrong and probably would have tortured me. But this? Life without magic? Without the island? And Grandfather . . ."

Coco shook her head and sniffed noisily.

"I saw what you saw. I know what he did, but all I can think is that he's not there anymore. He's not watching over me. It feels . . ."

"Scary," I said.

Coco nodded.

"But the protection I had . . . the money . . . It was stolen," said Coco. "Stolen from the island and the spirits. And that makes it worse. It's not just that we lost it, it's that we never should have had it at all. My whole life."

"I know," I said. "All my life I've wanted what your family had. And now . . ."

We fell silent.

"Miles said . . ." I said. "Your grandfather made us all part of this. We benefitted from it, depended on it. Even me. But he was the one who did it, really. All of it."

"No." Coco's voice was flat. "We're guilty, too. We wanted it, even if we didn't know. We could have known. If we wanted to, we could have. The spirits, they were slaves, and we never thought about it. And Ivo . . . he knew. He helped him. All those years. He knew what he was doing. Maybe he wanted to die for it."

"Don't say that," I whispered.

Coco wiped away a tear, but her face was hard.

"What do I do now, knowing this about myself?" she asked. "At least Ivo got to atone for it. With your help."

Her tone was bitter enough that it sounded like an accusation.

Miles climbed up onto the deck with three steaming mugs in his hands. He handed one each to Coco and me and stood with us. I took a drink of the hot cocoa. It scalded my throat on the way down.

Good. I deserved for my throat to be scalded.

"It's not true," said Miles. "What you said in there. It's not your fault Ivo's dead."

"Yes, it is," I said.

"No—"

"Miles, don't," I said. "He wouldn't have gone back for Alasdair if I hadn't asked him to."

"We both asked him to," said Miles.

"And do you think he agreed for your sake or for mine?"

"Don't be vain, Mae," snapped Coco. "None of this is about you. Ivo didn't save Alasdair for you. He didn't die for you."

I was stung into silence.

"You didn't even like him," said Coco. "Neither of you did."

Coco was crying again, silently, wiping tears off her face.

I clutched my hot chocolate and tried to swallow against the tightness in my throat.

Miles put a hand on my shoulder. It wasn't like before, in the cabin, when clinging together had been as necessary as the blanket over our backs. There was something tentative about it now. Something complicated. Something fragile, teetering on an edge.

"I wish he'd had the chance to be happy," said Coco. "That's all."

"It wasn't Mae's job to make him happy," said Miles.

Coco shot a sour glance at Miles's hand on my shoulder.

"Clearly not," she said bitterly.

I knew at once, from the twitch of his fingers on my shoulder, without even meeting his eyes. Whatever there might have been between us was over.

He pulled his hand away.

Coco didn't have to say more. The damage was done. We both understood. But it wasn't Coco's style to stop at merely enough.

"He didn't die so you two could live happily ever after, either, if that's what you're telling yourselves," she said.

"Coco, please," I said. "Please forgive me."

Coco didn't answer right away. She cleared her throat messily and took a deep, rattling breath.

"Maybe I will," she said. "If I ever manage to forgive myself."

EPILOGUE

One Year Later

I woke up late in the afternoon to silence.

Or near silence. Taxicabs honked outside my flat. Chairs dragged across my ceiling as the couple upstairs sat down to their tea. If my landlord ever fixed the sash on my window, I might open it and hear the birds. Or more likely, the sound of passing traffic.

A year later, and I still woke up expecting to hear the spirit music. Every morning, there was a feeling of falling through empty air when I remembered. I was saving up for a Victrola, like the one Coco had used to fill the quiet when she first went away to school. It would be another few months yet before I could afford it, if nothing went wrong. The newspaper didn't pay me much.

I pushed myself to my feet, then went to the washbasin and splashed water on my face. I looked into the cracked mirror above it, scooped my hair into the asymmetrical part I always wore it in now, and pinned one side down. I went to my closet and looked at the dress I had bought last month. It was a nice enough dress. Stylish, though a little cheap. I doubted all the beadwork would survive the night. It wouldn't have been good enough for First Night, not by a long way. But tonight wasn't First Night, even if it was the same day.

I put on the dress and suddenly realized it should not have been green. Especially not this vibrant shade of emerald green. Prosper green. Poison green.

Too late. I twisted the aether-stone ring on my finger, a nervous habit now, and dabbed some pot rouge onto my cheeks and lips. I needed it. My tan was gone, and I hadn't had sunburn on my face in months. Living in this dreary, rainy city had turned me from a wild-looking outdoor child into a regular, pale working-class girl.

I wondered if Miles would notice the change.

I walked slowly, taking the long way to the café along the slow-moving, fetid river. I stopped a block away. There was a little patio outside the café, but Miles wasn't sitting there. I looked through the grimy window and saw a dark-haired figure in a black coat standing by the counter. He turned, only slightly, but it was enough.

Miles.

I clutched my coat tighter against the shivers that ran down my back.

I hadn't seen him since we docked after that horrible night. We had walked off the boat into a crowd of sobbing, shouting partygoers, and by the time I had worked my way to the other side, Miles was gone.

He hadn't even said goodbye.

I took the letter out of my coat pocket and looked at it one more time, glanced down and realized I held the wrong one. This one was from someone who wanted to meet with me tonight about the article I'd written. Flat white paper and typed print. Not signed. Whoever this was, he wasn't the first editor who'd wanted me to turn the article into a salacious tell-all book, but he certainly was the most mysterious about it. I still hadn't decided if I was going to keep the appointment. I slipped that letter back and pulled out Miles's. His was in a cheap, flimsy envelope covered in foreign postage in a script I couldn't read. I didn't need to open it to recall what it said.

Dear Mae,

I'm coming to the city for Apollonia's party. I feel I have to, for some reason, though I don't want to see any of them except you. I'll understand if you don't feel the same way. But if you'd like to give me the chance to say sorry, I'll be at Café Marion at six o'clock, the day of the party.

Miles

I smoothed my hair, already frizzy from the fog, and crossed the street. Miles turned to me as I opened the front door. His eyes sparked, and his face brightened. He smiled like he was truly happy to see me.

I couldn't help it. I smiled back.

I crossed the café, and he folded me into a hug. He smelled familiar under the damp city scent that clung to his coat. I wanted to stay there, in his embrace, and skip the rest of it— the tea, the apology, the party. This was the part I had come for: the fleeting feeling of belonging with Miles, the stir of desire that would keep on going unfulfilled but that I still couldn't resist.

Even so, I pulled back first and was surprised to see Miles blinking back moisture in his eyes.

"How are you?" I asked.

"I'm—" Miles let out a little laugh and shrugged. "It's good to see you. I didn't realize how much I'd missed you."

I laughed, too, at that. I, of course, had known exactly how much I missed him.

"I wasn't sure what to order for you," said Miles. "I ordered coffee . . . Is that all right?"

"Coffee is fine," I said.

"Do you usually take tea?" Miles asked, looking abashed. "I guess I should know that, shouldn't I?"

"No." My smile wasn't even sad. "How would you? Coffee is fine. Thank you."

I picked a small table by the window and watched Miles bring the coffee tray. Just watching him was such a pleasure. He was a little less broad in the shoulders. Probably because he was out of school now and not playing rugby. But he had never needed all those muscles to be beautiful. Miles set the coffee down in front of me.

"Cream?" he asked and stirred a little in when I nodded.

I took a sip of my coffee. I usually did drink tea. Ivo would have known that.

He cleared his throat. He was about to apologize.

"Did you find your mother?" I asked.

"I did," said Miles. A smile tugged at his mouth. "She's much better. It was hard at first, when she was coming off the pipe. But she was so relieved to have their voices out of her head."

"The spirits' voices," I said.

Miles nodded. "She told me about it . . . about what it was like. I think it was a relief to her to talk."

"Where is she now?" I asked.

"Still in the east," said Miles. "She isn't ready to move back here yet. And the money stretches further there. We could make it last for years . . . though not forever."

I nodded. I'd heard secondhand that the lavish allowances the Prospers used to have had already dwindled. There was nothing new coming in now, and Vivian and Stephen had liquidated a good deal of the principal to pay off Alasdair's shockingly enormous gambling debts.

"And you?" Miles asked. "What have you been doing?"

"Working, mostly," I said. "I work the copy desk at the *Daily Sun*. Sebastian helped me get the job."

"Did he?" asked Miles. "That was nice of him, after Apollonia . . ."

"He knows better than to blame me for anything Apollonia does."

"And you like it?" Miles asked.

"The job?" I asked. "I do, mostly. It's long hours, and it doesn't pay much, but I've written a few stories for them. Sebastian thinks they might give me a regular reporting job if I keep it up."

"I saw your article about last year," said Miles.

I took a drink of my coffee and tried not to look desperate to hear what he thought of it.

"'The Last First Night,'" said Miles. "It was . . . something."

"When I wrote it, I wasn't planning to publish it," I said. "I wrote it down for myself, mostly. To try to understand it,

right afterward. But when I heard the islands were gone . . .
it felt safe to publish it."

"Safe," said Miles. "You mean . . . safe for the islands?"

The Royal Navy had organized an expedition to look
for survivors on the islands after the last First Night. They
sailed out and found . . . nothing. When I heard the news
that the islands had mysteriously vanished, I had no doubt at
all what had happened. The spirits knew us now. They were
never going to let humans near them again.

"Safe for the spirits," I said.

Miles nodded. He took a sip of his coffee and then set it
down.

"It was powerful, no doubt," said Miles. "Coco's furious
about it."

I looked up at him sharply.

"You talk to Coco?"

"We've exchanged a few letters," said Miles. "She sent the
first one. I was impressed she found the address."

"I haven't heard anything from her," I said. The pain of
it clutched at my heart again. Coco had left me on that dock
without a backward glance. "And I haven't been hard to find."

"Neither has she," Miles pointed out.

And that was certainly true. Coco had used the fervent
media attention after the First Night disaster to launch her
career as a celebrity pilot. She'd been doing shows all over
Europe and was supposedly preparing for a long-distance
flight. I had seen Coco's face on advertising posters in the
past year, though never in the flesh.

"Why didn't she like it?"

Miles pressed his thumb to his lip, thoughtful.

"Do you really want me to tell you?" he asked.

"No," I said. "I'll ask her myself. Tonight."

"Probably best," said Miles. He cleared his throat again. "Listen, Mae . . ."

"Don't," I said. "I didn't come here for your apology. I don't need it. I understand."

"I shouldn't have left you there like that," said Miles anyway. "But after what Coco said . . . I felt like there was nothing I could do to make it better."

"And you were right." I had only recently come to terms with this. "If you didn't want to stay with me, it was better for you to leave. You didn't owe me anything. None of you do."

"That's not true," said Miles. "You shouldn't have been left on your own like that; no money, no help. You were like family to us."

"I wasn't. I wasn't even staff, really. It was nice of you to feel guilty about that, but we all had enough to feel guilty about. I don't blame you for going." I looked fondly at the pained expression in Miles's beautiful brown eyes. "Truly, Miles."

"Part of me did want to stay with you," said Miles. He reached his hand across the table toward mine. I picked up my cup with both hands and sat back to take a drink. Miles pulled his hand back, astonished.

"Is it . . . ?" He let out a breath. "Oh. You're seeing someone else, aren't you?"

"No," I said. Though I was, in a way. I saw Ivo, sometimes. A face in a crowd, a hunched figure with messy, tied-back hair. It was never really him. Just my mind refusing to believe he was gone.

"Then . . . what . . . ?"

"It took me a while after you left to know what I felt," I

said. I remembered those long, blank days with a shiver. I had felt like I'd been split open, hollowed out, and sewn up empty. There was so much loss, so much loneliness and longing that it swallowed up particulars. "I missed you," I continued. "I missed the island. I missed—everything. But after a few months, I realized the one I missed the most was—"

"Ivo," said Miles quietly. He sat back and ran a hand through his hair. "I see."

"I spent so much time blaming him for things that weren't his fault," I said. "I hated him for keeping me from magic, when all the time, he was protecting me. I didn't really know who he was until the end."

"None of us did," said Miles. His shoulders slumped a little. By just the amount that I had disappointed him. "How could we? He never got to be who he really was until the end."

We stayed a little longer. Finished our coffee, talked about my work and Imogen and what the various Prospers were up to. And then the sun was setting, and it was time to go to the party. Miles flagged a cab.

Apollonia lived in the posh part of town. This party was the first she was throwing as a married woman, and it was sure to be wildly extravagant. Everything mainland money could buy would no doubt be bought. And everyone who had never been to a real First Night would say it was the most wonderful party they had ever been to.

I wouldn't say anything of the kind. I had no idea why I had been invited.

We stopped at the tall, wrought iron gates. Lord Darby's family coat of arms blazed in gold across the center.

Apollonia had married a lord, of course. A very rich one.

Miles climbed out of the cab first and offered me his arm.

"You're still wearing it," said Miles as we passed through the gates. He was looking down at the ring.

"I've been afraid to take it off," I said. "I'm not sure what will happen to my memories if I do."

"It's not as bright as it used to be," said Miles.

"No," I said. "The magic is fading. I can feel it."

"And have you noticed anything in your memories changing with it?"

I shook my head.

"Then you're probably fine, aren't you?"

I shrugged. I hoped so.

We went up the long walkway, past topiary hedges. Loud jazz music spilled out from the house, which was lit up from the inside like a bonfire.

"I thought maybe you wore it for him," said Miles, tentatively. Like someone pulling at the very edge of a bandage. "In his memory."

I looked down at it. I said nothing, and Miles didn't press.

And then we were inside.

It was loud. It was crowded. A butler took our coats, and almost immediately after that, a waiter pressed glasses of champagne into our hands and another swooped by with a silver tray covered in little blinis with caviar. I took several, shoving them into my mouth two at a time. I didn't get food like this anymore, now that I was paying for what I ate myself.

"There's Alasdair," said Miles. I followed Miles's contemptuous glance toward the ballroom, where Alasdair was dancing with a blond young woman with a soft, round face and a very expensive dress.

Miles and I went the other way, through the great room and into the courtyard. There, holding court and smiling with absolutely no real pleasure, was Apollonia.

"Mae!" Apollonia pulled her arm away from a solicitous mustachioed man at her side and waved. "Miles!"

To my astonishment, Apollonia ran toward us and kissed us both on each cheek.

"You came!"

"You asked me to," I said.

I didn't add that I still didn't understand why.

Apollonia took my hand and pulled me toward the mustachioed man.

"Mae, this is my husband, Lord Anselm Darby," she said, then turned to him. "My love, I simply must speak to my dear friend Mae. You'll excuse us, won't you?"

"Naturally," said the lord, who kissed my hand as though he couldn't even tell my dress had come from the discounted section of a store his wife wouldn't be caught dead in.

Apollonia pulled me away, back into the house, up a flight of stairs, and into the first room she found.

"Mae, I'm sure you know why I asked you here," said Apollonia.

"No," I said. "I don't."

Apollonia sighed in exasperation.

"You want me to say it?" she said. "Fine. Sebastian. I know you see him at work."

It made sense once she said it. Of course, she hadn't really wanted to see me.

"He isn't returning my letters," said Apollonia. "Does he get them?"

"I don't know," I said truthfully. He hadn't mentioned anything about letters to me.

"I know he was heartbroken, after—" Apollonia's jaw tightened, and a slight tremor passed over her bare shoulders and arms. "But he must understand—how could I possibly marry him if *neither* of us had any money? If we still had our fortune, that would be one thing—"

"I think he does understand," I said.

Apollonia's eyes widened with hope.

"Then why hasn't he answered my letters? Is it—" Her eyes narrowed again. "Is there another girl? You would know, wouldn't you, Mae? You always made sure you found out such things."

I pulled my shoulders back, and a ghost of a smile crossed my lips.

"There is another girl," I said.

"What?" said Apollonia sharply. "Who is she?"

I had only seen her once—a redhead from an artistic set. Nothing like Apollonia, which was surely the point. And not someone Apollonia was ever likely to meet.

"Not you."

Apollonia's face tightened. She turned away from me and put her hand on the morning table behind her.

"Did you really think he was going to spend the rest of his life waiting around for whatever scraps you might throw to him?" I asked. "He has too much pride for that."

"Get out," said Apollonia.

"You did him a favor, marrying Lord Mustache," I said. "He couldn't keep believing you really loved him after that."

Apollonia wheeled. Her hand flew at me, but I was ready

for it this time. I caught it in the air and held it easily. Apollonia wasn't especially strong.

"Learn to live with your choices, Apollonia," I said. "The rest of us have."

I dropped Apollonia's arm and went to the door before she could try to hit me again. I was done being smacked around by Prospers. I turned, hand on the doorframe.

"Is Coco really coming tonight? Or did you just put that in your invite to lure me here?"

"How should I know Coco's schedule?" Apollonia spat. "Ask her publicist."

I went back down the stairs and outside, my pulse throbbing in my temples. Miles stood in the courtyard talking with Lord Darby, a bemused look on his face. He glanced up and around—looking for me, I realized. But he didn't see me, and I stepped back inside, out of view.

I had been here barely fifteen minutes, and it was already time to go.

I pushed back through the crowds toward the front door, popping any canapés that I passed into my mouth.

"Mae!"

I groaned through a mouthful of salmon mousse.

"Mae Wilson!" Alasdair said again, laughing.

I didn't stop until Alasdair's hand was on my arm.

"Ah, come on, Mae, you weren't even going to say hello?"

He was still laughing. My fist tightened. I had never punched anyone before, but it seemed like such a natural thing to do. I imagined my knuckles sinking deep into Alasdair's face. But I knew enough about violence to know I would probably do it all wrong.

"Hello, Alasdair," I said. "I hear congratulations are in

order. You've found some unsuspecting rich girl to take you."

"Ha!" said Alasdair. He let go of my arm and took a swig of champagne. "You say that like it was difficult."

He looked worse than he had a year ago. Doughier around the face and the middle. His poison-green eyes were bloodshot already, and the party had barely started. Still, he was handsome enough to tempt most women. I looked past Alasdair to the round-faced blond girl he had abandoned in the ballroom. She was staring after us with a pinched, worried expression on her face.

"Poor thing," I said. "Though I suppose she must have some idea what she's getting into."

"Oh yes," said Alasdair. "I'm famous for my bad character. Speaking of famous, I wanted to thank you."

"For saving your life?" I said.

"No, no. For your article! The fuss had almost started to die down after the disaster. And then your salacious tell-all came out and—BAM—" He slapped his hand against my arm. "Everyone was talking about us again! It helped me quite a bit with Simone, actually." Alasdair glanced over his shoulder and winked at his fiancée. "Nice rich girls love a celebrity bad boy."

"I didn't write much of anything about you," I said. "You weren't particularly important to the story."

"What?" Alasdair exclaimed, mock-outraged. "Without me, your tragic hero doesn't get to nobly sacrifice himself!"

I bit down hard and thought again about punching. I'd heard there was something you had to do with your thumb when you made a fist, but was it supposed to be inside or outside?

"But really, it's that cloud of blood magic you threw over all of us," said Alasdair. "Everyone knew about the disaster, but no one knew what caused it until your story. Now it's all so much darker and more . . . fascinating."

My face contorted with disgust.

"The rest of your relatives aren't as happy to be known as a family who did blood magic on their own women and enslaved spirits."

"You mean Coco?" Alasdair shrugged. "She might say that, but if anyone's benefitting from the free publicity more than I am, it's her. You should send her a bill, really."

"What a good idea," I said bitterly, turning away. "The perfect way to win back my best friend. Thank you, Alasdair. You're a delight as always."

"You're not going already, are you?" said Alasdair. "Stay and have a few more drinks, then you can work up the nerve to throw that punch you've been holding in."

I stopped. Alasdair's laughing air had vanished. His voice had changed.

"I want you to," said Alasdair. "It might help, to get some little part of what I deserve."

I stared at him, astonished.

"Everyone wants to tell me it wasn't my fault, except you," he said. "You know better than that, don't you?"

He wasn't smiling now. There was nothing mocking about the slight frown that creased his still-handsome face.

"It feels good, the way you hate me," said Alasdair. "Or, not good. Right. It feels right. I want more of it."

"You'll have to find it somewhere else," I said. "I don't plan to see you again."

I hadn't guessed that Alasdair could feel that way. I had

thought of him, living his dissolute life, never thinking of what his survival had cost. Never grateful for it. A man who didn't care who suffered or how much as long as he could live the way he wanted couldn't have that much remorse in him.

Could he?

Still, I kept moving. If he enjoyed my hatred for him in some way, then I would vanish. He was by far the easiest Prosper to swear off.

But he followed me through the crowd until I reached the front door and had to stop to ask for my coat.

"Come on, don't you even want to talk about it?" Alasdair asked.

"With you? No."

I folded my arms across my chest and tapped my foot.

"Do you have nightmares?" Alasdair asked. "Maybe not. You didn't see him at the end, like I did. Running into that fire . . ."

"Shut up, Alasdair."

"You're right, though, you did save my life," said Alasdair.

"Ivo saved your life," I said.

"And you. That's a bond we have now. You can't just ignore it."

"I can, as soon as the butler brings my coat," I said.

"I wouldn't have killed you, you know," said Alasdair, a hint of pleading in his voice. "Or Sebastian. I just wanted to scare you both away. Put you back in your places."

"I don't care."

"It's that easy for you, is it?" Alasdair said.

"It is *not* easy for me," I said. "But talking to *you* won't make anything better."

Alasdair reached for my arm, and I decided I could do

without my coat. I threw the door open and jerked away from Alasdair's outstretched hand. I ran down the steps with my eyes lowered and my teeth clenched and didn't look up until I saw someone standing in my way.

Coco was wearing the tweedy suit I'd seen in all the posters, along with her bright red lipstick. Her hair was cut short and more stylishly curled than I had seen it before. It looked almost lacquered. She stared at me with her mouth pressed into a straight, bloodred line, like she was trying to keep something from coming out of it.

Alasdair's footsteps slowed behind me.

"Well, hello, Coco," said Alasdair. The serious, almost pleading note in his voice was covered again with his usual mocking tone. "We were just talking about you."

"No, we weren't," I snapped.

"Yes, we were," said Alasdair. "I was giving you excellent advice on how you might win back your best friend, remember?"

"Go away, Alasdair," I said.

"You sure you don't want me to stay so you have someone to blame when this doesn't go well?"

"You heard her," said Coco, glaring past me at him. "Scram."

"Fine, fine. But do try to kiss and make up, girls. Surprising as it might seem, considering . . ." Alasdair trailed off, and Coco's flushed cheeks told me what kind of smile he was making. "Your friendship was the only pure thing on that whole damn island."

Alasdair draped my coat over my shoulders.

"The butler brought this just as you were fleeing," he said and left.

Coco looked at me then glanced quickly away.

"Were you leaving already?" she asked.

"I didn't think you were coming," I said. "And there wasn't anyone else I needed to see."

"Did Miles not come?" Coco asked.

"He's here," I said.

"Oh," said Coco. She rolled her shoulders and rocked back on her heels. "Listen, I'm sorry about blowing you two apart on the boat. I probably shouldn't have said what I said."

"It was what you thought," I said, raising an eyebrow.

"It was what I felt," said Coco. "But that doesn't mean I should have said it. I don't like to think about you being alone because of something I felt."

"I don't blame you for scaring Miles away," I said. "There was nothing between us, not really."

"I don't know about that," said Coco. "He likes you."

"Not nearly as much as I liked him," I said. "And I'm finished trying to wring more love from your family."

Coco straightened, pulling her shoulders back.

"Oh," she said.

Coco's eyes were wide with shock and hurt, and I felt and then suppressed my instinctive desire to apologize.

"Miles stayed away because he wanted to," I said. "And so did you."

"Yeah, well," said Coco. "You didn't come find me, either."

"Did you want me to?" I asked.

Coco looked past me again, to the house and the party. She sighed, a loud, dramatic sigh. Like she was projecting for the audience in the back.

"I did and I didn't," she admitted.

"I guess you haven't forgiven yourself yet," I said.

"What?"

"You said you'd forgive me when you'd forgiven yourself."

"Did I?" said Coco. "I guess I don't remember that night very well."

"Really?" I asked. "I remember everything."

"Oh, I know," said Coco. Bitterness crept into her voice. "I read your article. It was extremely detailed."

I nodded, chin up. I wasn't going to apologize for that, either.

"People deserved to know what happened," I said. "There were people who died there whose families had no idea why. What they died for."

"And you think telling the world what Grandfather did was the answer? Telling them that he stretched me over a chasm and almost did magic on me that would have destroyed my life—"

"I didn't write anything about you being stretched over a chasm," I said, nearly rolling my eyes.

"No, but you told them what he was going to do. You told them my own grandfather almost sacrificed me for . . ."

"For magic," I supplied.

"Yes, and for the money and power that came with it. For everything we've lost. You made me a victim, Mae."

"I didn't," I snapped. "Your grandfather did that."

"But you told everyone! The whole world!"

"And that's so terrible?" I demanded. "You hate the attention, do you?"

Coco stared at me.

"Spheres, Mae!" she exclaimed. "So I like attention. That doesn't mean I like every kind!"

"You're right," I said. "I'm sorry."

Then I winced.

"No, actually, I'm not sorry," I said. "Not for the article, anyway. I still care about you. I've missed you every single day I've been in this wretched city. But I've gotten through a whole year of it on my own, and I can get through the rest as well. I'm *not* here to beg for your forgiveness. And I'm not here to beg you to be my friend."

I met Coco's wide-eyed, helpless stare until I couldn't anymore. Then I buttoned up my coat.

"I'm going to go," I said.

"Where?" asked Coco.

"Someone wanted to meet to talk about my article," I said. "I think they want to turn it into a book. I can be a bit early. I didn't think I would have much to say to all of you, but it turns out I have even less than I imagined."

"Mae—"

I waited, eyes on the fastenings of my coat.

"I've missed you, too," said Coco.

I nodded and finished doing the last button.

"Right," I said. "Well, you know where to find me."

"I do," said Coco. "When I forgive myself."

I looked up then. My throat tightened. The corners of my eyes filled.

I told myself I wasn't going to cry. I cleared my throat.

"And when will that be?" I asked.

"I don't know," said Coco, wiping her eyes. "Maybe any day now."

I nodded again, eyes down, and started to walk past Coco and out the gate.

"Maybe tomorrow," said Coco.

I stopped.

"Could I take you to lunch tomorrow?" Coco asked. "I

have a favorite spot. Nobody bothers me for an autograph there. I'll come by your flat."

I swallowed again. I didn't turn around.

"That sounds good," I said.

"Right," said Coco. "I'll see you then."

I nodded to myself. Then arms circled around me from behind, and Coco wrapped me in a backward and somehow extremely Coco-like hug. There wasn't much for me to do, other than pat Coco's hands around my waist and hope the gesture felt at least as affectionate as it was awkward. Coco laid her face on my shoulder and sniffed loudly.

"I'm sorry I didn't come," Coco said. "It was easier to pretend none of it ever happened. I didn't want to think about any of it. But we lost so much . . . I don't want to lose you, too."

"You didn't," I said. "You won't."

Coco squeezed me tight, sniffled again, and then let go.

I went through the gates wiping tears from my eyes and smiling.

I walked through the streets, toward the pub where I was supposed to be. I picked a booth in the corner and ordered a beer and roast beef. That was the main benefit of meeting with these publishers. They always picked up the tab.

I would probably write the book one day, but for now, that article was all I wanted to say about that night. I had written it for myself, and for Ivo. To remind myself why it had been necessary for us to do what we had done together. To remember him as he had really been. Not a saint. Not even a hero, really. Not after all the magic he'd done, all the damage he'd helped do for so long. But he was brave. He wanted the best for me. He wanted to do the right thing, and in the end, he did. It cost him his life, but he wouldn't have chosen differently if he'd known it would. I was sure of it.

I looked down at the ring I had used to help the spirits bring it all down. It was brighter than it had been before the party. I polished it with my sleeve, then held it closer to my face to be sure.

It was brighter. Almost as bright as it had been before, on the island.

I felt it, too—the crackle in the air of magic.

Someone was standing by my table. I was almost afraid to look up. I took a deep breath and smelled metal. I closed my eyes and breathed it in. My hands shook. I didn't want to look up and see some publisher. I wanted to stay like this and imagine it was him. Alive. Smiling. Finally free.

I would have to stop this one day. It didn't do me any good to have fallen in love with a ghost.

I steeled myself and looked up.

ACKNOWLEDGMENTS

Most fervent thanks to:

My agent, Bridget Smith, and the team at JABberwocky Literary Agency. I will never stop being glad you're on my side.

My editor, Jennie Conway, for loving this book and helping me make it what it is.

The team at Wednesday Books: DJ DeSmyter, Meghan Harrington, Chrisinda Lynch, Brant Janeway, Rivka Holler, and Manu Velasco; Kerri Resnick and Jack Hughes for my dazzling cover. I'm not sure how you don't get tired of kicking so much butt all the time, but I'm glad you don't.

Ken McCall. Dad, thanks for beta-reading even though there's kissing in it!

Coral Jenrette, for reading this book so many times in its awkward preteen phase. It never would have grown up without your help.

Derek Reiner, for loving this book with what at the time seemed like an unreasonable degree of fervor. I have come around to your point of view.

Catherine Egan, for giving me back my confidence in this story.

Ren Hutchings, for an incredibly thorough, adoring, incisive, and correct edit letter, as well as my first-ever fan fiction.

My Critters: Oz Spies, Kellye Crocker, Coral Jenrette, Derek Reiner, and Lisa Hernbloom. Hopefully by the time you read this we'll be back at Annie's eating nachos together!

Shannon Doleski, Jenny Elder-Moke, and Prerna Pickett, for helping me keep my feet aboard this pitching ship that is publishing.

Amos Cohoe, because I forgot to thank him in the acknowledgments for *A Golden Fury*, the book he actually beta-read. Sorry, man.

William Shakespeare and Evelyn Waugh, for loaning me some vibes and most of the names.

Grama's house, which was my island.

Isaac, Davey, Una, and Caleb. You are my life and my home.